THE GAME OF THIRTY

THE GAME OF THIRTY

WILLIAM KOTZWINKLE

All the characters and events portrayed in this work are fictitious.

THE GAME OF THIRTY

A Felony & Mayhem mystery

PRINTING HISTORY
First U.S. edition (Houghton Mifflin): 1994
First U.S. paperback edition (Bantam): 1995
Felony & Mayhem edition: 2007

ISBN-10 1-933397-68-3
ISBN-13 978-1-933397-68-9

Manufactured in the United States of America

ACKNOWLEDGMENTS

For assistance in matters of police procedure, private investigation, and surveillance technology, my thanks to Frank Johns, Managing Director, Pinkerton Risk Assessment, and Tim Jameson, p.i. extraordinaire.

And special thanks to Bronson Platter, Danny Morell, Lisa Pete, Len Levinson, Jessie Hamilton, Irene Williams, Camille Hykes, Henry Dunow, Ron Bernstein, Dan Wakefield, and Richard Bausch.

The icon above says you're holding a copy of a book in the Felony & Mayhem "Hard Boiled" category. These books feature mean streets and meaner bad guys, with a cop or a PI usually carrying the story and landing a few punches besides. If you enjoy this book, you may well like other "Hard Boiled" titles from Felony & Mayhem Press, including:

Satan's Lambs, by Lynn Hightower
Season of the Monsoon, by Paul Mann
The Ganja Coast, by Paul Mann
Death of a Dissident, by Stuart Kaminsky
Black Knight in Red Square, by Stuart Kaminsky
The Lime Pit, by Jonathan Valin
Yellowthread Street, by William Marshall
One of Us Is Wrong, by Donald Westlake writing as Samuel Holt
I Know a Trick Worth Two of That, by Donald Westlake writing as Samuel Holt
What I Tell You Three Times Is False, by Donald Westlake writing as Samuel Holt
The Fourth Dimension Is Death, by Donald Westlake writing as Samuel Holt
Belshazzar's Daughter, by Barbara Nadel

For more about these books, and other Felony & Mayhem titles, or to place an order, please visit our website at

www.FelonyAndMayhem.com

or contact us at

Felony and Mayhem Press
156 Waverly Place
New York, NY 10014

THE GAME OF THIRTY

"**S**OMEBODY'S GOING TO TRY and knock me off today." Saul Feldman stood across from me at his counter in the heart of New York's diamond district. He had a diamond-studded pen worth a thousand dollars in his lapel pocket. The pen I carried in my lapel was also worth a grand; it contained a radio transmitter that could send a signal a quarter of a mile.

"I had one of my feelings." Saul was stacking money into a briefcase, beside bags of diamonds, "Today is the day I get popped."

The aisles around us had been created by display cases, and the facets of thousands of diamonds sparkled like the suns in an elf's galaxy. Saul's cases were protected by motion detectors outside, and by weight detection devices inside. I'd installed them for him, along with overhead cameras and monitors, in which his roly-poly form now appeared as he cleared his counter. It was near closing time, but the other merchants were still haggling with customers, in accents that went from Brooklyn to Beirut.

Saul put his diamond-studded pen back in the display case, then pivoted the trays in the case so that they showed nothing but velvet backing. "It started with my morning omelette. It jumped out of the pan. I looked down, part of it is on my shoe, I said, Saul, when the omelette jumps

1

out of the pan, it's a sign. This isn't your day." He reached under his counter and brought out a holster. "So I bought this. Then I thought better of it and called your office."

I removed the stun gun from its holster and examined the pair of electric prods sticking out of it like the horns of an angry snail. "This is not you, Saul."

"I know, it's like something from a Wagner opera."

I switched it on. Blue electricity leapt from one horn to the other. "The problem with this—" I switched off the stun gun and slid it back into its holster. "—you have to be close to your attacker."

Saul put it in his briefcase. "I'll use it to boil water when I'm on the road." He led the way through the aisles of the miniature Milky Way, its jeweled planets rotating on carousels, floating on invisible wires, resting in skies of black velvet. One of the other merchants reached over his counter and grabbed me by the sleeve.

"I know what you're looking for. A present for your wife. Am I right?"

"Right," I said, even though the last time I saw my wife was eight years ago in divorce court.

"Don't look at the price," he said, angling a diamond necklace toward me under the light. "Only look at the colors in those stones. Every shade is there."

I pointed past the necklace to the Metropolitan Security sticker on his display case. "Your system is old, it's oxidizing, it's filled with dust. You probably couldn't set it off if you tried." I handed him my card, on which was printed *James McShane, Private Investigation.*

"I need a private investigator to install a burglar alarm? There's all the security I need." He pointed to a weary rent-a-cop who stood near the door, hands crossed in front of his crotch, as if he were holding himself up by his balls. I said, "Fifty percent of the crime in New York is perpetrated by security guards. They're the greatest security risk there is."

Saul and I walked on. At the front of the store there was gold on both sides of us—chains, bracelets, crucifixes, and modest cuff links made from Krugerands, one ounce of fine gold for each cuff. I stepped with Saul onto Forty-seventh Street. The August sun was a huge, boiling Krugerand in the sky, and the heat from the sidewalk came up through my shoes.

Hasidic diamond merchants in full beards and black suits and hats were in the crowd, starting to head for home. A week ago, a diamond merchant had been pulled into a van, robbed, beaten, and dumped naked in a bombed-out section of the Bronx, where he'd wandered like Neanderthal man, armed with a stone, until police found him.

Saul hurried nervously along, forehead already covered with perspiration from the heat of the unshaded street. "My wife wants me to go white-water rafting in Colorado. With the whole family, which is about sixteen people. First we ride donkeys all day, then we sleep on the ground, then we go down the rapids." He wiped his sweating brow with the back of his hand. "This is what I get for marrying an environmentalist. She has to save the great outdoors. She should be on a golf cart in Westchester."

My eyes were moving from doorway to doorway, and to the cars parked at the curb. Anybody making a move on my client would broadcast it. I'd protected brass and other senior government officials when I was in the U.S. Air Force, and I'd been on hundreds of simulated military exercises, but any old day in Manhattan could provide action that wasn't simulated.

"When she went after that plastics manufacturer in New Jersey, it was fine," said Saul. "We drove out, we looked at some polluted water, we had a nice lunch. In Colorado, I'll be lunching with a donkey."

"What's she going to be saving there?"

"Dinosaur beds." We crossed to the other side of the street, Saul gripping the briefcase tightly, keeping it close to his leg. He gave me a mournful look, and asked, "How is your fiancée these days?"

"She broke it off."

"I've never understood women. I say this in all humility. I don't understand their thinking. You probably don't understand it either."

"No, I don't."

"Precious gems I understand." Saul patted his briefcase. "Which is fortunate because protecting dinosaur beds costs, big time. The checks I write, Jimmy, to stop uranium miners from digging up dinosaur beds. And trees. My wife is also protecting something called an Engelmann spruce. It sounds like it might be Jewish but with trees you never know. The dough I forked out, they should call it the Feldman spruce." He pointed with his briefcase to the underground entrance of the Manhattan Parking Corporation. I accompanied him across the concrete, oil-stained floor to the elevator. He hammered the button. "Come on, come on." He glanced anxiously around the lot. "How many murders are committed every day in this town?"

"Nine and a half."

"To be half killed is a terrible thing. It's the half I'm worried about." The elevator shuddered down through the shaft and clanked to a stop. Saul shook his head despondently. "When our grandparents were kids, people slept in Central Park in the summer. For the pleasure of it. Can you imagine sleeping in Central Park tonight? By morning you'd be fertilizer. Why isn't this door opening?" He jabbed the elevator button and the door responded, creaking slowly open. We stepped inside and rode to the third floor. We'd grown up together in Hell's Kitchen, where I'd occasionally had to punch somebody in the nose on Saul's behalf, as he never backed down in an argument, despite being half the size of everyone else. Now he stepped out of the elevator and looked around anxiously. "Where did I park my car, there it is, over there. Do I seem nervous to you?"

"No, not at all."

"Calm my nerves. Tell me how you used to protect nuclear missile sites."

"I used to protect nuclear missile sites."

"Did anybody ever try to steal your atom bomb?"

"A couple of Cheyenne Indians."

"What would Indians want with an atom bomb?"

"I don't know, but if they had one they could sure as hell get a better treaty than the last one they signed." I swept my gaze along the tier of cars and connected with the face of a young pillar of the community, wearing a baseball cap turned sideways. I looked the other way and saw a second gentle citizen standing by the doorway to the stairs in a red T-shirt with gold lettering on the chest, and it spelled trouble.

"What's wrong, Jimmy? What—" Saul saw them, and swallowed.

"Nothing to worry about."

"I knew it. Today is the day." Saul was digging in his pocket, trying to find the keys to his Jaguar.

I shifted thy gaze from one young man to the other, meeting a look I know so well, the we-got-your-ass look. "Find the key, Saul."

"I got it, what do we do?"

"Hey yo!" One of the young men called to us.

"Yo yourself," I said, waiting as Saul got behind the wheel and started the car.

The two young men were coming toward me now. "Hey yo," said the first one again, "we got a dead battery. Could you give us a jump?"

"Jump this." My Beretta came out, leveled at their heads. With my other hand, I pulled out my wallet and flashed my tin, holding it high. They probably couldn't read, so the fact that it was a State of New York investigator's license and not NYPD didn't much matter; it was bright, it was official, and I had them backing up.

"Hey, officer, we was just having car trouble, you know?"

"You're going to have trouble," I said, waving Saul's car forward.

"Ah shit, man, we ain't done nothing."

I yanked up their shirts and removed a Colt Diamondback .38 from one of them, and a double-action .22 from the other. "Into the elevator." They turned and shuffled toward it. I pressed the button and the door opened. They looked at each other and signaled with their eyes, so I gave them a shove between the shoulder blades. They bounced off the back wall of the elevator, and turned, dazed from the impact, but one of them decided he wasn't going to take that kind of shit from a cop. He lunged, and a second later he was on the floor of the elevator, clutching his McNuggets. The second one made a sideways grab for my gun, and received my elbow rammed at medium velocity into the three major aortic branches of his solar plexus. He made plaintive little croaking sounds as he struggled to breathe. I leaned over him, my Beretta under his nose. "Would you repeat that for our viewing audience?" "Eat...my...crank..." he gasped. You had to give him credit for hanging in there. I reached inside the elevator and pressed the button to the top floor of the parking lot. The door closed on the young men's wholesome forms, and Saul eased the car in alongside me. I got in, tossed the pistols on the floor, and slammed the door. "Home, Saul."

Saul stared at the pistols for a second, then floored the accelerator and swept around the yellow exit arrows. He squealed onto the circular ramp, and slowed only when he was rounding onto the next floor.

"I've perspired through my underpants down into my socks." He came off the last ramp and drove toward the ticket booth. He handed his ticket and his money to the parking attendant drowsing there. "I was almost robbed up above."

The parking attendant nodded, made change.

"Robbed," repeated Saul. "Upstairs in your facockta parking lot."

"I don't think he speaks English, Saul."

"No, of course not. Why should he speak English?" Saul took his change, closed the window, and edged out toward the street. "So I was right, Jimmy. Today was the day. The omelette didn't lie."

"What's for breakfast tomorrow?"

"I never plan. Maybe French toast." Saul moved into traffic. "My briefcase! Where is it, here it is, I've got it, Jimmy, I've got my briefcase." He took out a handkerchief, patted his forehead. "They would have shoved my stun gun up my ass. They would have electrified my kishkas."

I took out a toothpick, peeled off the wrapper, and put it in the ashtray. "I'm parked a few blocks away, I'll ride with you."

"It's not the money or the diamonds I care about. It's my kishkas. I can always get more diamonds, but I can't get more kishkas. At least not at a good price. Does that make me a coward?"

"Wounds to the genital area are the greatest concern to combat veterans. Polls show it ranks way above dying."

"Already I'm a combat veteran. In the battle for Manhattan." Saul returned his crumpled handkerchief to his breast pocket. "Jesus Christ, what an environment. Kids have ruined this city, Jimmy. The lawless little fuckers are everywhere. They're like some new level of evolution."

We drove toward Fifth Avenue. I tossed my toothpick in the ashtray and opened a new one. I'd recently given up smoking. The car phone rang. Saul picked it up as the Jaguar came to a stop on the corner. I pocketed the pistols and opened the door. Saul put his hand over the phone receiver. "I'm in my overpriced automobile, and I'm safe. Right?"

"Right." I slammed the door and stepped out behind a bus that covered me in hot exhaust fumes. I found my Dodge Shadow, with a ticket on it, and got in, reaching automatically for the glove compartment, until I remembered that the medicine bottle full of gin wasn't there anymore. Along with smoking I'd stopped drinking. I had nothing in the glove compartment but mint-flavored toothpicks, some more parking tickets, and an extra gun. I pulled into traffic and started down Fifth. My cellular rang, and I picked up.

"McShane."

"*Jimmy, is that you?*"

"At your service, Saul."

"*I think I've steered some business your way. That call I took when you were getting out—it was a friend. She owns a very high-class antique store. She has a problem. I told her I was sure you could help her.*"

"What's the problem?"

Saul's voice faded in and out for a few moments, and all I heard through the static was the word *murder*.

"TELL ME ABOUT TOMMY RENNSELER."

"A wealthy antiquities dealer. He got knocked off a month ago in his apartment." Detective Sergeant John Manning sat across from me in a Hell's Kitchen topless bar. He laid a folded *New York Times* in the empty seat beside me. Through the folds, I felt a thick manila envelope of official police documents. Manning said, "Everything I know about the case is in there. Who's hiring you?"

"The dead man's daughter, Temple Rennseler. I'm auditioning for her tomorrow."

"And you want to look prepared." Manning turned toward the girls grinding on the stage nearby. Surrounding the stage were arched mirrors, smudged with body prints, grease, and cosmetics; the dancers' swaying forms were multiplied into a chorus line to infinity. Reflected in the background were Manning's face and mine. When we were sixteen, Manning and I had both apprenticed to a Hell's Kitchen housebreaker named Willy the Wire, the best lockpick alive. I could still pick any lock ever made, and so could Manning, but we'd wound up going through unexpected doors, Manning into the New York Police Academy and I into one of Uncle Sam's blue suits.

Manning turned back to me, swirling the ice in his glass. "Tommy Rennseler owned Antiquity International up on Madison, renowned for its Egyptian collection. Now here's an interesting little bit of business information for you. The Egyptians never liked foreigners robbing their tombs; they figured they'd do the robbing themselves. So they made it illegal to export ancient artifacts out of Egypt. But Tommy Rennseler had a shop filled with them. None of these dealers could stay in business if they didn't buy under the counter. It's one of those things that everybody does and nobody talks about. But when you buy under the counter from an Egyptian gangster, maybe things get nasty." Manning looked at my dealcoholized beer. "You don't drink anymore, you don't smoke anymore. What the hell do you do?"

"I chew toothpicks." I stuck one between my teeth.

"I always said you forgot to open your parachute."

"I wasn't a paratrooper."

"Whatever the fuck you were. Jumping out of helicopters on a rope." Manning's lips had a cupid's bow to them, which gave him an innocent smile he used to great effectiveness in getting information. His head was well sculpted, with dark brown hair that fell onto his forehead in curls that had made the West Side mothers sigh when we were kids, but his nose had been broken a few times since then, which served as a warning to tough guys who thought this handsome cop might not want to get himself damaged in a fight. He belonged to the knighthood of the NYPD—a detective in Homicide. You needed to solve fifty-five percent of your cases to stay in Homicide, and Manning was known for an uncanny intuition in running down suspects. From time to time, he had me helping him. There were people on the street who wouldn't talk to Manning but they'd talk to me, and whatever I learned I passed on to him, free of charge, of course.

I asked him, "Where did Rennseler get whacked?"

"In his apartment. Fifth Avenue near the Metropolitan."

"Anything around the body?"

"No fingerprints, no hairs, no blood or torn skin under his fingernails. The Crime Scene Unit got some cotton fibers, which don't mean squat. But they did vacuum up a few grains of sand from his carpet. It matches the composition of sand clay from Luxor. We found correspondence between Rennseler and a dealer from Luxor named Hamid. They had some kind of falling-out over a deal Rennseler pulled, details unknown. Interpol said Rennseler also dealt with some other Egyptians who had deep criminal backgrounds, that he'd do anything to get the artifacts he wanted, and that he didn't always pay his bills. The ragheads don't like to be treated that way, especially by Americans." Manning pulled at his earlobe, as if trying to switch on a listening device that would let him hear the whispers in the walls. "Rennseler was eviscerated. Is that the word I'm searching for? They cut out his lungs, stomach, liver, and several lengths of his intestines. And took them away." Manning raised his glass. "So here's to ragheads. The case is on inactive status now. I suppose Temple Rennseler wants you to poke around some more in the shimmering sands. She's got the money to pay for it."

"She inherited?"

"The wife got most of the money, but Temple got the business." Manning stood. "So you could make some dough."

"Thanks for the file, John."

Manning gave me an indifferent shrug. He saw murder victims every day, had seen thousands of homicides over the years, and indifference had become his style. If a Homicide detective doesn't learn it, the blood sticks to him and he gets as crazy as Lady Macbeth. I watched him go, past mirrors lined with red and blue lights flashing in sequence like an iridescent caterpillar.

A topless waitress brought me some unshelled peanuts in a dish. I shelled one and the peanut within looked like it had been mummified in 2000 B.C. I signed the tab and walked to my car. Once inside it, I opened the file on Tommy Rennseler of Antiquity International. There were drawings and photos of the Rennseler apartment and a brief biography of the family, including the maid. There were canvass reports from the building, from all the doormen on the block, and from cabbies who'd had a fare in the neighborhood that day. There were statements from Rennseler's clients. There was a copy of the mourner's book from Rennseler's funeral, and photos of those who'd come. The coroner's report gave the temperature of Rennseler's body at the time it was found, taken to determine the time of death based on a degrees-lost-per-hour formula. There was everything you could want, except an arrest. And Manning had forgotten to mention one interesting fact: Rennseler had been killed by a lethal injection of snake venom.

TEMPLE RENNSELER was dressed in an oversized blazer, with matching baggy pants and a simple, tailored, silky blouse. She was tall, and her short dark brown hair was sprayed tight to her skull Valentino-style. She was appraising my office, which went well with her style—my furniture is 1920s antique—rounded on the edges and highly glossed. She was seated beneath a pair of fan-shaped twenties wall lamps, their orange tint casting a flattering light on her prominent cheekbones. She'd angled her chair so she could check out my degree in criminal justice, along with my license from the state, and plaques identifying me as a member of the World Association of Detectives and the Society of Private Investigators. She seemed satisfied.

"My father's been dead for a month," she said, running a hand through her sleek helmet of hair. "I no longer have any hopes of the police solving the case."

Her eyes were the blue of a dancing gas jet, with a faint halo of gold. Beautiful women make me want to smoke. I picked up the office toothpick, a little number in eighteen-karat gold Saul Feldman had sent down to me after our walk to his car. I held it between my fingers like a long-lost cigarette, and said, "It's a fact, Miss Rennseler—a case is stale in forty-eight hours, and if thirty days roll by, it's probably not going to be solved."

"Saul was positive you could solve it."

I slid a finger along my red lacquered desktop, toward the NYPD file on Tommy Rennseler. "I have to tell you—New York Homicide is the best there is. I don't know what more I could bring to the case."

"I want to know who killed Father." Her eyes softened, and I saw the little girl she'd been, with a big soulful gaze of the kind that's disconcerting for adults to deal with; there was something unreasoning in it, and stubborn. And then the look passed. Miss Rennseler blinked, almost sleepily, and she glanced around my office again, as if she'd just woken up and needed a moment to find herself. She said, "You have interesting taste."

"I like the wood they used in the twenties." I pointed to the table beside her, on which my chessboard sat. "Makassar ebony." I omitted mentioning that it was my ex-fiancée who had, at her insistence and my expense, decorated my office. Before she came all I had was government surplus furniture and a Security Police desk set; if you'd hummed The Star-Spangled Banner everything in the place would have stood and saluted. Now my ex-fiancée is gone, and I'm mistaken for a man of taste.

"You've got a game in progress." She nodded at the silver pieces on my chessboard.

"I'm playing by a computer link. At the moment, I'm kicking my opponent's butt."

She said, "Somebody's kicking mine. I'm coming apart at the seams."

"Why?"

She uncrossed her legs, crossed them the other way, with a sound of whispering nylon. "I'm doing my best—

but I work where Father worked, and the atmosphere is unsettled. His ghost is all around me."

"Ghosts aren't my title." I tapped the file folder. "Some folks think your father was involved with Egyptian smugglers and wound up on the short end of a price war."

"My father wasn't killed by Egyptian criminals."

"What makes you think so?"

"I know it, that's all." She paused, lowering her eyes to the floor. She stared at the big red and brown rectangles in the carpet, tracing them with her eyes. I waited, which wasn't hard, with her perfume in the air. It was *Spellbound*. I know perfumes pretty well, because following rich women to their hideaways is something I get paid for.

She raised her gaze again. "He was killed by a person we know, a person close to us. That's my gut feeling."

"Do you have somewhere for me to start? Someone I could start watching?"

"Everyone loved my father."

"The Egyptian guy your father did business with—Mr. Hamid—didn't seem to love him all that much."

"Their correspondence made it seem that way, but Hamid is an old family friend. He was hurt by Father's death, emotionally and financially."

"Your father was killed Middle Eastern-style."

"It was made to look that way."

"You think the mutilation was a screen?"

"If this were a horse race I'd bet everything on it."

"A private inquiry can be worse than a horse race. We could eat up ten grand in no time."

"Don't worry about the money, Mr. McShane."

"I'm not worried. But you could spend the ten and still be no further than you are right now."

"I'll chance that."

"It's also intrusive. I'm going to have to talk to family and friends, and people you do business with. We'll be opening up all the wounds again."

"I don't care. I'm either heading for a nervous breakdown, or I'm on to something."

I was taking in her earrings: a pair of gold coins with an emperor's head on them. She was turning a ring back and forth on her finger, like the dial on a safe that wouldn't open. Her smile had a masklike quality now; her cheekbones were strong, and her jawline was as smooth as jade, but she looked as though at any minute this flawless countenance would collapse.

"I'll need an advance."

"How much?"

"Five thousand."

She opened her black leather clutch bag and took out her checkbook. The checks were gas-jet blue, to match her eyes. She wrote a check and slid it across the desk. Her wristwatch was a gold chronograph, with three little dials turning inside a big one, and that was my impression of her—little dials turning inside a big one.

"My father's murder laid life bare." Along with the scent of *Spellbound*, there was an emanation of fear around Temple. She gave me her business card and a brochure from Antiquity International, printed in color on heavy, expensive paper. "Come to the store. Madison and Seventy-first."

I put the card and brochure in the Tommy Rennseler file folder. "What do you mean, it laid life bare?"

"The ancients laid life bare too. That's why so many of their statues are of monsters." She closed her bag with a sharp snap. "I used to think those monsters were quaint. Now I look at their evil little faces and see reality."

"Tomorrow afternoon? Two o'clock?"

"Fine." She opened her bag again. "Here's a videotape of Father's sixtieth birthday party. Mother is on it, in white, trying to look twenty. You'll also see Father's brother, Richard, and his wife."

"Thanks, I'm sure it'll be helpful." I stood, and Temple held out her hand. She was just a couple of inches below my six two, with an athletic frame; when people give me their hand, I gauge their energy; Temple's energy was wiry and nervous, and she was strong, but I couldn't imagine violence ever being a solution for her. She was gentle, and there was unusual kindness in her eyes. She would let others hurt her, and never dream of hurting back.

I walked her to the door, and stepped out into the hallway with her. My secretary, a high-caste Hindu who treats me with Brahminic disdain, looked up and smiled at Miss Rennseler. Mrs. Ranouka Maharaj is a fashion plate and appreciated Miss Rennseler's style. I was learning about fashion from Ranouka. The key, she said, was understatement. She had me weaning suits by high-caste Italian designers, which I was able to purchase from a Hell's Kitchen high-jacking mob. They always stole something in my size.

I accompanied Miss Rennseler to the outer door, beneath a surveillance camera that sent its image to monitors back in the hall. My own security setup is more show than substance, but if you'd like thirty-five thousand dollars worth of state-of-the-art surveillance and protection, let me know. If you live in the suburbs, I can wire your sidewalk with sensors that tell you when somebody's approaching your door. If you want a Gothic touch, I can put a spring-loaded platform in your backyard, with a pair of pit bulls on it, and when intruders come over your fence they launch the pit bulls onto themselves; so far I've had no calls for the pitbulls, but I'm hoping a rock star will want the installation.

I opened the iron gate that guarded the basement offices, and Miss Rennseler stepped into the bright summer sun, which made her sleek, dark hair shine. As she climbed the stone stairs to Christopher Street, her baggy slacks tightened up a little. When she turned back to me, I quickly lifted my eyes to hers. "Have a good day."

"Yes, thank you." She hesitated for a moment as if she'd felt my stare and been disturbed by it. In turn, I felt guilty, so we were even.

I closed the gate, and watched her through the bars as she walked up the street. A drunk was coming the other way, waving his arms angrily at a world that had double-crossed him. As the drunk passed her, he lashed out, and Temple tilted her body, just enough. The drunk lost his balance and collided with a NO PARKING sign, while Temple glided on, not missing a step. Reflexes, excellent.

I returned to the waiting room. I was met by Dr. Ann Henderson, the chiropractor with whom I shared the basement offices.

"Well?" Her arms were crossed over the front of her starched white blouse. Henderson was petite, with auburn hair, and had the best legs in Manhattan, in my prejudiced opinion. I'd been in love with her since we'd opened the offices, which may be one of the reasons my fiancée walked out on me.

"Well, what?"

"So who is she? I saw her on the monitor. She's gorgeous, Jimmy. I feel she has a story."

"Henderson, you know my cases are confidential."

"This is different." Henderson was in the push mode, and bearing down on me. She was wearing *Obsession*.

I filled a paper cup with water from the waiting room dispenser. "I wish I could satisfy your curiosity."

"Jimmy—" Henderson peered at me as I drank, her eyelids narrowing. She was five feet two and full of gunpowder. She rarely stopped talking and had a photographic memory for everything she'd ever read. "I told you about my patient with the extra nipple."

"What patient with the extra nipple?"

"Ranouka, did I tell Jimmy about the patient with the extra nipple?"

"Yes, you did. We were sitting in the back garden when you told him."

I crushed my paper cup and tossed it in the basket. "Sorry, I don't remember a thing."

Henderson turned back toward her office. "This is far from the end of my investigation, Jimmy." She slammed her door behind her.

I turned to Ranouka. "Get Vaughn Steed in Athens. It's late over there, but he owes me a red-eye call." I returned to my office. I had a new toy to play with—a Nagra subminiature recorder that gives conviction-level recording in stereo and has the same radiation frequency as a quartz watch, which protects it from scanning devices that look for hidden recorders. I was playing with it when Ranouka connected me with Vaughn Steed. Steed's a p.i. who works in Greece and has contacts all over the Middle East. "Sorry to wake you, Vaughn. I need an Egyptian p.i. who can help me with a murder case. An American antiquities dealer got rubbed out, and he had strong connections in Cairo."

While I was talking to Steed, Ranouka entered with a fax in her hand and a puzzled look on her face. She laid it down on the desk in front of me. There were no words on the fax, just a little drawing of a cobra.

I worked late clearing up paperwork so that I could roll with the Rennseler case. Some p.i.s in this city are just licensed guns for hire, and they can do well working for the Mob, though occasionally they turn up dead. Legitimate private investigation has lots of paperwork. My computer was spitting out information from my info broker, while I studied the transcript of testimony given by a client who was sitting before a judge I knew hadn't drawn a sober breath in ten years. The State was trying to put my client away until the middle of the next century. The judge was trying to keep his eyes open. I'd been trying to find a friendly witness, living, dead, or invented, but there was none.

My last task for the day was at my chessboard. I had a game going against the Electronic Mole—that's what my info broker calls herself. I sent her my move over the modem and hoped she'd crumble. Then I closed my office. Ranouka had gone, and so had Henderson. The outer hall was empty, except for traces of spruce oil in the air, which Henderson used in her aromatherapy treatment. I shut the gate and went up to street level. Across the street was McNulty's Tea and Coffee Company. Huge wooden chests of tea leaves and sacks full of coffee beans were giving off their aroma. Henderson had advised me to give up caffeine, had told me it congested my kidneys, and

I'd believed her because I'm in love with her. Eliminating smoke, alcohol, and coffee had pretty much ruined my nervous system, but there's little I won't do to impress a woman. I stood in the heavy cloud from McNulty's and attempted to imbibe some caffeine breezes. Henderson had advised a foul-tasting herbal tea to purify my blood. She told me I tended toward liver stagnation because I was the aggressive type. I don't know why she thought I was aggressive; if I could just have a goddamn cup of coffee I'd be fine.

My apartment was above the office, four flights up. I entered the lobby and stopped at my mailbox. There was no personal mail. There was a Victoria's Secret catalogue. Somehow, it seemed personal.

I walked down the hall, looking at the catalogue, and started up the stairs. My neighbor Viola was resting on the second-floor landing, wheezing, a cigarette between her fingers. Viola was seventy-five, overweight, and took an hour to climb the stairs each day. She'd been in the building all her life, and the landlord wanted her out, but I'd threatened to bury him in building code violations, and he backed off: Viola would be wheezing up the stairs until she croaked. A half inch of ash was dangling from the end of her cigarette, and I looked at it hungrily. Viola looked at me, eyes squinting through the curling smoke. "Sonsofbitches." She turned slowly toward the open window that led to the air shaft between the buildings. She placed her hands on the windowsill and carefully leaned out; tired leg veins peeked from beneath her skirt. "Turn off that fan!" Her voice was lost in the loud hum from the kitchen of the bar below. She leaned farther out, cigarette hanging from her lip.

"Turn it off or I'll kill you!" She pulled her head back in and looked at me. "That fan vibrates my ovaries."

"I know, Viola."

"I can't sleep at night." She flipped her cigarette out the window. It landed in the dry grass near the door of the bar's kitchen. "You're a cop. Arrest those guys for disturbing the peace."

"I'm not a cop. I'm a private investigator."

"Sonsofbitches. They don't care if a beauty queen can't sleep."

"They care, Viola. But they've got to have a fan."

"But does it have to be on full blast?"

"Why don't you have a talk with the cook?"

"You think I haven't tried? He thinks I'm nuts. He doesn't have ovaries." Viola stared toward the darkened window of the bar. "I should go in there topless. When they're quivering with lust, I'll make my demands." She picked up her two shopping bags and turned herself on the landing. "Which way was I going?"

"Probably up."

"Yeah, okay." She took a labored step and paused. "G'wan by me."

I continued up the stairs to my apartment, disarmed the electronic alarm, unbolted three locks, and entered, the floor bar sliding up the door. I stepped into the 1920s, into rooms my erstwhile fiancée had decorated. Tinted seashell lamps framed the door.

I entered the living room and flicked on a lamp shaped like a female athlete holding an oval shade which illuminated her naked form. It was the correct light by which to look at a Victoria's Secret catalogue. The walls were faint blue, and there was a couch of soft brown leather. The black lacquered bookcase was flanked by two art deco chairs whose glossy sides were covered with intricate scrollwork designs. My ex-fiancée had shopped for months for these things, and just before she left me she'd declared the place period-perfect. I've never had occasion to doubt it.

I took off my jacket and removed a wad of hundred-dollar bills from the pocket. Many of my clients preferred paying in cash, which was fine by me, but it meant I always carried a lot of money around. However, I also carried the Beretta, which I now hung on a wall hook. My bedroom has pyramid-shaped enamel lamps on the wall; when lit, they cast a tango orange glow onto the padded satin headboard of my twenties-style bed, where my ex-fiancée used to lie, imagining she was Jean Harlow. I don't know who she imagined I was. The chairs and bureaus are red lacquer. On the wall is a color photo of the Malmstrom Air Force Base Security Police, with blond Airman McShane towering over everybody else.

I changed into loose slacks and shirt, then ran through some punches, kicks, and elbow strikes toward a tinted mirror on the door of the bedroom closet. I've got good reach and I'm the same weight I was at twenty, just under one-ninety. My ex-fiancée told me that whenever I looked at myself in the mirror I scowled. What do I look like? If I said Robert Redford, would you believe me? Let me lower the tights a little, then you'll catch the resemblance.

I finished my punching and kicking and followed up with fifty push-ups on the bedroom rug, half of them on my thumbs. Like many Irishmen, I have a fanatic in me. The telephone rang in the midst of my fanaticism.

"McShane."

"Jimmy, it's Henderson."

"Hello, Henderson, what's up?"

"I cooked way too much seitan bourguignon. Want some? With brown rice? But let's do it at your place, I'm tired of my four walls. Bye." She was just three blocks away on Perry Street, and she'd be roller-blading over, so it wouldn't be long. As a gesture of hope, I straightened the sheets and put my Beretta in a drawer. I checked myself out in the mirror again and tried to stop scowling.

Viola's voice sounded in the air shaft. I walked to the living room and looked down. She was now one flight below me, with her head out the landing window, shouting down at a waiter from the bar on the ground floor, who'd stepped out for a smoke. "Turn off that goddamn fan!"

The waiter smiled, waved back to her, and said something, but the sound of the fan covered his voice.

I stepped back from my window and flopped down on the deep leather couch with the file on Rennseler. The photographs showed him face up on the floor. His shirt was open and his midsection was empty. "Somebody was very pissed at you, Tommy. How could you have slipped up like that, a sharp guy like you?"

Rennseler's eyes stared upward, points of light reflected in them from the camera flash, giving them a false life, like a pair of expressive marbles. This is what he'd got for screwing with Egyptian gangsters. Certain law-abiding citizens like to have flirtations with the underworld. They usually miscalculate, letting their romantic notions guide them, and for a while they may succeed. But finally those they've romanticized cut them down with sudden ferocity, smiling at their naiveté.

The downstairs buzzer interrupted my reading. A few minutes later Henderson appeared at my door, roller blades and plastic containers of food in hand. She wore a tank top and black bicycle shorts with neon inserts to make her glow in the dark as she skated through traffic. A cotton sweater was tied around her waist. "Roller blading gets the turbid winds out of the head, Jimmy. You really should try it."

"I don't like going around on little wheels."

"You're afraid of looking foolish, but I think you'd be good at it. You're basically well coordinated. And if you got a smooth piece of pavement, you'd feel those flying dreams you had as a kid." She put her foot on the edge of my kitchen chair, and the neon inserts shimmered around her perfect thighs as she retied the laces on one of her sneakers. "You start coordinating so much information, you get conjugate vision."

"Conjugate vision?"

"Horses in teams have conjugate vision. I was almost hit by a taxicab this week, but my conjugate vision saved me. I turned at exactly the correct moment." Henderson smoothed her laces down and stood up. "There. What perfume am I wearing?"

"Eternity."

"Correct. Now, I'm ready to cook for my dear friend and colleague."

"I know why you're here, Henderson. You're not getting anything out of me about Temple Rennseler."

"Jimmy, have I asked you anything about her? When your liver stagnates, it certainly sends up little flares of belligerence." Henderson walked to the windowsill and examined the large potted plant growing there. "Your false aralia needs a tepid spray on the leaves." She opened up a cabinet under the sink, took out the spray bottle, and demonstrated. "A light mist. I showed you this last week." She'd swept her auburn hair back in a ponytail this evening. She had the pixyish pointed ears of an elf, and when she smiled her eyelids narrowed into a squint. I kept my desire in check. She was a woman who'd let you know if she was interested. Until you got the go-ahead, you were going to get your ego bruised.

She emptied her bourguignon into a pot. "I won't give you any peace until you tell me about Temple Rennseler. And I can be as annoying as a mosquito." She dumped rice in a pan, and began to stir it around. "Do you want my analysis so far? Based on my seeing her for just a few seconds?"

"Sure."

"I think she studied ballet, because she has the posture and some of the wrist action, but she didn't take it so far as to consider it for a profession. Women who take it all the way get very specific calf formations, and they tend to toe out when they walk. Temple doesn't, so the question is—why did she quit? She's athletic, she's strong, she has the body of a ballet dancer. Wasn't she good enough? Or was it a matter of confidence? I'd say confidence, because in spite of her beauty and aplomb, there's something shaky about her."

"Henderson, you amaze me."

"At first I thought she could be a young lady of leisure who had lots of opportunities to study but no real ambition. But then I caught the tension around her eyes, and I had to switch gears." Henderson turned back to the rice pan and. stirred briskly. "She does work that requires concentration, and it's not about where she should have lunch, or who should sit next to whom. Right?"

"Right."

"So she does a lot of reading, or maybe research on a computer. Anyway, something with lots of visual detail. On track?"

"On track."

"Then I thought about that twenties hairdo. She wears it perfectly, and understands it, and we already know she has artistic sensitivity, to which we can now add an affection for the past." Henderson stirred her stew. "So that could point to a number of professions. Interior decoration? Let me take a wild guess. She restores old paintings. Am I close?"

"Close enough."

"After work, she takes a dance class. Or yoga. No, wait a second, I bet it's more like Feldenkrais or the Alexander technique because she realigned herself in your doorway as she turned toward you—head, shoulders, and pelvis. It wasn't the kind of posture correction most people make, it was much more complete. She has remarkable muscular control. Look, I can keep on going, but there's one very good reason why you've got to take me into this case."

"And what's that?"

"Because she's in danger."

"As a matter of fact, she's not."

"Yes, she is. She may not have told you, but she is. Very real danger." Henderson gave an approving sniff to the dark red concoction in the pot. "Seitan is made from wheat and it's a perfect meat substitute for stews. The mushrooms I used are shiitakes, because they lower cholesterol and yours is much too high." She got out two plates and ladled the bourguignon over the rice. We sat down across from each other, beneath the enamel radiance of the oblong kitchen lights. Henderson smiled at me, her eyes crinkling up at the corners, and her head bobbing in an expectant little movement. She began to chew each morsel eighty-seven times, as was her practice. "The onions and garlic have antiviral properties, and you'll notice I added carrots even though they're not traditionally in the recipe, because with all the smoking you've done you need a lot of beta-carotene to protect you against lung cancer. Now tell me about Temple."

"She runs Antiquity International on Madison."

The smile of satisfaction continued to spread across Henderson's face. "I was better than close, Jimmy. I nailed it."

"All right, you nailed it."

"So what did she come to you about?"

"Her father owned Antiquity International. He was murdered."

"How awful. By whom?"

"The police think he might have crossed an Egyptian connection and the connection killed him. Temple doesn't think so."

"What do you think?"

"I don't know. But whoever killed him took his insides along with them when they left."

"Ugh."

"After injecting him with cobra venom."

Henderson nodded, and took a forkful of seitan. "Complex proteins."

"What, seitan?"

"Snake venom. It's a complex protein that attaches to the neural tissues of its victim." She was off again, flaunting her photographic memory of flashy facts. "I did a snake project in high school. I loved it. It made me feel I was peeking into Mother Nature's darkest secret. I mean, the snakes *created* that poison."

"Well, somebody stuck some of it in Rennseler."

"What a bizarre way to kill a person."

"Venom from an Egyptian cobra."

"They're actually asps. This is significant, Jimmy. The murderer *could* have used cyanide, which would be much easier to get. And cyanide kills a lot more quickly. Like in one minute. The cobra venom would take much longer. So I wonder why it was used. Of course, Cleopatra killed herself with an asp. I'd think about that, if I were you."

"What do you mean?"

"Well, it was done for love. Cleopatra got involved with Mark Antony. He was a violent man, and they died together, practically in each other's arms. So death by cobra has historical meaning. It's bound up with misguided love. Okay, who are the suspects?"

"An art dealer named Hamid. Rennseler pulled a fast one on him."

"No, he's not involved."

"Just like that?"

"It doesn't resonate with the Cleopatra motif. I'm getting the entire vibration." Henderson had a hand to her forehead. "It's a romantic murder and it was done by a lover. Tell me about the family."

"You'll see them all." I nodded toward the living room. "I've got a home video."

"We'll watch it while we have our infusion." She slipped out from behind the table. "Home videos are so wonderfully bad. Everyone looks terrible, and they speak the worst lines." Henderson filled the tea kettle from the bottled spring water she insisted that I buy.

When she swung toward the stove with the kettle, her tank top pulled tight across her chest. I can't feign indifference to such things. My ex-fiancée considered it a character flaw.

"What's in the infusion collection this week?"

Henderson opened the kitchen cabinet and reached up to the shelf that held the various Chinese herbs she'd given me. "We'll have some astragalus to boost our immune system. And some ginseng for our mental clarity. And peony for our complexion. It makes it soft as a petal."

"I don't want my complexion going soft." All of Henderson's infusions tasted the same. In my air force drinking days, I'd gotten my head into an aquarium, and I remembered the taste. It was the taste of infusions.

Henderson laid out the cups and saucers, and said, "Scald the inside of the teapot."

I scalded it. "Will there be anything else, your grace?"

"I'm convinced that most of the world's crimes are caused by bad digestion," she informed me as she anxiously timed her infusion. Like many health care practitioners, Henderson was a hypochondriac. I switched on the VCR, loaded the Rennseler video, and joined her on the couch. She unlaced her running shoes, kicked them off, and drew her legs up underneath her.

I pressed the remote, and the video started to roll. Henderson's *Eternity* sailed my way; I imagined it being launched from some pulse point on her throat, an exquisite little area of her delectable skin, which I knew she treated with a variety of New Age emollients. Life, with all its lures. And now, for the dead man:

The victim appeared on screen, intact, enjoying himself at his sixtieth birthday, a man who can't see Death waiting for him. I froze the frame. Henderson squinted toward the screen. "He's very attractive, if you like the Claus von Bulow type. I mean, the blazer and the ascot?"

I looked at Rennseler's frozen form, his hand in a gesture toward his guests. My take was con man, with the same studied respectability the S & L bankers had. Rennseler continued his gesture to the camera, over a long table set with sparkling crystal. He said, *"It's a pleasure to have my nearest and dearest here on this inglorious occasion."* He pointed to a cake glowing with candles. *"At sixty a man is either a stoic or a satyr."*

"Now that's a strange thing to say," observed Henderson, placing one finger against her cheek. "Okay, who's this?"

"The wife."

Mrs. Helen Rennseler came into view in an ivory satin evening gown, the bodice fastened with three bows that left several patches of bare skin at the midriff. "She's too old for that outfit," said Henderson. "Her self-image is distorted. Stop it there."

I froze the frame and Henderson studied Helen Rennseler. "Her right collarbone is low, I'd love to get an X-ray. She probably has a slight secondary scoliosis."

I pressed the PLAY button and the film continued, Temple Rennseler coming into the frame, on the other side of her father. Henderson leaned forward. "She's ethereally damaged, but she's lovely and she knows what she looks good in. Funny that the mother is floundering. Maybe the birthday was too much for her."

We watched Rennseler and Temple cut the birthday cake together, her hand over his. *"I need Temple to steady me,"* Rennseler was saying. *"Next year she'll have to feed it to me, too."*

"Daddy, you're still the best-looking man in town."

"Well," said Henderson, "she certainly adores him. See how she looks at him? That's why she can't let the murderer get away with it. The best thing in her life was killed."

The cake was cut and served, and the camera pulled

back to include the others at the table. "That's Rennseler's brother and his wife. Richard Rennseler's a stockbroker, I don't know her story."

"Anyway, her dress is perfect for her. She has better sense than the other Mrs. Rennseler."

The tape continued on as Henderson had predicted, with everyone looking slightly distorted by the lens, and speaking awkwardly toward the camera, of whose presence they were painfully aware. Only Tommy Rennseler maintained an easy self-mockery. After fifteen minutes it was over. "I knew I'd like Temple," said Henderson. "The rest of them I could live without."

"What's your take on Tommy?"

"I'd say he's carrying chronic tension around C-1."

"He's permanently stiff, Henderson. It's too late for a neck adjustment. What about his character?"

Henderson picked up her teacup and sipped her infusion, both hands wrapped around the cup, and both legs still tucked under her. "He's got all that *savoir-faire*, and he's perfect for selling expensive artifacts, but there's something about him..." She looked into the depths of her infusion. "For one thing, he's been cheating on his wife for years. That's obvious from her attitude. She's remote, she watches everything from a little distance. She's made other arrangements with her emotions, and they don't include her husband."

"Is she having an affair?"

"At the moment? Not in that dress. That dress was desperation. But I'm sure she's had affairs. I mean, why shouldn't she?"

"Say she was having an affair. Say she wanted to get rid of Rennseler. Could she have killed him?"

Henderson set her teacup down, stretched her legs out

to the coffee table, and rested her feet there. "He hurt her, I'm sure of that. That's why her face is a mask. And I don't mean the little bit of cosmetic surgery, which is very good, I wonder who did it." Henderson turned toward me. "He hurt her, and she was out of love with him, and maybe she even hated him. He had the kind of charm that could drive you crazy after a while, because he was so conscious of it. She might kill him just to get him to stop being charming." Henderson tossed her ponytail back over her shoulder and turned toward me, her head cocked to one side. "You see how valuable my analysis can be, and I haven't even *begun* to think about the case. What I've always wanted to do is ride around in a surveillance van with earphones on." She put her arms behind her head and stretched. "Goodness, that tea made me sleepy."

Her breasts pressed up through her tank top as she arched her spine and tilted her head back against the leather sofa. She sighed, though I should have been the one sighing. She caught my look, and said, "Jimmy, we'd be very foolish to start getting serious about each other."

"Why?"

"Because our chakras don't line up."

"Would you mind explaining that one?"

"Your chakras have a very aggressive, erratic spin. Mine spin much more gently. We're not romantically compatible." She sat forward. "But we'd still make a good detection team. Will we ride around in a van with earphones on?"

"If we have to."

"I've always been the nosiest person. Sometimes I get into a frenzy." She stuck out her lip and blew upward, the fringes of her bangs lifting lightly. "Helen Rennseler could have killed him. What about the brother? He acts like one of those brokers who'd give you a song and dance in bond land."

"I'll be talking to him."

"And I'll be coming with you. Won't I?" She leaned toward me. "Please, Jimmy? It would be cruel to show the world's nosiest person this much and no more."

"And what do I get?"

"A neck adjustment? I could do it right now. Here, lie down." She got up and made me stretch out on my back, with my head hanging off the edge of the sofa. "Now relax. Just give your head to me."

"It's yours, sweetheart."

"Stop trying to be macho."

I was looking up into her elfin face. Her ponytail fell forward and its edges landed on my forehead as she cradled my head in her hands. Her breast was nearly touching my nose. If you had to have a neck adjustment, this was the way. Suddenly her hands moved, twisting my head. A sharp crack sounded in my neck; it felt as if she'd just unscrewed my skull. "I've been wanting to do that for months," she said smugly, then slipped her feet into her running shoes. "And now I have to be going. Am I your partner in crime?"

I followed her into the kitchen. "Why don't we go for a drink somewhere?"

"You gave up drinking."

"Why don't I walk you home?"

"Because I'll be roller-blading. I'd leave you behind in the dust." She pulled the door, and the police bar slid up the face of it with a metallic scraping. "Watch the tape again. To a man like Rennseler, every woman is a sex object. Very unevolved." She reached over and squeezed my hand. "I'm so glad you're not like that." She backed into the hallway, put her fingers to her lips, and threw me a kiss. "'*Night*," she said in a whisper.

I watched her go down the hallway. She turned onto the stairs, and I listened to her quickly descending step, the disappearance of a sprite into the earth. I locked the door, bolted it, and armed the alarm. There was some infusion left, which I poured down the sink.

Then I watched the tape again and froze the frame on a close-up of Temple. She had just run both hands through her hair, drawing it back tightly against her scalp. That, and something peculiar in her eyes, gave her a masculine air—streamlined, handsome, but coarse in the style of her father, and ruthless, which surprised me. When I pressed the PLAY button, the hair loosened around her face, and the look was gone.

I LIKE MADISON AVENUE, and I'd spent many hours in its shops with my former fiancée searching for the 1920s. Tommy Rennseler's killer had slithered up against this shimmering bubble of bright and expensive illusions, and slipped inside. The bubble had repaired itself, with no indication that a poisonous intruder had gotten through.

The glaring summer sun shone into the window of Antiquity International. Thousand-year-old bottles without price tags rested there, on red cloth. They'd survived the ages, and if you had the money you could buy one and travel with its genie, back to Ur. My reflection was laid over them, like the genie himself, updated in an Italian suit.

I rang the bell. A woman looked up from a desk at the rear of the gallery, checked me over, and rang the buzzer that admitted me. "Yes?" she asked coldly, the inquiry seeming to come from a Tron Tek transmitter inserted under the bridge of her nose.

"You're wearing *Joy*."

"Are you a perfume salesman?"

"The name's McShane. Miss Rennseler is expecting me."

"You're the private detective," she said. She was in her fifties, with eyes that protruded slightly, much white showing. Her body was long and angular, and her face round and pale, with a little chin; she was the moon on a pin. The black dress she wore made her pale skin seem paler, and I saw a faint smile of scorn playing on her lips. I said, "You're Gladys Groome. You knew Mr. Rennseler very well."

"I've worked here many years." Her voice yielded no emotional content, as her large, keen eyes looked past me.

"It must have been awful for you when he died."

"Yes, it was a terrible misfortune," she said, again without emotion, but I saw a spot of color come into her pale cheeks. She rose from her desk. "I'll tell Miss Rennseler you're here." She went into the back office, and I attached a wafer transmitter under her desk, powered by a flat Polaroid battery. I don't ordinarily bug my own clients, but I wanted to have an ear inside this place, to listen in on the aloof Miss Groome, and the workings of the antiquities trade.

After attaching the transmitter I took a look around. The walls were lined with display cases, and the ancient world was inside them. On a pedestal by the door was the statue of a naked woman, identified as Fortuna, goddess of fate. Her sightless marble eyes stared at me coldly, not unlike Miss Groome.

I bent to look at a less imperious figure—a bottle with two heads shaped into it, back to back.

"That's Janus, Mr. McShane." Temple Rennseler's voice came from behind me. "First century A.D."

"Always look both ways, right?" I straightened up and found her smiling at me. Miss Groome stood beside her in silence, holding us in her impassive gaze. It was hard to know what was going on behind those eyes, but my guess was disapproval. She sat back down behind her desk, and Temple held out her hand to me. "Thank you for coming so soon. I know you're busy."

"I've cleared the books. The only thing I have to do is escort Saul to his car at five o'clock."

"He told me how you rescued him."

"I just held the elevator door for him."

"He thought he was going to be killed."

"As I said, you've got to look both ways all the time." I stepped toward the next display case. She moved with me and pointed to a tall, large-mouthed vase. "That's another double figure. They're brother gods, Ephialtes and Otus. They personify the nightmares of sleeping women. But they've been kicked out of dreamland and sit back to back on the chair of forgetfulness."

"How much?"

"Actually it's not for sale at the moment." She was wearing another loose-fitting blazer, this one the color of honey, and a short honey skirt, which interested me more than the chair of forgetfulness. She brought out Ephialtes and Otus and set them on the counter, running her fingers along the handsome, carved faces that haunted women's sleep. "I'm having trouble parting with this piece. Maybe it's because I have too many of my own nightmares. I guess I'm hoping these guys will ease off if I treat them right."

"They're too good-looking to be nightmares."

She stroked the gleaming head of Otus. "Women's nightmares are often about good-looking men."

"I learn something every day." I looked back into the display case, at a circle of perfume bottles, identified as Late Period Egypt, 700–332 B.C. They were shaped like clusters of purple grapes, with a soft luminescence in their curving forms.

"You asked about price," she said, and turned back toward the case. "They're five thousand dollars each."

"Any perfume left in them?"

"I expect it evaporated around the birth of Christ." She pointed to a pale blue-green cup. "That's an important cup." She knelt to unlock the case, and her skirt slid several inches up her thighs. I, like most men, when asked to choose between lovely legs and an important cup, will waver.

"This is one of the few pieces from the ancient world that carries a signature." She stood back up and placed it on the countertop. "The inscription is Greek. It says *Ennion made me*. And over here, *Let the buyer remember*"

The light in the display case was muted, and the pieces seemed in a kind of slumber, waiting for their next owner. I was trying to concentrate on them, but what I was feeling instead was Temple's fear, that intangible scent in the air again, of a woman who feels herself being stalked. But her expression revealed nothing of this, and her manner was enthusiastic, as she said, "My father was very lucky to have gotten Ennion's cup."

"Who did he get it from?"

"A young man who has the habit of selling off family valuables. Whenever he gets involved in a new love affair, all of which are costly, he pops in with another piece. I've made you a list of people we've bought important pieces from. Shall we go into my office?"

We stepped past Miss Groome, who glanced toward Temple, the scornful little smile playing on her lips again. "Should I hold your calls?" She clearly disapproved of me, and perhaps of Temple for hiring me.

"Yes, please say I'm in a meeting."

"Of course." Miss Groome looked back toward the papers on her desk, and the hand she laid upon them was long, thin, and very white. Henderson would say poor circulation, but I felt it was Miss Groome's soul that was pinched and cut off from life. As I closed the door, I caught her glancing toward me again, and it was with something more than disapproval; I saw a will of iron in that mummy.

The furniture in Temple's office was massive, suggesting heavy respectability. Just what you want when buying a two-thousand-year-old cup. The room was in good order. No business clutter, no personal items. She handed me a computer printout. "These are the collectors and dealers we've purchased from."

"What about Miss Groome?"

"She was with Father before I was born. She knows as much as most curators. Father hired her straight out of college and taught her everything. Her work is impeccable."

"I get the feeling she was in love with your father."

"Yes, I suppose so. Poor Miss Groome."

"Her love was not reciprocated?"

"I doubt it."

"How does she feel about you?"

Temple looked away, but I could see her discomfort. "Oh," she said, "Miss Groome's all right. I couldn't run the business without her. But you can imagine her feelings: she saw me in my baby carriage and now I own the business, and I'm her boss. But we're working on it."

"Your office could pass a military inspection. You're just as on top of things as the gloomy Miss Groome."

She smiled and ran her hand over the roof of a miniature temple set on a pedestal beside her desk. "This is the Egyptian goddess Maat. She's called the goddess of truth. She keeps order in a chaotic world. Very important." Inside the open doors of the temple was a bronze female figure with a feathered crown. "Watch," said Temple, and she touched the base of the pedestal with her foot. My eyes remained on her legs until I heard a faint noise from inside the column of the pedestal; it was the sound of shifting tumblers. The doors of the little temple started to close, activated by weights that must have been moving inside the pedestal. The doors met in the center in a seamless line, and the temple was sealed. I hadn't seen anything that slick since the false ceiling in Willy the Wire's apartment, which lowered to hold stolen goods.

"Father built it. It's a copy of a life-size temple that once stood in Luxor. The doors opened and closed by hidden mechanisms. It must have been pretty impressive to the uninitiated."

"Your father was a clever guy. Forgive me for asking, but did he have any girlfriends?"

"He was attractive, and he and Mother never got along well. They stayed together for convenience."

"Mutilation fits with crimes of passion. And the injection of snake venom. Do you see anything feminine in that?"

"No."

"I get the image of a ministering angel in white."

"Mother always refers to herself as an angel. Obliquely, of course. But the implication is clear. She finds it painful to be with those who are so much less developed spiritually."

"You think she killed your father?"

"I'm not accusing her. I don't know who she is or what she's capable of."

"What do you mean, you don't know who she is?"

"She still wears the same George Washington ponytail she wore as a debutante, held by the same black ribbon, and I've never seen her without her make-up on. She doesn't let her guard down for a minute."

I was trying to feel Tommy Rennseler in the shop, the man who bought and sold the ancient world. But the works of art overpowered any lingering impressions of a mere human who'd gotten himself killed; he'd been shattered, and they'd survived.

"I'll need a client list."

She took another printout from the drawer and gave it to me. "They were contacted by the police during their investigation."

"All wealthy?"

"Most of them."

"I'll do some quiet checking."

"How will you do it? Quietly, I mean."

"Information about all of us is moving from one computer to another a dozen times a day. An information broker can dip into that stream and find out plenty. He can tell us—" I ran my eye down the list. "—where Jeremy Trowbridge III does his banking and how much he spends on clothing, restaurants, travel, jewelry, and art. We can get his medical records and find out if he's had an HIV test, what drugs he takes, and whether his wife has had her tubes tied. For the sake of convenience, people have opened their lives."

She sat down behind her desk with a guarded movement, as if to escape the scrutiny being described. I sat down in the chair beside her. "Tell me about your father."

She leaned back in her chair and ran her hand through

her hair, lifting the short straight strands off her neck. She had the kind of expression you see on the faces of New York City marathoners as they come down the last hill in Central Park—determined, but in a kind of dream.

"My father was a perfectionist. Unsatisfied. He never had enough. And he tended to be critical, but he had to be. It's very easy to buy a fake in this business. Father used to speak of the times he'd walk into someone's house, and they'd show him a beloved piece of antiquity which he recognized as a forgery. It gave him a jaundiced view of the art world."

"Have you been stung by any forgers?"

"I would have been, very recently, but Miss Groome stopped the sale at the last minute. She'd known from the beginning it was a forgery, but allowed me to continue with negotiations. I suppose she wanted to teach me a lesson."

"Thoughtful Miss Groome."

"I was grateful to her, but her timing was bad. A very good client of ours was involved, and he was present when Miss Groome exposed the fake." A strand of hair had loosened itself from her slicked-down helmet and fallen onto her forehead. "So I came away looking like a dummy, which I'm not. I know as much as Miss Groome. But I'd gotten myself into a manic state, and it clouded my judgment."

Before I could question her further about her relations with Miss Groome, she questioned me: "Tell me about yourself."

"What part are you interested in?"

"How did you get into investigation?"

"My father was a longshoreman, Local 824. Most of its members were felons, including my old man. I grew up with stories about Legs Diamond and Killer Madden, the Duke of the West Side. My second home was the Forty-sixth Street pier. I ran errands for crooks and cops. I wanted to be somewhere in the middle."

"Is that what you are—between a crook and a cop?"

"Not anymore. I served twelve years in the air force."

She gave me a quizzical look, as if trying to find the traces. "An officer and a gentleman?"

"Staff sergeant and wild man."

"Did you fly a plane?"

"I was in base security. Sam paid for it so I also got a degree. After that, I was transferred to the Office of Special Investigations. We did for the air force what the FBI does for the general public, everything from bank robbery to murder."

"Why did you leave?"

"They wanted to take me off the bricks, make me an officer and a leader. All I wanted to do was carry tin and be an investigator."

"So you became a detective. Do you enjoy it?"

"A lot of the time it's loose ends and lost causes. But yes, I enjoy it."

"Do you like following people around?"

"That's a strange question."

"Is it?"

She was wearing a gold ring set with a carved carnelian satyr. It seemed a peculiar accessory for a woman, considering the sexual appetite of satyrs. I asked, "When can I see your mother?"

"Wait, I want to hear more about following people."

"That's enough. That's everything."

"You don't like talking."

"I'm successful in my business because of one important fact: People talk too much. So there are no secrets."

"And you want to keep yours." She came out from behind her desk, and I let her open the door for me. Miss Groome smiled her half-dead little smile again. People who bought ancient crockery must expect it. But within that smile I saw again her scorn not only for me but for Temple, and her determination to humiliate her, ruin her even. Miss Groome was still in love with Tommy Rennseler, and she saw Temple as his usurper. We walked through her icy atmosphere, back into the heart of the shop. Temple said, "I want to tell you something about ancient artifacts. I think it's relevant to Father's death."

"I'm here to listen."

"These things—" She touched the statue of Fortuna. "—exert an influence that's almost sexual. Most dealers, if they're at all sensitive, can tell you about it, because we feel it ourselves, and we see it in our clients. Serious collectors are like lovers. The piece starts to speak to them, because ancient works of art have powers we don't understand. They get inside our minds, just like a sexual obsession. Once that happens, we have to own them. The satisfaction of finally possessing one of these things is enormous. And the feeling doesn't die. The piece keeps on revealing itself, because it has thousands of years stored in it. That's why collectors collect, and sometimes they get a little crazy."

"You're saying a collector could have killed your father to get hold of an artifact?"

She nodded, and I tried to feel what her clients felt, the pull from the stone figures that surrounded us. There was no denying their presence. I pointed to a small stone statue of a well-shaped woman. "Who's she?"

"Aphrodite. Wearing her magic girdle."

"What's magic about it?"

"Anyone looking at it will fall in love with her."

"Some girdle."

"Can you come to Mother's tomorrow night at seven?"

"I'll be there." I handed her the fax with the little cobra on it. "I received this at the office yesterday, about an hour after you left. Who knew you were coming to see me?"

"Miss Groome."

"It didn't come from your fax machine. It was sent at a midtown copy shop."

She slipped her hand into her pocket and handed me a computer-printed note. "I found this on my desk this morning."

It said *Dump McShane. If not, you die.* It was signed Rex.

"Who's Rex?"

"I...don't know."

"You sound a little uncertain."

"It's just that the message frightens me."

"Who has the key to your shop?"

"Miss Groome. No one else."

I looked back toward Miss Groome, whose eyes lifted to meet mine, but now her gaze expressed only indifference, as if I were a transitory human figure among the statues of eternity she served.

I turned back to Temple. "I'll check the security system on the door."

She had an old-fashioned plunger switch in the doorjamb. These can be defeated by slipping a thin piece of steel through and holding the plunger down, so the plunger will think the door is still closed. There were no scratches on it, and there would have been if it'd been defeated. "Nothing here. Whoever came in had a key. This is a lousy security installation, by the way. The movement of the door is always wearing the switch down. You should have an ultrasonic system."

"Can you recommend someone to do that?"

"I'm glad you asked." I sold her on a McShane installation, made my goodbyes, and left her shop. When I turned back, she was still looking at me through the window, her body at an uncertain angle, as if she'd tried to reach out after me, to say something, but had been restrained. Now, as our eyes met, her gaze was as expressionless as the statue of Aphrodite.

I walked across the street and switched on my pocket receiver. I was getting a static-free transmission from inside Antiquity International, Temple's voice coming through:

"That's a very interesting man."

"Do you think so?" said Miss Groome. *"Isn't he a little on the wrong side of the tracks?"*

"That's the interesting part."

A review of my pedigree was not my objective. I switched off the receiver and walked up Madison. I stopped at the Whitney Museum and looked over its granite moat to the people dining below, behind the high glass wall of its basement restaurant. Their lips moved silently, their forks and spoons making no sound as they touched their plates. Tommy Rennseler had walked past here each day, leaving his shadowy imprint. The museum, the art galleries, the antique shops, had been his reference points, his familiar sights, the background against which he strolled, unsatisfied with his fortune. A man who dealt in two-thousand-year-old objects might have known better than to want more; the ancient king who held Ennion's cup had wanted more too, but the cup finally slipped from his hand. Rennseler had caught it, and somebody caught him. The precious cup slipped from his grasp, and time spilled out, along with his kishkas.

I continued along Madison, certain that someone was following me.

Saul Feldman sat across from me in the window of a hole-in-the-wall restaurant, one flight up, at the edge of the diamond district. There were only two of us for supper, but somewhere on the street below there was a third. I didn't mention it to Saul, as I didn't want to spoil his appetite. On the table between us was a maple syrup container, filled with an orange liquid. Saul said, "Pour it on your bread, Jimmy. Go ahead."

We poured the golden liquid on, as Saul continued: "I'm completely relaxed, now that I have my own detective. Everyone should have their own detective." He bit into his dripping bread. "Now I can enjoy chicken fat again. Now I am a man."

"Chicken fat?" I set my bread down.

"Don't be afraid of it. It soothes the nervous system. I'd better have more." He sloshed another layer onto his already swimming bread. "Rita's bought me a life jacket for our white-water rafting trip in Colorado. She said it's the latest design for comfort. When I'm being swept downstream to my death, I'll be able to make comfortable arm movements." He put the bread to his mouth and bit into it. "However, I've been given an alternative. We go up the Amazon. I told her they've got a worm there that swims into your schlong and opens an umbrella."

"What's she going to save in the Amazon?"

"Something called a strangler fig. I ask myself, is this a plant I want to save? It sounds like it's going to come after me in the night."

"Maybe it only strangles other figs."

"I'm making inquiries. But it's not a trip I'm looking forward to. I tell her this and she tells me the boat is air-conditioned. An air-conditioned boat ride up the Amazon. All right, maybe it's not so bad. But then we have to get into canoes. A Jew in a canoe in Peru. This is in Peru, Jimmy. They land airplanes there by flashlight. My wife says the guy who's leading the expedition is a botanist, so it'll be educational. I'll receive an education while I'm dying of malaria. I can see me lying in my canoe, racked with fever, listening to a botanist describe the sex life of flowers. It's not a pretty picture."

"Tell me about Tommy Rennseler, Saul."

"Rita and I bought some pieces off him. He probably screwed us, but now I own the dish some pharaoh ate off after beating my ancestors with reeds."

"What sort of guy was he?"

"Well, he sold old bottles, but a junk dealer he wasn't. I mean, he wore a navy blazer with gold buttons, he had the silver hair, the prominent chin, the distinguished air. A perfect gentleman of the kind I never trust."

"He was an operator?"

"Put it this way—he says the dish is old, and it looks old, it's got the pharaoh's last meal in the cracks, but I'm saying to myself, Saul, watch out. However, my wife wants it and I'm hoping it'll forestall a trip in a rubber raft. So I buy it,"

"But you think you got taken?"

"Look, the dish has papers. You ever buy a dish

comes with papers? Tommy Rennseler had papers for everything in his store. He printed them himself, but he had them. And the fucking pharaoh probably did eat off the dish, but there was something about Rennseler that troubled me, finish your chicken fat, Jimmy."

"A little goes a long way."

"You're afraid of cholesterol? It's a myth. The only vegetable my grandfather ever ate was grated radish in chicken fat and he lived to be ninety-six."

"Tommy Rennseler, Saul."

"He was an intelligent man. He knew how to sell. His dishes had papers. But he was not my favorite person."

"Why?"

"Why, why...it wasn't because he was taking large amounts of my money. I knew I was there to spend. And he was very nice to us, in fact he was wonderful to Rita, very attentive, very charming. Like I said, a perfect gentleman. But there was something underneath that wasn't so perfect. I never did pin it down because I figured why bother? But now you're asking, and I can't answer."

We ordered food no sane person should go near. While we waited for it, the waiter brought chopped liver to hold us, and Saul tried to tell me more about Rennseler: "I felt I wasn't good enough for his dishes. And to tell you the truth, I've neglected the pharaoh's breakfast bowl. It's in my house, displayed prominently, but I never look at it. A bowl's a bowl. Am I getting through?"

"What about Temple?"

"Temple is a different story. A fine person. Sensitive. This murder thing has disturbed her very deeply. Of course a father is murdered, it's terrible, the family grieves. When my head is cut off in the Amazon, the blow will be felt by my family. But in time they'll forget me and go on another trip somewhere. But Temple isn't going anywhere. She's stuck in her father's death. And I'll tell you something—he wasn't worth it. I was not surprised when he turned up dead."

The waiter brought a plate of carp in more chicken fat, and meatballs with raisin sauce. Saul said, "This is food," and I stared at my meatballs, which looked like land mines submerged in used motor oil. "Of course," continued Saul, "Rennseler raised Temple, she's imprinted with all his aristocratic bullshit, and she feels one of the great men of the age has died. It's a powerful illusion, from which my children don't suffer. I already told them: all I do is buy diamonds from Antwerp and sell them in Manhattan—" He sighed. "—so their mother can save the strangler fig."

"Rennseler knew somebody called Rex. He has a key to Temple's shop, and he left her a threatening note."

"What did he threaten?"

"To kill her if she didn't get rid of me."

"What's so bad about you?"

"I'm a snoop. Rex's afraid I'll uncover something."

"All right, so who's Rex?"

"He might be working for the Egyptians. He might've worked for Rennseler. Whoever he is, he's a lowlife. And there must be some big money still out there, from something Rennseler pulled."

"It wouldn't surprise me. Rennseler was a sharper. One of those lean and hungry types. He probably never ate carp in chicken fat."

"It reduces crime?"

"It sedates the mind." Saul cut into his carp. "Now you've got to find Rex, yes?"

"I think he's found me."

"What do you mean?"

"I got a threatening note too."

"What did it say?"

"It was a drawing of a cobra."

"Jimmy, have I gotten you into a dangerous case?"

"I'm not worried about it."

"You're not worried? Maybe you're right. I always worry about the wrong thing. Eat your meatballs."

"*Them* I'm worried about."

"They're delicious. Afterward you drink some seltzer and burp your way back to equilibrium." Saul wiped his brow with his napkin and laid it back on his lap. "What else can I tell you about Temple? She's a fine athlete. I've seen her play tennis. She could drill a ball right through my head. Not that I play tennis. Or anything, for that matter. For sport, I open a can of tuna fish." Saul paused, setting his knife and fork down beside his plate, and a silent belch undulated through his chest. "When Rennseler was selling me the pharaoh's dishes, he had us out to his place on Fire Island, which is where I saw Temple play, in a little white tennis skirt. Oh boy, what a pair of legs. And when she finished with tennis, she went jogging. I would have had two heart attacks. No, she's an impressive human being. Not all that easy to talk to, I admit. She's a little mixed-up, maybe. But a real diamond, not a fake like Tommy. How she could have respected him the way she did is beyond me. She idolized the prick. But you know what? Once or twice, I caught a look in her eyes, and it wasn't love."

"What was it?"

"It was like she wasn't there at all. It's a look I see in a customer's eye when she decides she's not going to buy, she's already gone. And Temple was gone, she wasn't buying Tommy's act. It was as if she saw right through him. And he got uncomfortable, it made him shift gears. He looked like he was afraid of what she might say, and he hustled us all out to the yard for cocktails. My kids give me all kinds of looks, they think I'm a nebbish, but they never look at me the way Temple looked at Tommy. All of a sudden, she was a different person. This is a very intelligent woman, so she probably saw through him now and then. But I guess she couldn't sustain it, because she loved him with a little girl's heart."

The window beside us was open, and the aroma from the kitchen mixed with steam from under the street, and with perfumes, colognes, exhausts, and faint essences of rodents and bugs. I'd known it all my life. It was the breath of the Manhattan dragon, coiling through the streets, a sagacious old dragon who lives off our dreams.

THE ELEVATOR OPENED directly into the Rennseler apartment. I was looking through a decorative iron gate protected by two Chinese temple dogs. Beyond the gate I saw a small vestibule. On the wall, lit by a brass fixture, was a Matisse. A young Haitian maid appeared, and I showed my tin. She opened the gate. Her eyes were anxious. She had her green card, I knew that from the report Manning had given me, but she might be afraid of losing it. I said, "Don't worry, Angelina, I'm just a private detective here to help Miss Rennseler."

She looked relieved by this, and said, "Miss Rennseler is a good person. She is like a sister to me."

"Right, I like her too."

"Would you come this way, please?" She led me through a book-lined den. On either end of a long library table were lamps in the form of rearing cobras, hoods spread wide to support softly glowing tulip shades. Tommy Rennseler had chosen them for their startling beauty, not knowing they were the advance guard of Death.

Angelina showed me into the living room. A wall of windows faced the reservoir; beyond it were twin-towered silhouettes of apartments along Central Park West, from the San Remo on Seventy-fourth to the glowing dome and cupola of the St. Urban on Eighty-ninth. The park lamps played on the dark mirror of the reservoir. The usually deafening street noise was muffled by thick walls, the horns and sirens having the decibel level of chirping crickets and droning cicadas. I was in the lap of luxury, into which Death had crawled. It's enough to make you stop believing in the advantages of Fifth Avenue co-ops.

I heard a footstep behind me and turned. Helen Rennseler had entered the room, on waves of *Narcisse*. At first glance, she appeared no older than her daughter; twilight and plastic surgery. "How do you do, Mr. McShane. I'm sorry we have to meet under these circumstances."

"So am I, Mrs. Rennseler." I stepped away from the window and followed her to a pair of sofas in the ancient Roman style, with large spirals in the armrests, suitable to the imperial household. The couches faced each other over a glass-topped table; under the glass was a scroll of papyrus, its hieroglyphs inscribed in black and red ink.

"Please, sit down, Mr. McShane."

On the end table beside me was a collection of carved miniature figures—jackals, baboons, frogs, snakes, birds, and a tiny pharaoh on his throne. The old pieces did talk, or so it seemed to me as I looked at the little group; they had presence, almost as much as Helen Rennseler had.

"Exquisite, aren't they?" She sat across from me. "And all of that fine work consigned to a tomb. The statues were supposed to get up and dance with the dead." Helen Rennseler was wearing a black silk blouse and a black skirt with large pink hearts. The skirt's long line accentuated her height, but the pink hearts and the dancing dead made me wonder; she seemed a little exuberant for a woman whose husband had recently been murdered. She wore rings on both hands, set with diamonds and rubies, but they weren't in the flashy style of Saul Feldman's stock; they were old jewels, with the stored light of another era. They had authority, like Helen Rennseler herself. The look she gave me was the sort you give to an umbrella stand on a sunny day: I was there, I was of no use to her, and I reminded her of bad weather. But private eyes have tough fabric on their ribs. I smiled, and went to work.

"Mrs. Rennseler, I'm going to go over some things you'd rather forget. But if I'm to be of any help—"

"I don't know that we need any help. But you may ask whatever you think is relevant." She had the kind of society voice produced by a light clenching of the teeth, which gives a tone of continuous disdain. A wall fresco behind her looked as old as Pompeii. A blue glass frame protected the ancient colors from the light. I felt that Helen had a similar glass around herself, to reflect noxious rays from the lower classes.

"Do you think, as the police do, that it was an Egyptian, connected to the antiquities trade, who—" I let the question hang. *Who injected your husband with cobra venom, watched him die of respiratory failure, and then eviscerated him?*

"Yes, it must've been." She looked past me toward the darkening skyline, where a low-flying helicopter was floating by like an illuminated bug. When she turned back to me, her face had composed itself into a smile, of the kind meant to charm by its sincerity and simpleness. Apparently she'd decided I could become an admirer, and she began to tell me about Police Commissioner Brady, whom she'd first met at a fund-raising function last year at Gracie Mansion. She'd found the commissioner to be a very intelligent man, unexpectedly cultured and bright. He knew something about antique art, and she, to his surprise, knew something about criminal investigation, but neither of them could have imagined they'd be meeting again, over a murder. "Commissioner Brady found me most cooperative. He remarked upon the thoroughness of my recollection of events on the day of my husband's death." She went on in this vein, the focus of the narration certain indefinable qualities in herself, which made her a delight to the commissioner and the investigating detectives. Apparently they'd never seen quite such a reliable and accomplished woman at the heart of a puzzling case. Her husband was strangely left out of the account, as if his death had been incidental to her fine performance for the commissioner.

"Would you mind, Mrs. Rennseler, showing me where—"

She pointed to a place on the carpet just beyond the couches. "There." It was as if she were pointing out a coffee stain to the maid.

I gazed at the spot, imagining Rennseler lying there, convulsed by the poison, fighting for breath, and the West Side skyline out beyond him, its towers twinkling for the last time. On all sides are his treasures of the ancient world, solemnly waiting for him to die, as have all their earlier owners, a habit humans have. He's gasping, staring up at his killer, and he has all the useless insight such last moments bring. *I zigged when I should have zagged.* Or something like that. An antiquities dealer fades. Detective John Manning says that murder leaves traces in the air. You imagine that the atmosphere is imprinted, and you take the print, you lift it off the air. I imagined an Egyptian hit man standing here, a specialist hired to handle the will of Allah.

And then I imagined Mrs. Rennseler standing over the body. John Manning says that if a member of the family kills you they'll usually cover you with something before they leave, out of consideration for you and the rest of the family. Tommy Rennseler had been left uncovered. And a good portion of his midsection was gone. Is this the act of a society matron? A woman involved in New York charity functions with the commissioner of police?

The elevator door opened again. Through the doorways of living room and den, I could see the Chinese dogs guarding the gate. They seemed to want to bark. Temple opened the elevator gate by punching the numeric code on a keypad in the wall of the shaft and entered. She was in an emerald linen dress with white and emerald pumps, and she came through the successive doorways with her long, athletic stride. "Sorry I'm late." She leaned down and kissed her mother's cheek, then sat beside her, facing me. "Are you two getting on all right?"

"Mr. McShane has asked some questions, darling. I've done my best to answer him. He seems satisfied. I was telling him about my acquaintance with Commissioner Brady."

"The police were impressed by Mother. Did you tell Mr. McShane about that?"

"We were discussing where your father's body lay." Helen fired that one sharply, and added, "I just hope it won't be too much of a strain on you, Temple. You know what your nerves are."

"Mother, I'd rather if we left me out of the discussion."

Like the concerned mother she was, Helen ignored what her daughter said. "Temple needs a long vacation, but she refuses to take it."

"There's no need for me to take a vacation."

"There's a fortune at stake at Antiquity International." Helen was looking at me. "But I'm sure you know that. I'm sure you know all about your client's financial position."

I was fascinated by the sight of this tigress and her daughter side by side. They both had the same high cheekbones, smoothly rounded chin, and graceful neck, but Temple's presence made comparisons inevitable for Helen, and I saw she wasn't happy with Temple around.

"Your mother's been very helpful, Temple," I said, sitting forward on the imperial couch. Temple's short dress had traveled up her thighs, and my animal nature surfaced for an instant before I kicked it back into its lair, but Mrs. Rennseler had spied the beast. A look of resignation crossed her face, of a woman who's been in a contest with her daughter for a very long time.

"Can you tell me if there was anyone in your husband's circle who had bad feelings toward him?"

"We had a loving circle of friends." Helen Rennseler's eyes were misting over, but it had the look of a practiced art. She put a handkerchief to the corner of her eye. "They've been wonderfully supportive. I can't tell you the concern they've shown. Every day I receive phone calls."

She said this as if addressing an audience on Academy Award night. In a way, she deserved an Oscar. "Had someone wished Tommy ill, we would never have anything to do with such a person. He was a kind, generous man. He was optimistic about people, about life. Do you understand?"

"I do, Mrs. Rennseler. And I appreciate your loss."

"It's, not my loss I'm speaking of. Out there—" She gestured toward the skyline, its ragged outline dark now.

"—there is so much that's awful, and I'm sure you've gotten used to seeing people who find it easy to hate. But Tommy moved in a world of beauty. He helped people find that beauty. He did it thoughtfully and conscientiously. His contacts were with people like himself. I only wish Temple were more like him."

"What the hell's that supposed to mean, Mother?"

"Just that your father and I created Antiquity International."

"Father created it. You had nothing to do with it. You've never had anything to do with it. All you do is shop for clothes."

"You do a bit of that yourself, darling, wouldn't you say?"

"I meet the public every day."

"Is that what you call it? It seems to me you hide from the public."

"Yes," said Temple, changing moods again, "maybe I do." She turned to me. "My first memory is of walking down the street, hoping no one could see me." She turned back toward Helen. "I wonder why a four-year-old should hate herself."

"I'm sure I don't know, dear." Helen stretched an arm languidly out along the back of the couch and looked dreamily across the room, her position unassailable; nothing Temple might say could perturb her. I turned my gaze back to the spot where Rennseler had bought it. I'd seen the police photographs and sketches. Rennseler's head had been facing the west wall. He'd had a view of a glass cabinet, in which a collection of small antique objects were contained, among them a snuffbox with the initial N on it, in jewels. It took me a moment before I recognized the fleur-de-lys. Rennseler had been able to see

Napoleon's snuffbox as he suffocated. Had the snuffbox been attentive? Had Rennseler taken comfort from its silent message, that all great men must fall?

I went to where Rennseler had lain. The two women were watching me. Here the family provider went down, deeply surprised, profoundly regretful, and soon to be history, the cold chemistry of cobras in his heart. "Was there anything disturbed in the room? Any sign of a struggle?"

"No," said Helen. "Nothing was out of place."

"Doesn't that seem strange? That he could be injected without a struggle? You've got stone objects all over the place. If somebody was trying to inject you, or me, we'd start throwing things."

"Tommy would never throw *these* things," said Mrs. Rennseler, gesturing at the collection on all sides. "Not even if it meant his life."

"Maybe he was taken unaware. Reading? Napping?"

"He never napped. He always had enormous energy. We were always on the go. I called us the Treasure Hunters." She stared out the window toward the shadowy towers beyond the park. "I made some remarkable finds."

I tried to bring her back to the point, which wasn't easy with someone for whom the only solid point of reference is herself. "How good was his hearing?"

"There was nothing wrong with it."

"So we have a very quiet intruder, or one he knew. What do you think?"

"I have no way of knowing." Mrs. Rennseler rearranged her skirt with an irritated little tug. "The police think it was an intruder. There are people who don't make noise, who are trained in attack. They're out there training right now. Security means nothing, locks mean nothing, they get in. They can wait for hours without moving. Sometimes they pretend to be homeless, and no one will dare ask them to get out of their cardboard box."

I had the feeling Helen was not overly sympathetic to the homeless. I asked her about the sand the Crime Lab found.

"Yes," said Mrs. Rennseler, "it was Egyptian sand." She rose suddenly, all the pink hearts shifting. "And I accepted that. As did Commissioner Brady, who certainly should know. He sent me a personal note." As Temple had implied, Helen was still a dizzy debutante at fifty-something, her development probably having stopped at her coming-out ball at the St. Regis.

Temple turned to me. "Something *was* changed in the room."

Helen interrupted. "The police weren't able to make anything of that, dear."

"Yes, Mother, but maybe Mr. McShane will." She pointed at the end table to my left. It held a wooden box, the sides carved and the top a playing surface, separated into squares, each of which bore a hieroglyph. "It's the Game of Thirty. The Egyptians played it. Father and I played it all through my childhood, and we'd started playing again recently, in the evenings when I visited." Temple opened a drawer in the box and pulled out a few pieces. "Father had the cobras, and I had the cats. You shake these—" She took out a pair of bone dice and threw them. "And then you move, trying to pass your opponent, which can be complicated, as you can divide your moves among your pieces. The night before Father was killed, we hadn't finished our game, so we left the pieces on the board. Father was ahead. Whoever killed him changed the position of the pieces." She pointed to a hieroglyph on one of the squares. "This is a penalty square. It's the square called Rebirth. It means your piece dies and has to start all over again. The killer had put Father's piece there."

"Would it be safe to say few people on earth know how to play the Game of Thirty?"

"In the gift shop of the Europa Hotel in Giza, you can buy a replica of the board King Tut played on. In Cairo, there's even a video arcade version."

The box had cracks in it, the wood twisted from its long sleep in the tomb. I liked board games, and I liked the look of this venerable playing surface. It wasn't difficult to imagine the hands of long-dead players hovering over it; or the hand of one more recently deceased.

Temple placed one of the little cobras on the board. "What's interesting about the Game of Thirty is that the Egyptians believed it reflected the state of our lives. The squares we land on correspond to what's happening to us at the moment. They played it not only for enjoyment, but to receive guidance from the oracle of the board."

I picked up the polished little cobra and moved it forward a square. Temple smiled, and said, "That's the square of Shu the Inquiring Wind."

"What's it mean?"

"An Egyptian would say that Shu will bring you an answer to some question in your life. Shu gets into things, uncovers them, blows things around." She nodded toward the window, where the drapes were moving gently, and I felt the moist evening air from the reservoir on my face.

Helen intervened: "All this is pointless, Temple. A strong person knows how to go on without looking back. What's important now is that we carry on Tommy's work."

"We, Mother?"

"I advised your father every single day of his life. You don't seem to understand how crucial my help was to him." She spoke as one long used to airing personal concerns before servants who were in no position to judge or benefit by what they heard, and I, obviously, was ranked with them. "I'm only your mother. You don't understand how important my contribution is to Antiquity International. But you'll find out. It's a matter of poise."

Temple looked at me. At the moment, her poise had been eroded. She was rubbing the back of her hand repeatedly along her lip, soothing herself with its slight roughness. I wondered if Helen had hated her from the beginning, in a kind of existential arrogance that refuses to acknowledge the legitimacy of another person's claim to a life, because the only life that mattered, the only real and proper life, was Helen Rennseler's. All others served that great and singular self.

Temple didn't respond to her mother, but instead pointed to the papyrus beneath the glass of the coffee table. "It's so fragile. When it was brought out of the tomb and unrolled, it broke into a hundred pieces." I had the feeling she was talking about her own fragility. "It was restored in Berlin. The teams wore surgical masks, so that not even their breath would disturb the pieces." The look she gave her mother seemed to contain a plea, but Helen seemed only annoyed, as if Temple's breath were disturbing the carefully arranged pieces of her evening. "I don't think, Temple dear, that Mr. McShane is interested in the details of restoration."

"It's an evocation of the goddess Wadjet," said Temple, running her hand over the glass that covered the papyrus. "She's the goddess of cobras." Her fingertip slipped from the glass to the little cobra on the board.

"She's one of the rulers of the Game of Thirty. It was her square my father's leading piece had reached that last night we played. He said to me, *'The cobra protects the ruler of Egypt. I can't lose now.'*"

"We don't have time for games, ancient or otherwise." Helen turned to face me. "Mr. McShane, I'll pay whatever costs you've incurred so far, and then some. But our lives must come back to normal. I say this for Temple's well-being, not my own. Commissioner Brady and his men saw what I was made of. But they saw, and surely you've seen, that Temple is a high-strung sort of person."

"Mother, must you?"

"Must I what, dear? I'm naturally concerned with a business it took your father and me a lifetime to build. The clientele of Antiquity are my personal friends. They're used to a certain atmosphere, of confidence and position."

"What position is that, Mother?"

"Scholarship isn't enough, Temple. What's required is an easy rapport. Your father and I visited his clients at their homes. We went sailing with them. We knew their children. You've neglected all of this."

"What matters is the art. If people want it, they'll buy it. I don't need to go sailing with them."

"How wrong you are, my dear."

"Oh for god's sake—" Temple interlaced her fingers in frustration, then unlaced them. A cruel look crossed her face as she reached toward her mother and brushed Helen's lapel, silently mouthing the word *dandruff.*

"Yes, dear, just the right amount." You had to hand it to Helen, she knew how to return a fast serve. I looked back at the Game of Thirty, whose rules had been known to Tommy Rennseler's killer. To kill Tommy and then arrange the board game so he loses—that showed a thoughtful mockery. Maybe

Tommy had still been alive, the poison killing him as he watched the move being made, the killer smiling and placing Tommy's little cobra back to the square of Rebirth.

"Mrs. Rennseler, did your husband ever mention someone named Rex?"

She pulled back, just slightly, and then recovered quickly. "No, I don't think so."

She was lying. I heard a faint tinkling sound and turned my head. In the hallway a wind chime of blue glass was moving gently in a breeze from a window at the other end of the apartment. Was the Inquiring Wind pointing something out? Angelina stepped into the hallway, underneath the chimes. I turned to Helen. "I'd like to speak to your maid."

"She's told the police everything she knows."

"But you have no objections?"

"I don't care what you do, as long as no one is intimidated," said the mistress of intimidation.

I left mother and daughter to fight it out, and joined Angelina in the hallway. "Excuse me, Angelina. Do you mind if I ask you a question?"

Her eyes darted fearfully, and I said, "You're not in any trouble, okay? Nobody's going to take your job away. I just have the feeling you might be able to tell me something that'd help me. I'm trying to find out who killed Mr. Rennseler. You liked him, didn't you?"

"He was a good boss. He treated me well."

"Did he ever do anything you thought might get him killed?"

Angelina's expression changed, and I saw her taking stock of me. I knew then that she hadn't opened up to Manning, despite his cupid lips. I glanced toward the bits of tinkling blue glass that hung behind her and listened to their tiny chatter, and suddenly she said, "Mr. Rennseler knew how the secret doors of the pyramids work. He told me himself." The look she gave me then came straight from Haiti and was that of someone who'd grown up in an atmosphere of magic. "That's what got him killed, messing around with those pyramids. *Les invisibles* were mad."

"*Les invisibles?*"

"The spirits. Look how he died. By the cobra. No clues. But somebody was here. Somebody came in easy, just like a *bokor*. A voodoo man." A faint shiver ran through her, and I saw that she'd taken an imprint from the air exactly as a Homicide detective would, only her imprint was made on a fabric rich with the weave of sorcery. She was here alone most days, and moved through the crime scene, back and forth over that spot on the carpet where Rennseler had lain, back and forth through the lingering atmosphere of his murder. She said, "A *bokor* has a rattle that makes an evil sound. You know what's in the rattle? The bones of a snake. It was snake power helped that killer get in here." She lowered her voice. "But Mr. Rennseler fooled that snake *bokor*. He was powerful too. A very powerful man. He'd already hidden what they came for."

"What did he hide?"

She looked at me, her eyes narrowing, as the blue glass shards behind her head grew more agitated in the breeze that moved through the hallway. "Something wonderful, I don't know what. He'd just come back from Egypt, and he was excited. He had a treasure. I heard him on the phone a few days before he died. He said, '*Don't worry, it's safer than it was in the pyramid.*' And he laughed. '*Safer than it was in the pyramid.*' See what I mean?" She turned away abruptly and walked back down the hall. Temple was coming toward me.

"Has Angelina been helpful?"

"Yes. So has the Inquiring Wind."

She smiled. "Are you going to become a Game of Thirty player?"

"It seems I already have."

We walked to the gates of the apartment, where the huge porcelain dogs were waiting. Temple laid a brightly polished fingernail on one of the enameled heads. "They're supposed to let their owner know if an evil spirit approaches"

I looked down into the grimacing face of the dog. "You were asleep, pal."

Temple pressed the elevator button. As we waited, I looked at the painting by Matisse, but I couldn't concentrate. I was thinking about snakes and the sound their vertebrae must make when they rattle together in a gourd. And I was wondering what it would be like living in a place like the Rennseler apartment with its temple dogs and treasures. Or dying in it. Especially dying in it. Would every coveted art object become grotesque? Devalued by a dying breath, would it all be contemptible, the ridiculous creations of a deluded species? Sometimes I find myself wondering how I can even carry on a conversation, given the fact of my inhabiting a ball of rock floating in an infinite void, but I muddle through and speak the necessary words. Rennseler's pad, with its art, its papyrus, its view of the park, made me acutely aware of my own tendencies toward wrapping myself in a cocoon of beloved assumptions. As for Rennseler, he'd thought he was safe, but he'd lost the Game of Thirty.

The elevator opened. I stepped inside, and I was surprised when Temple stepped in with me. The elevator doors closed and we rode down together. She said, "Mother wants the business. She and Miss Groome think they can push me out."

"Why should your mother want it? Hasn't she inherited all the money she could ever need?"

"*Lobby*," said the computerized voice of the elevator. The doors opened and we stepped out, into the replica of a Spanish courtyard with a marble fountain bubbling at its center. We walked over to the fountain and sat down beside it, our conversation masked by the water's bubbling. "Mother wants the business because it would give her satisfaction to be known as an authority in ancient art. But she wouldn't know Janus from Neiman Marcus." Temple put her hand in the water and brought wet fingertips to her forehead. "Miss Groome wants it because she thinks I don't know what I'm doing. She's spying for Mother and trying to undermine me."

"Fire her."

"She loved Father, and she gave her life to helping him build the business. I can't fire her." She rubbed her shoulder, then rotated it slowly, as if working out a kink in her neck. "Sometimes when I get anxious, I feel as if another person were wearing my body. It doesn't feel like it's the right size."

"It looks like the right size to me."

The lobby door opened, and a woman entered with her dog. It was a poodle, and it walked at her heel with a subdued gait. Temple said to me, beneath the fountain's patter, "Dogs in Mother's building have to be interviewed by the co-op board. If they're not well behaved, they don't pass the interview, and their owners don't get into the building. I'm surprised they let me visit."

The dog gave us a guarded glance. He looked like he'd

stored up a lot of barks. I turned back toward Temple. She was staring into the lights beneath the swirling water of the fountain as if she wanted to swim away. The damp air from the fountain was heightening the smell of gun oil and neat's-foot from my Beretta and its holster.

She said, "I never should have gone into the business. But antique art is powerful. I couldn't turn my back on it, it was the only warmth I'd ever had. I huddled beside it."

I turned my gaze toward the fountain as she talked, and traced the shiny black tile with my eyes. Whenever a woman employs me, she inadvertently helps me. With what? My assumptions about women; it always comes as a sudden jolt when a woman's real presence shines through the veil I unconsciously lay over her at our first meeting. With Temple, I was still waiting for that presence to shine through. She was a very nice person, very sympathetic, and that's who I was playing to, but I kept feeling that our conversation could be very different. I looked back up at her. "Angelina said your father was killed for something valuable. Something that he hid from the killer."

"How would Angelina know?"

"She's observant, but she knows how to fade into the background. Your father was comfortable with her. And he was excited about something he'd gotten in Egypt. She heard him talking on the telephone about an object that he said was as safe as it was in the pyramid. What would that be?"

"I don't know. Most Egyptian pieces come from tombs."

"Any idea where he'd hide something unusually valuable?"

"You saw the little temple he made, with its hidden

mechanisms. He could hide something under your nose and you'd never know it was there."

"Do you think your mother would know anything about this valuable object?"

"If she does, she'd never tell me." Temple's mood changed suddenly, and I felt her fear, as tangible as the moist air of the fountain. She said, "That note I got, about dumping you or dying. Am I really in danger?"

"If your father's killer didn't get what he wanted, you probably are. Do you want me to put security around you?"

"No! I couldn't stand to be watched."

"We're talking about friendly forces."

"It doesn't matter. Being watched would be awful for me."

"Why?"

She didn't answer. Instead she said, "I'm worried about that fax you got, with the cobra. I don't see how I can let you continue if you're in danger too."

"I know how to watch my back. It's you I'm concerned about. And though your mother is not one of my favorite people, I'm concerned about her safety too."

"Somehow I don't see Mother as a victim." She stood then, her reflection lengthening in the fountain. "Tell me honestly—by hiring you have I put us all at risk?"

"The risk is there with or without me." I took her hand, and we made our goodbyes. I crossed the marble tiles of the lobby to the exit, and stepped onto Fifth Avenue, into the noise from which I'd known temporary escape up above in Rennselerland. Traffic rolled by swiftly, with no mercy from kamikazi cab drivers. Sirens wailed in the distance, announcing various transgressions and emergencies. I let my gaze travel up the side of the building, past its stone floral pilasters and balconied windows, counting floors. Helen Rennseler's drapes were still open, and I could see the light from the living room. The quiet up there had been unnatural. I walked a few blocks to where I'd parked my car. Someone had spit on the window. That was more like it.

SPENT A RESTLESS NIGHT.

When I did sleep, I had nightmares. I arrived at the office feeling less than rested, and Ranouka noticed.

"Out late, were we?"

"I couldn't sleep. Somebody's following me."

"How very upsetting. You should biff him one in the head."

"If I catch him, yes, I'll biff him one in the head."

"Jolly good. Meantime, here are those insurance forms you wanted copied." Ranouka was wearing a ruffled red and gold silk blouse over red and gold striped slacks. A red silk scarf lay against her dark brown throat. The insurance forms were a day late. I was reluctant to say anything about it, as she was more Henderson's secretary than mine, and even that connection was tenuous; she'd told me that the only reason she worked for us at all was because she felt she had a karmic debt with Henderson: "The moment I see Dr. Henderson safely married, I will quit." She laid the forms on my desk, her long silver earrings tinkling as she bent forward. There's music wherever she goes. Her husband's father had been a king in India, hence the name Maharaj. So I had a princess for a secretary. I watched the round form of her royal ass depart in her understated slacks. My gaze was not an attempt to devalue her as a person.

I was still looking over the insurance forms when she buzzed me on the intercom. "I've got an Egyptian detective on the line. Mr. Rafeek Shaddi from Cairo."

I picked up. "McShane."

A thin, nasal voice came over the line. "Hello, Mr. McShane, I have some information for you."

"How much will it cost and where do I send the check?"

"Two thousand U.S. to the Riggs Bank in Washington, please, for deposit in the account of the law firm of Lowell and Connors."

"It goes out today." I opened the terrarium lid and dropped in a dead fly along with a few crumbs from a bagel. My lizard looked up from his heated rock, my little spy from hell.

"Mr. Hassanein Hamid of Antiquity Luxor is most certainly doing business with an individual of violent reputation, a man named Alsahir Azar. I obtained hard facts of interest from Azar himself though I feared for my safety several times."

I closed the lid of the terrarium and sat down at my desk. "What did you find out?"

"Your dead man, Tommy Rennseler, was well known to Azar. They did a bad deal together"

"Without Hamid?"

"Hamid introduced them, at a very wonderful dinner party held by the Antiquity Society at the Nile Hilton. Tremendous business was being done there, all hush-hush."

I nodded. Rafeek Shaddi's voice was as sticky as a fig, and I imagined hush-hush deals were his specialty. "What kind of business?"

"Azar had the ceremonial scepter of Pharaoh Akhenaten up for sale. Solid gold, containing the face of the pharaoh and his wjfe."

"Two heads for the price of one."

"That scepter is worth ten million dollars and your dead man, Tommy Rennseler, stole it from Azar."

"How?"

"He borrowed it to have it tested for age. But when he failed to return it he proved to be a scalawag instead of a scholar. I am being very impressed by your dead man, even though he is dead."

"And Azar got mad."

"He likes to say that his family has been robbing tombs since 1414 B.C. It is a hard fact that for sure they stole the mummy of Amenhotep's son when it was uncovered in 1881. No one, until now, has robbed anything from them. So he was most upset with your dead man, as much for insult as for injury. After all, family pride counts for something"

"So he killed Rennseler?"

"His ancestors have killed with cobra venom for centuries. It is the family trademark."

"Right, people like to keep a nice tradition going."

"For this reason he is known affectionately along the west bank of the Nile as Haja Naje—the Cobra. But he told me that he did not kill Tommy Rennseler. He only wants his scepter back. Someone, he said, has tried to make it look as if he did the murder"

"What happened to the scepter?"

There was a long pause from Rafeek Shaddi. "But isn't that what you are looking for, Mr. McShane?"

I looked into the terrarium. My lizard was nibbling his bits of bagel. Rafeek said, "Mr. McShane, if you find the scepter of Akhenaten, you could be squatting in tall flowers. The Cobra will pay handsomely for its return. By the way, who is employing you?"

"Sorry."

"Of course, I'm only asking," said Shaddi, cheerfully. "Well, just remember, the Cobra is the rightful owner of the scepter"

"Rafeek, are you by any chance also working for the Cobra?"

"Cheerio, Mr. McShane."

Rafeek hung up and I looked back into my terrarium to consult with the lizard. He stared at me, his neck pulsing gently. He'd been partial payment from a pet store where I'd installed some security surveillance equipment. The lizard was worth a hundred bucks. He was a good lizard. I looked at him, and asked, "Who's got the scepter?"

He stared at me, noncommittally. I tapped on the glass. "Ten million bucks. That's what got Rennseler killed."

After lunch, I went to Central Park, where I walked from the Seventy-second Street boathouse along the south shore of the lake. The water sparkled brightly around some teenagers trying to kill a duck with an oar. Joggers were out circling the park, while drug addicts hallucinated along the pathways, their fuzzy kingdoms floating in the warm air. The earth under my feet seemed softer for being surrounded by steel and cement in all directions. I went through a stone underpass, my footsteps echoing as if in a labyrinth of the dead; stone is solemn, and helps reflection. I was reflecting on the scepter and its passage down through the centuries. Akhenaten had commissioned a dream in gold, thinking it would sink with him into eternity. But tomb robbers have dreams too.

I reached Bethesda Terrace and crossed its faded brick toward the crowd gathered around the fountain. She was already there, gazing into the spray. She looked up at me and smiled. Helen Rennseler was dressed in white slacks with a white linen jacket over a lacy little nothing that showed off her trim figure. She held out her hand to me. "Thank you for coming."

"My pleasure. Is this a favorite spot of yours?"

She pointed at the sculpted figures of the fountain. "Health, Peace, Purity, and Temperance." She said this as one who possessed the attributes.

"What did you want to speak to me about, Mrs. Rennseler?"

"Please, call me Helen. If we're going to be friends—"

"Are we?"

"Going to be friends? I hope so. You took me by surprise when we first met, and I couldn't find quite the right response. Perhaps I seemed reticent. I hadn't expected you'd be a cultured man, which you obviously are. Nor had I expected you to be quite so attractive." She said this with a look that might have been called seductive, except for the air of manipulation that accompanied it, which Helen hadn't learned to mask. "Temple told me you were in the air force. I might have guessed it from the way you hold yourself—very erect, very formal. It's not unbecoming."

"Well, Helen, I like the way you hold yourself too." Jimmy McShane is always polite, even when ladies are manipulating him.

"Why, thank you, Mr. McShane. You've cheered me up already."

"Anything else I can do for you?"

"I'm concerned about my daughter's health."

"I wasn't aware there was anything wrong with her health. I understand she's a wonderful athlete."

"Oh yes, she's very strong—physically. But I'm referring to her mental state. Temple has never been emotionally robust. I won't tell you what I've suffered with her through the years, but I'm sure you've seen how unstable she is."

"She's young, Helen. She's allowed to be a little unstable."

"She's not that young. But that's not the point. There are sides of her you haven't seen. You haven't seen her riding a motorcycle at a hundred miles an hour, as if the only thing she wanted in the world was to kill herself. And she's an alcoholic."

"Are you sure about that?"

"Well, she drinks far too much. It gives her Dutch courage. She goes skydiving, she's raced stock cars. She does it to irritate me, of course."

"Maybe she enjoys it."

"Temple now owns an important business. She'll destroy it if she doesn't control herself. Her...mood swings—let's call them that—exhaust her. And me.

This investigation she's begun is one of those swings. It's another of her fantasies, like skydiving. A handsome private investigator, helping her to solve a murder. My god, what's next?"

"Maybe it's a way of grieving for her father. Maybe this is the only way for her."

"She needs to trust me. I can help her to grieve. I can help her with so many things. I have experience, and some people even think I have wisdom. Temple needs guidance. She needs my loving concern." Helen gazed up toward the winged Angel of the Waters atop the fountain, as if to take counsel with another such as herself. "I believe I can make her well."

"So where do I come in?"

"Has she told you that I'm trying to take over the business?"

"What she says to me is confidential."

"I don't want the business. My first concern is Temple. She needs rest, and safe surroundings."

"What safe surroundings did you have in mind?"

"A private clinic. It's not far out of New York. The doctor who runs it is a friend. With your help—"

"I'm concerned, of course."

"Temple trusts you. In a lifetime I've never gained her trust. If I'd had it, things could have been different for us, because I have an unusual energy, Mr. McShane. People often comment on it. I want to share it with Temple—my intuitions, my ability to resonate with others. She needs that. The business needs it. When Temple was a very small girl, we had such fun together. I cherish those memories. That's what's at the core of our relationship, and I want to get it back, for both of us." She looked up at the Angel of the Waters again. "If you knew how many times over the years I've asked myself how I could have prevented Temple's illness. And all I can think is that I should have gotten her to a psychiatrist sooner. That might've done some good."

"Is she seeing one now?"

"No, but I've talked to the doctor at the clinic. He says he can help Temple, but it has to be on a round-the-clock basis. Therapy must be intense, and there are drugs that are necessary also, powerful drugs that have to be monitored. He's suggested a year's program."

"He sounds like a thorough man."

"He's a very good man. A true healer. I've given him a complete emotional picture of Temple. I don't know how much you've seen of her erratic behavior, but I've seen all of it. She can't be reasoned with. It's a chemical problem."

"You've held up under it very well."

"I've a resilient nature. I admit I was terribly upset about your coming on the scene, but once I met you I realized it could be a blessing in disguise."

"If we could get her into the clinic."

"Yes."

"And calm her down a little."

"Exactly. And then start anew."

"And who'd run the business?"

"I'd look after it, of course, along with Miss Groome, and Temple would supervise from the clinic. I don't pretend to be a scholar. It's Temple who has all the art degrees. That's her true calling—not motorcycles, or skydives, or god-knows-what-else. She has a wonderful understanding of art. Shouldn't that be enough? I'd never dream of taking the business from her. She needs it. It's the best thing for her. But she needs to see that clearly, and the only way she'll be able to is if she gets professional psychiatric help."

"Sounds like a great plan to me."

"I'm so relieved you think so."

"I think it's the way to Health, Peace, Purity, and Temperance. I really do."

"Are you mocking me?"

"It's that or push you in the fountain, Helen." I turned and left her there, beside the bubbling waters.

I sat in Temple's store, watching her work. I'd come for an hour and ended up spending the rest of the afternoon. Unless your consumerism is pathological, almost any store loses its excitement after a few hours, as the illusion of the merchandise wears thin and you find yourself in a room with a lot of shelves and a staff of mildly dazed sales personnel. But Antiquity International was a little museum, and Temple was its curator. She was a hypnotic salesperson, her manner enchanting because she herself was enchanted. Miss Groome was in no way enchanted, and had as much charm as a mummified ibis, but she had authority. Clients respected her, and Temple deferred to her. But it was Temple who brought the statues to life. As she spoke about them, the marble forms seemed to soften, releasing their ancient radiance. When the shop closed for the day, I had an odd sensation that something old and venerable had been present with us, and that Temple had evoked it, and that now it would sink back into the stoppered glass bottles and statues for the night, until she called it out again.

There was a Game of Thirty in the shop, and I'd been amusing myself with it. The rules for the game were in a leather-bound book, which contained a reproduction of the board and the meanings for each square, with a brief description of the deity who ruled that square. I'd played a few moves against an imaginary opponent and had progressed from the Inquiring Wind to the square of Maat, the goddess of truth, and there the dice had held me until the lights were turned off and Miss Groome had gathered up her bag and her *New York Times*. "Will Mr. McShane be here again tomorrow?" she asked, as if I weren't there.

"That's up to him," said Temple.

"The shop is very small," said Miss Groome.

"Oh, I think there's room for Mr. McShane," said Temple, with gentle humor.

"Of course, you know best," said Miss Groome, moving past us toward the door, newspaper under her arm and her bag clutched between her long white fingers. She went out, and turned in the uptown direction, enveloped in her malevolent atmosphere. I watched until she turned the corner.

"Cheerful soul, isn't she."

"She lives alone. Father was everything to her."

"So now she's filled with hate?"

"She's not filled with anything. She's empty. And lonely."

"She doesn't wish you well. I'd pitch her gloomy ass out of here."

"I'm hoping to resolve it some other way."

"Right, *you'll* be working for *her.*"

"It feels like that already."

"Give her a year's severance and glowing references."

"I'm bound up with her, through Father. It's hard to explain."

"I saw you at work today. You don't need Miss Groome."

"Perhaps. But she needs me."

Women have feelings that astonish me sometimes, especially in regard to each other, their sympathy cutting through surface irritations to deeper accord. But Temple's feeling for Miss Groome persisted in the face of the woman's obvious design for ousting her. I sensed I'd get nowhere pushing the point, so instead I asked, "Was your father as good as you are at the antiquities business?"

"Much better. He'd traveled more and seen more. For him, 2000 B.C. was yesterday. I've never met anyone more sensitive to the past."

"Your father dealt with a man called the Cobra, whose trademark is injecting people with venom."

"I know about the Cobra."

"You do? And you didn't tell me?"

"I didn't want you wasting your time."

Clients who make decisions for me never help the situation. All I could do was ask, "So what do you know about him?"

"He's an art collector. Wealthy and powerful. But no one ever meets him. Everything happens through intermediaries."

"Your father met him and ripped him off for ten million dollars."

"Who told you that?" The corners of her mouth turned down, and for an instant it looked as if she'd aged ten years.

"I was told by an Egyptian colleague. He seemed in a position to know. Your father took a solid gold ceremonial scepter from the Cobra. It belonged to Pharaoh Akhenaten."

"Father stole Akhenaten's scepter?"

"More or less. Do you know the piece?"

The tension slowly left her face, as she became the curator once again. "The Germans are supposed to have found it when they found the bust of Nefertiti in the 1912 expedition. You know that bust, I'm sure; the woman with the greatest profile of all time."

"I'll take yours any day. But yes, I know about Nefertiti. She was Akhenaten's wife."

"You've been doing your homework, Mr. McShane."

"The history of the world is on computer disk, Miss Rennseler. But I couldn't find any trace of the scepter."

"That's because the scepter was never catalogued. Nefertiti is in the Berlin Museum, but the scepter vanished. The Germans say the scepter was never uncovered at all, that all they found was a painting of it on the throne room wall. But one of the expedition logbooks describes the scepter three-dimensionally, with detail you couldn't get off a painting."

"Well, it wound up with the Cobra. And he was ready to sell it. To your father. But your father stole it instead."

"That's what the Cobra says. You don't know what kind of deal he and Father were cooking up.

Ten million dollars is a bargain for Akhenaten's scepter."

"What do you mean, a bargain?"

"It'd be worth five times that much to a museum like the Metropolitan, but the Egyptian government would never issue export papers for it. If it ever surfaced at the Met, or any other museum, the Egyptians would demand it back. So it had to be handled by someone like Father who could find a private buyer for it."

"You don't think the Cobra killed your father?"

"I know he didn't. Why would he kill one of the few men in the world who could help him?"

"You're not talking fact, right? You're talking feelings?"

"Feelings can be very informative."

"I'm not denying it. But I can't put an intelligence gathering device on feelings and get an audible playback."

"Trust me then. The Cobra didn't kill Father."

"Do you think the killer was the guy who left you the threatening note? Rex?"

"Father went to Egypt just before he was killed, and if he did acquire the scepter, he would have needed help getting it out of Egypt and into America. There are people who facilitate such things. They're not exactly criminals, but they walk a fine line. They're all through the art world, especially the antique art world, where smuggling flourishes."

"So Rex is a smuggler?"

"He might be. Or he could just be someone who knows a certain sea captain, or a certain customs official. These international intermediaries do very well."

"You seem to know all about them."

"Father made sure I did, just in case there was something I really wanted, and couldn't bring in legally. But I didn't have the nerve for it, and I told him so. So he let the matter drop. I never knew who his contacts were."

"My picture of your father is rapidly changing."

"Yes, all right, he did play on the edge. It was foolish of me to give you an idealized picture of him. I'm sorry. But I loved him. I still do."

We were standing over the Game of Thirty, and Temple saw where my piece had landed, on the square of Maat, goddess of truth. She smiled and said, "The Game of Thirty is always right. You heard the truth today."

"I'd like to hear it every day."

"But you might be on a different square tomorrow. Or even a minute from now. Shall we see what's next?" She handed me the bone dice, and I rolled them. I counted the squares and moved my piece, to a square on which another female figure was depicted. Temple put her finger in the square. "Hathor, the cow goddess of love."

"Sounds good to me."

"I want you to have this."

"Have what?"

"The Game of Thirty." She put the dice and the playing pieces away in their little compartment.

I said, "I can't take something so valuable."

"Yes, you can. You're at risk because of me. I wanted to give you something anyway, and you like board games." She closed the drawer and slipped the latch—a thin piece of bone carved into the shape of a jackal's head. "Here—" She placed the ancient box in my hand. "Better than owning Boardwalk."

"Thanks. Thanks very much."

"One square at a time," she said with a smile. "Now, don't you think we should close this shop for the day?"

We did, and stepped out onto Madison. "Where are you headed?" I asked her.

"Just walking home."

"Want some company?"

"Love it. But what about Saul? Don't you have to take him to his car?"

"He's not carrying anything valuable today. His wife's meeting him. He's being outfitted for the Amazon."

She glanced sideways at me, her eyes playing with some thought I couldn't read, but it had to do with me, and I felt the cow goddess of love mooing in my brain.

Temple matched her stride to mine, and our bodies drifted together for a moment, both of us set slightly off balance by our proximity. She looked at me again. "I want things to be normal. I want to have a life."

"You will."

"When does it start?"

"Why not right now?"

"Right now everything is suspended." Our bodies swayed together again; neither of us tried to correct the balance, and I felt the cow goddess of love nudging me with her soft snout. We reached the corner and came apart as we stepped off the curb; even love has to look both ways when crossing against the light. I said, "Yes, things are suspended," but what I wanted to say was that I was suspended there with her, and that her viewpoint was slowly becoming my own. The NYPD had missed something about the murder, she was correct in that, and I felt I'd uncover it. But I wanted the suspension to last. I wanted to dangle with Temple. The problem in working with women is that beauty has its own purpose, to rivet our attention to it and obscure everything else.

We continued on down Madison. Our swaying resumed, and I was mesmerized by the clicking of her heels on the pavement, by the whisper of her clothes and the tiny whirlpools of *Spellbound* that came my way, a part of Temple's own essence blending with the scent as it floated off on its mission, to cloud men's minds.

"Are we going to be friends?" she suddenly asked.

"Your mother asked me that."

"Oh god, I hate being like her. Anyway, what was she doing talking to you? Was she trying to enlist you in her cause?"

"I guess you'd call it that. She thinks you need psychiatric help."

"Did she say why?"

"She thinks you shouldn't jump out of airplanes. Or engage a private investigator. It's peculiar, but you engaged one of the few private investigators in Manhattan who's jumped out of an airplane."

"Did you like it?"

"It has its moments."

"She thinks I do it to spite her."

"Do you?"

"Maybe I do."

"You're a sweet, kind person. Why do I sometimes get a wave of anger coming from you?"

"We all have angry thoughts. It's from living in Manhattan."

"Is that what it is? I think you'd feel a lot better if you fired Miss Groome."

"I can't take my anger out on Miss Groome. She's lonely and sad."

We were crossing another intersection, in front of a car that was inching forward like a nervous bull in a stall. The evening sun was sending shafts of bronze light between the buildings, onto Temple's face. You can't be as beautiful as she is without knowing your place in the hierarchy, yet she hadn't claimed what should have been hers. I had the feeling she'd been knocked around emotionally by guys vastly inferior to her.

"Do you ever lose it?"

"Lose what?"

"Your temper."

"Never. I don't think I've ever raised my voice at anyone. Except possibly mother."

She looked at her reflection in a shop window and ran a hand along her hair. It was a simple enough maneuver, but I found it provocative. I was in the square of Hathor, goddess of love, and the day was ending very differently from the way it began.

She saw me staring at her in the window, and turned toward me. "I want to hear more about you," she said. "I want some of those secrets of yours."

I thought of my secrets, which were really the things I felt people wouldn't understand about me.

I said, "When I was a kid, I'd sit on the fire escape and listen to the voices of people passing on the street. What they said didn't matter. It was the way their voices came close and then faded away. I remember thinking, with a kind of shock, that life was a mystery and the fading voices on the street were clues. And I thought that I was born to solve mysteries." I paused, as crosstown traffic crept by us at the corner, anxiety-ridden drivers craning their necks for a hole they could shoot into. Her hand came into the crook of my arm, resting with a discreet pressure, emotionally still tentative, but it helped to bring the next words out of me. I said, "When you told me about the ancient artifacts and the power they exert, I understood. They were your fading voices."

The sky was turning reddish gold and the windows along Madison were becoming pools of shimmering fire, as if a great Siamese fighting fish were reflected beneath their surface as it swam through the neighborhood.

She said, "Do you remember that game children play—The Cheese Stands Alone? One kid in the middle of a circle of playmates? I had a friend who said that's who I was, the cheese who stands alone. He wasn't talking about dates, or a love life, or any of that. Just about the cheese, standing alone."

"You're not alone."

"I can't expect you to remain around indefinitely. You'll have other cases. There'll be other fading voices."

We continued walking. Our strides were

matched, and we probably looked as if we were a couple, and the Game of Thirty seemed to think we were. But it was murder that had accelerated our feelings. Only when I'd solved the case, and its intensity had been lifted, would we really have a chance to know each other.

SAT IN MY OFFICE, playing the Game of Thirty against Ranouka. Temple had told me that the game trains players for the crucial match they have to play against Death in the underworld with dice made out of their own bones. I figured I needed lots of practice. I had the cats, Ranouka had the cobras, and she had me blocked. "I think, Mr. McShane, that you must remain on that square for a while." It was the square of Tayt, the goddess of weaving, who weaves the strands of our lives from birth until death.

Barbara "Bytes" Jensen looked up from behind her computer as I entered her office on Avenue A. Monitors, modems, computers, and printers sat on a circular desk, where Bytes spun in her posture chair, while beyond her the walls were cracked, the windows filthy, and the floor was covered with tile that was chipped, ripped, and in some places completely missing. Bytes didn't need period-perfect decor, she lived and breathed in the multicolored glow from her Super VGA diwsplay terminals. There was nothing on the directory in the hall to identify her office, and nothing to identify her in the office itself, because like everyone who deals in the illegal buying and selling of information, Bytes is paranoid. She knows that the surest way to stay out of harm's way is to have no identifying numbers of any kind attached to your name—no address, no social security number, no credit card.

She looked up at me now through her large horn-rimmed glasses. It'd taken me awhile to realize her face was actually pretty, because she had no sense of style. Her clothes had the worn-out look of things bought at a thrift shop and were always unflattering; her haircut appeared to have been done at home using a bowl for the outline. Her gestures were awkward and robotic. She was a nerd, and mildly irritated at my dropping in on her now, preferring human encounters to be filtered through a modem. In her business, it was more elegant to handle everything electronically. But I liked going to her office, to watch her move her tentacles. She worked with fiendish glee, hired by private investigators, corporate spies, lawyers, and anybody else playing the information game. Her form of relaxation was to hack her way into a credit card company's files, find some perfect stranger who was deeply in debt, and doctor the account so that it came up paid in full; she called this *mainlining*, as in, "I mainlined somebody's American Express today." She also liked to hack into high school computer files, find the kid who was flunking everything, and make him an A student. This she called *accelerated learning*. Now, without turning away from her terminal, she muttered, "What's up?"

"I want the world, Bytes. I want the secret of existence."

"No problem. All we need is the password." She continued hacking away. Passwords are the key to every computer program, because they block unauthorized entry to government, bank, or corporate files. Bytes has security-cracking programs that strip passwords from the systems she dials into; she has programs that test an entire dictionary's worth of words on a system, racing words past the electronic security gate until the right one turns the key.

"What insidious move am I looking at?" I asked, peering over her shoulder.

"I'm running the names of key executives in this company, because key executives will often, in true modesty, use their own name as the password." Bytes had a list of the honchos of the company she was cracking, gotten from a master file called the Guide to Corporate Executives and Directors, and she was typing them in, one at a time. "Maybe they couldn't think of any other word but their own name. Maybe, like many executives, they don't *know* any other words. Wait—here we go. Bingo." The gateway had just opened. Bytes was inside the brains of another company. If she can't find a password electronically, she'll bribe someone to go into an office and check display terminals, on which passwords are often taped. But she feels this is a crude solution to be used only as a last resort.

I dropped Richard Rennseler's name on her desk. She glanced at it, and asked, "How soon?"

"I'm standing here."

"Instant gratification costs."

"The trail is growing cold."

"Stand back."

Though it's perverse, I enjoy the sensation of seeing intimate details of a person's life called up electronically. The modem on Byte's desk was already dialing its way into the web of information available on all of us, the many threads that weave our image and our destiny. The Game of Thirty had known where I should be today, with the weaver goddess.

It didn't happen instantly; we were able to send out for sandwiches and eat them while Bytes worked. We had time to discuss Bytes's view of the twenty-first century—a prison of data erected around everyone in the name of law enforcement, each of us born with a number that would follow us all our life. Contemplating it made Bytes feel good. "Our government cares for us, and watches over us like our own mother. That's why it keeps gathering data about us. Okay, here comes Richard Rennseler. He banks at the Bank of New York. Started by Alexander Hamilton in 1790, did you know that? It was Alexander Hamilton who said there should be a line separating honest men and knaves." Bytes continued typing. "I bought the bank's password from one of their greedy little assistants. A knave, if you will." Bytes dialed again. She was asked by the program for the Bank of New York's password, typed it in, and watched the screen. "Excelsior." The gate lifted, and the electronic gatekeeper quietly escorted us into the banking records of Richard Rennseler.

"Trouble," said Bytes, pointing to the screen. "Federal tax lien on him. Delinquent on his mortgage payment—look at the size of that payment. Where does he live?"

"Townhouse off Park."

"He can't afford it anymore. Let's look at his credit cards." She brought up Richard Rennseler's Visa, MasterCard, and American Express accounts. "Your man's tapped out. He's running scared. What's he do for a living?"

"Stockbroker."

"Okay, who's in the shit on Wall Street at the

moment..." Bytes piggybacked her way into the data-banks of the Securities and Exchange Commission, following a legitimate caller's access. In very little time, we had a most interesting picture of Mr. Richard Rennseler, brother of Tommy, deceased. It seemed that Richard Rennseler was something of a knave himself.

"Jimmy, why do the windows of your car have that transparent tape on them?"

"It makes them shatter-resistant."

I found a parking spot on Fifth and backed the Shadow in. Henderson pulled the visor down and checked her face in the mirror. "Do I look like a detective?" She was wearing what she called her investigator's uniform, tailored navy pants and jacket. She raised her wrist for me to sniff.

"*Poison.*"

She nodded. "I felt it was appropriate."

We got out, and walked north to Seventy-ninth Street. My former fiancée was a member of the New York City Landmarks Preservation Commission; on our walks together I'd picked up a lot of peculiar information on Big Apple architecture, which I'd made it a point to remember; if I have to watch a building for hours on end, it helps pass the time to know what I'm looking at. I pointed to the old van Horn Stuyvesant residence on the corner. "Few know, or care to know, but that's a French Gothic palace." Its four-story face was alive with concrete sculpture, the windows framed by winglike decorations soaring upward. Concrete webs and curlicues trimmed its balconies and peaked dormers. "See the little gargoyle up there on the end? He protects the palace. An early security system."

"A little gargoyle all alone up there. He's like you. The one who watches." Henderson put her arm through mine, and we continued east to Madison, where I stopped us again. "Postmodern. The chromium cylinder makes it take off."

"Jimmy, this is the Hanae Mori Boutique, for goodness sake. We *shop* here, we don't look at the architectural details. Do you like that black dress in the window? Black is the most psychologically protective color you can wear. Yves Saint Laurent said all a woman needs to be beautiful is a black dress and a man on her arm who loves her."

"So all you need is the dress."

"You only think you love me. What you really love is your solitude. And I love mine. Why would we want to become a couple? I mean, we're in the same office all day long. We'd never be away from each other."

"I'll get another office."

"You have nice broad shoulders and you're good to look at, and I enjoy your company. And after a few more neck adjustments your head will be properly aligned with your torso. But in spite of all this—"

"Yes?"

"Every woman should have five years alone. It's important to personal growth."

We crossed Madison, as Henderson continued:

"When I come home at night I'm exhausted and I feel like nesting. I couldn't do that if you were there."

I pointed to the building that housed the Greek consulate. "A nice piece of Neo-French Renaissance."

"A lot of women are afraid of those five years alone. But not me."

We turned up onto Park, and then onto Eightieth

Street. The trees were encased in squares of sculptured cement, pointed like the teeth of a shark coming out of the ground. The Richard Rennseler residence had a garden in front of it, protected by a wrought-iron fence and ADT Security. A flowering vine was growing up the limestone face of the building and had entwined itself over the first-floor balcony. "Neo-Georgian Regency," I said, and rang. An elderly Irish maid with an attitude answered. "Yes?"

"McShane Investigations. We're expected."

The maid allowed us in with undisguised reluctance. "Come this way," she said, icily. Henderson and I followed. I could see that Henderson wasn't used to being treated like this, and I said to her softly, "Unless they're armed and dangerous, it doesn't mean a thing."

The maid led us into the living room, which was dominated by a massive chimneypiece in marble up to the ceiling. The hearth had large blue and white urns on either side of it. A baby grand piano was set against a wall of Tiffany glass. Crimson brocade covered the other walls as well as the backs of the chairs and couches, in one of which Temple Rennseler was waiting for us. She rose when we entered, and I introduced Henderson.

"That's a wonderful pin," said Henderson, pointing to a pair of twin gold figures on Temple's collar. Temple unpinned it for her. "It's Egyptian. Shu and Tefnut are the Egyptian version of Gemini."

"Are you a Gemini?"

"No, but I should be. I've always felt I had a twin somewhere." She pinned it onto Henderson's collar. "Wear it for a few weeks. If you like it, I can give you a very good price. The Egyptians wore them for protection. There are lots of fakes, dead amulets, the Egyptians called them. The real ones are supposed to be powerful. Let me know if you think it's real."

"It's real, I can feel it."

"I felt it too." Temple turned to me. "Have you been playing your Game of Thirty?"

"Henderson and I are playing. I'm on the square of Deception. What do you think it means?"

"That someone is lying to you." She turned toward the creaking staircase and lowered her voice. "Uncle Richard's coming down. He hates the idea, of my hiring you. He and his wife are on the outs, so he's in a lousy mood. She's at their place on Martha's Vineyard."

On which I knew Rennseler had taken a second mortgage. Did the wife know that Rennseler was starting to circle the drain? Was she clearing out while there was still something to get? I slipped my radio fountain pen into a container of other pens on a small writing desk in the corner of the room, just as Richard Rennseler appeared in the doorway. "Good evening," he said to me coolly, but when he got a look at Henderson his manner improved. I said, "My associate, Ann Henderson."

"A pleasure to meet you." Richard Rennseler held out his hand to her. "I hadn't expected a lady detective. Is it common?"

"Women are very well suited to investigative work. We're more observant than men, and more meticulous." Henderson is never short of confidence, but Richard Rennseler's smile was confident too, and I saw the resemblance to the brother then, in the easy charm, the avuncular manner, and the sexual hunger. Some guys never quit. He arranged the seating, putting himself across from Henderson, in the circle of living room couches and chairs. Then he looked at Temple. "Well, this is your show, my dear."

"They know my feelings, Uncle Richard, and so do you. I believe we can go deeper than the police did."

"I'm all for anything that will bring you peace of mind." Rennseler spoke to her, but his gaze came back to Henderson and lingered. The maid came behind him with a silver tray on which a liqueur glass and a single chocolate were presented. Here you lifted your hand and whatever you wanted was placed in it. How would it feel to have it slip away? Would it make you want to kill? "Anyone else care for something? No? Forgive me if I indulge. I made a promise to myself long ago that nothing was going to interfere with my happy hour."

I said, "You go ahead and be happy, Mr. Rennseler."

"I've found that simple pleasures restore the soul." Rennseler popped the chocolate, not as one who is going under financially, but with an air of deep contentment. Maybe he was trying to trick the gods.

"Mr. Rennseler, you were close to your brother?"

"Very."

"Did he have any sort of quarrel going with anyone?"

"Certainly not."

"An enemy from earlier days?"

"Tommy dealt decently with everyone. He made a great deal of money, but he made it fairly." Richard Rennseler said this with his gaze on Henderson.

I continued: "Did your brother ever mention a man called Rex? Someone who could help him get things quietly into this country?"

Temple intervened: "Father brought things in illegally. I'm sure this is no surprise to you."

"Tommy never discussed business with me."

Temple leaned forward impatiently. "Richard, don't be ingenuous. Father smuggled artwork. You knew it. Mother knew it. We're trying to find out who helped him."

"I'm sure I don't know."

I said, "It might help you if you remembered, Mr. Rennseler, because it's possible that Rex thinks you have something valuable, something Tommy entrusted to you."

"I don't know what you're talking about."

"Don't you? Well, that's too bad. Your brother was killed for it."

Rennseler did not react to this, his gaze remaining steady, and then it returned to Henderson, appreciatively, as if he didn't have a concern in the world, except how to get to know this young woman better. But Temple intervened again: "Richard, Father did something very stupid. He stole an extremely valuable object. And he had help, from someone who may have then killed him in order to get the object himself."

"And what object was this?"

"An ancient Egyptian scepter. Please, Richard, do you have any knowledge of it?"

"None."

"Because if you do, Mr. McShane thinks you might be in danger."

"I appreciate Mr. McShane's concern. I'm sure he cares a great deal about me." After firing this off, Rennseler softened again, remembering that what mattered in this meeting was the charming young woman seated across from him, a welcome addition to his happy hour. Henderson matched his smile with a big one of her own, which made her look like a mischievous Pekingese. She said, "We know so little about this last acquisition your brother made. It could be the key to everything." She put her hand out, a peculiar movement, as if she were brushing aside an invisible web between them.

Rennseler said, "I know nothing about any irregularities in Tommy's business. His world was museum functions, gallery openings, charities. He didn't call himself the owner of Antiquity International. He called himself the host. Your host, Tommy Rennseler. That was how he conducted business, as if he were entertaining friends. He would find something for you which you'd treasure, and which would also be a sound investment. If you were wise enough to take his advice, you'd never regret it. I never detected the slightest hint of anything criminal in his activities."

Still smiling her Pekingese smile, eyes crinkling, Henderson asked, "What about Hassanein Hamid?"

"Mr. Hamid was a friend of Tommy's, and is still a friend of Helen's. I certainly did *not* think of him when I heard about Tommy's death. I've accepted the police conclusion about a network of underworld suppliers in the Middle East." Richard Rennseler turned to his niece. "I'm sorry, Temple, but I don't think anything can come of this investigation."

He was lying. The only real information we'd get from him would be through the bug I'd stuck in his pencil box. But it might not hurt to shake the lion's cage a little and see if a mouse ran out. "Mr. Rennseler, what's your connection to Gordon Ferriter?"

Rennseler's expression registered the first genuine emotion of the afternoon, total surprise, tinged with alarm. "Why...he's...he's a client."

"Business okay, is it? You're giving Mr. Ferriter good advice?"

"That's none of your business." Rennseler was rebounding fast. He turned to Temple. "I think we've gone far enough."

She said nothing for a moment; it seemed as if she wasn't there, and I certainly didn't blame her. Then she moved with a little jolt, as if her uncle's anger had only just touched her. She said, "Have I upset things?"

"Yes," said Rennseler, "you've certainly upset things." He was on his feet. She rose with him, as if on a string. They both seemed unconscious of anyone else being in the room. I'd pulled the plug on Rennseler's happy hour, and anger was contorting his face. "To bring this person into my home—he's nothing more than a blackmailer. You might be able to do this sort of thing with Helen, but not with me. I won't stand for it. Do you understand me?" He was cracking, poor slob. Financial ruin can make men crazy. He grabbed her by the shoulders and shook her as if she were the cause of his ill fortune. Temple went rigid for an instant, and then her body seemed to lengthen—that peculiar adjustment in her posture that Henderson had noticed. It was like the movements some birds will make, to appear larger; but she did nothing else to defend herself, which only made Rennseler crazier. He shook her again, and shouted, "I won't be treated this way by you!"

"How about by me?" I grabbed him by the wrist and twisted it backward.

"How dare—" His words were choked off by the pain of my thumb on the nerves at his wrist.

I said, quietly, "Temple's my client." I had him bending forward in an awkward bow toward Temple. She watched, fascinated, and made no attempt to interfere with my putting her beloved uncle to the floor. I found that interesting.

"Brigid!" he cried. "Call the police!"

I let him go before he fell. "That won't be necessary, Brigid. Your boss doesn't really want the police, do you, Mr. Rennseler?"

"Get out!" He turned to Temple. "Are you satisfied?"

She looked away from him, toward an antique marble head of a woman, its features almost totally worn away, and for an instant Temple appeared worn out too, by the imperial Rennselers. I headed toward the door, with Henderson beside me, and Temple behind. Brigid looked smugly satisfied now that her suspicions about me had been confirmed. I said, "You remind me of my sainted mother."

"That'll be all, Brigid," said Temple, and when the maid was gone, she said, "Can I go with you? Somewhere? Anywhere?"

"Come on," said Henderson, and put her arm through Temple's. We walked out together onto Eightieth Street. The night was warm, and the smell of Rennseler's flower garden was in the air, only slightly cut by bus exhaust and other floating poisons. I said, "Sorry if I upset things, but you shouldn't have to stand for that kind of treatment. Are we still in business?"

"Yes, still in business."

Henderson kept her arm through Temple's. I let them get ahead of me, and checked my pocket receiver, through which I got a good signal from the radio pen I'd left in Rennseler's living room: "*You're getting the last of my money and want you to get this detective off me... His name is McShane... What do you mean, let it go? I want him stopped.*" On the phone with his lawyer. Or someone heavier. I heard him slam the phone down, so I put away the receiver and caught up with Temple and Henderson. The night sky had a silver radiance from low clouds absorbing the light of the city, and against these clouds the dark shapes of high apartment houses seemed to move like hulking giants from another planet. A gentle breeze blew over us as we reached Lexington. I noticed we were passing the old Vincent Astor residence. It has some nice travertine limestone on it, which I refrained from commenting on; Akhenaten's architect would have appreciated it, but Henderson didn't care, and Temple was too depressed.

We walked over to Third Avenue and went into a bar. "I look a wreck," said Temple, straightening the shoulders of her jacket as we passed the bar mirror. She was wearing one of her soft silk blazers and a soft blouse with large lapels, which her uncle had crushed. Henderson led her to a table, while I made a phone call to a stakeout man I worked with. He was expensive and usually hired only for high-paying corporate espionage cases, but now that ten million dollars had been stirred into the pot I figured we could afford his expertise. Bobby Booker answered from his apartment in Harlem, with the sound of his parakeets in the background. "Yeah, what?"

"Bobby, it's Jimmy."

"Oh, okay, wait'll I shut these fuckin' birds up. Shut the fuck up!" The birds quieted down. "Sorry about that. What's happening?"

"I've got a bug in number 170 East Eightieth. It's in a room on the ground floor facing the street, so you'll get a good signal. Stay on it every evening between seven and midnight until I tell you to shut it down."

I hung up and joined Henderson and Temple at the

table. It was beneath a slowly turning ceiling fan; the lights in the fan cast reflections on Temple's dark, slicked-down hair. She turned her head toward the mirrored wall beside us, still trying to straighten her outfit; as far as I could see it was already straight, but her sense of herself had been dislodged. She turned away from the mirror and looked at me. "What was the point of your question about that client of Richard's?"

"Your uncle handles his investments."

"And?"

"There's an SEC investigation going on. It's confidential, but my info broker pulled it up. Your uncle handles accounts on what's called a discretionary basis, which means he makes all the moves and doesn't have to consult his client. But for the past year, he's been buying stocks for clients and journaling the trade to his own account. In other words, he's been the one making the dough. But this particular client finally got wise to it, and now the whole thing is falling in on your uncle. It's noteworthy that he got away with it for as long as he did in the most regulated business there is. He was making false entries and issuing dummy statements. He really is a brilliant guy." I was drinking some kind of sparkling fruit essence. If it weren't for Henderson reforming me I'd be drinking dry martinis and getting lushed to the nuts. In the presence of two females this could only end badly. I lifted the fruit essence bottle. It was tinged a cool, pale blue, the color of virtue. "So that's the story on Uncle Richard."

I was looking for a reaction from Temple, but I saw nothing. She might've been hearing about the activity in an anthill.

"Your father is murdered at a time when your uncle is

in trouble. I don't understand the situation, but my motto has always been—when you don't understand a situation, look for the profit motive." I watched the shadow of the turning fan cross her hair. "So how does Uncle Richard profit from your father's death?"

"He's in the will, naturally. He and my father had joint investments, of many kinds. The police knew all this. It didn't constitute a motive for them because Uncle Richard is—or was—so successful."

"So what do we do with him? Do I look for proof?"

"If he did it," said Temple, "I want to know." She paused a moment, then continued. "I have nightmares about Father. In the nightmare he begs me to catch his killer." She had torn her napkin into little pieces and was trying to fit the pieces back together again, like a jigsaw puzzle. "He tells me to remember Canopus. Canopus was a god of the Nile delta. I have four Canopic jars from the mortuary temple of Ramesses III. They once contained the pharaoh's mummified organs. As you know, Father's organs—" She let it hang. "I didn't see Father's body. Mother contacted me after the police had removed him from the apartment. But in my dream, I'm with him in the living room. I'm staring down at him, and he comes to life and begins to talk to me. It's horrifying."

I was studying her face, with its flawless features that went so rapidly from animated to dead flat. She said, "I'm afraid of this Rex person. I'm certain he's watching me."

"Yes, I think you're right, he is watching. But you don't have the scepter, so you don't have to worry."

"Why are you looking at me that way? I told you I don't have it."

"Sorry. I'm on the square of Deception. It makes me think everybody's deceiving me. Uncle Richard certainly was."

Temple turned to Henderson and nodded to the amulet she'd pinned on her collar. "It looks very good on you. Please keep it."

"Oh, god no," said Henderson, "I couldn't."

"Yes, I want you to have it." Temple reached across to Henderson's collar, and settled the pin more carefully.

"Thank you," said Henderson. "I don't know what else to say."

"I know you have good feelings toward me. And the pin does do something for you."

"It'd do something for anyone," said Henderson.

"No, it's a match. I know when my pieces are happy. It wanted to be on your collar."

I sipped my sparkling water. Temple was rubbing the rim of the glass along her lip, the way she'd earlier rubbed her hand there, with a nervous sawing motion. "We have a house on Fire Island. It's almost always empty. If either of you ever want to go out for a weekend, let me know." She had a need to reach out, to give. She was the cheese who stands alone, and it was getting to her. I wondered if she'd give her whole store away eventually. Maybe that's what Helen and Miss Groome were worried about. She finished her second Scotch as soon as it arrived and set the glass down with a smile. "Screw them all, right?"

"Who?" I asked.

"All the great ladies. My mother's friends. I've disgraced myself with them dozens of times. It's been almost my only fun in life."

I knew she wasn't joking, but it's hard to accept suffering in the rich and beautiful; you think they shouldn't have to struggle with anything more serious than hair and make-up. I felt, like every idiot since time began, that all she needed was my company. But when those strange blue eyes fell on me, I saw the painful depths of her solitary nature. She read my thoughts, and said, "The only really suicidal thing I do these days is maintain contact with Mother."

"Break off with her."

"I could never do that!" She suddenly sounded a little prissy, and very much like her mother. She pushed away her empty glass. "I suppose I'd better get back. Richard will be expecting me whether or not—" She stood. "—he murdered my father."

I stood with her. "Temple, did your uncle ever knock you around before?"

"No. We've been very close since I was a child. He took me to museums every Sunday." She turned toward the wall mirror again; its glass was overlaid with a design of gold threads that caused a fine fragmentation of her image, and it gave me an uneasy feeling.

I took a computer printout from my pocket. "This is a rundown of Uncle Richard's life-style. He's been spending a million bucks a year on his townhouse in Manhattan and his house on Martha's Vineyard; his kids are costing him two hundred grand a year at Hotchkiss and Yale. His dues and bills at the Racquet, Brook, and Piping Rock Clubs are another two hundred grand. He has a hundred-thousand-dollar speedboat anchored at the Seventy-ninth Street marina, and the little things add up. Now he no longer has a license to buy China Light and Power at four bucks a share and sell it for six. Maybe he thinks about killing someone. Give it some thought."

"All right, I will."

"Your father liked hiding places. Here's a list of his safety deposit boxes."

She ran her eyes down the list, then looked back up at me in surprise. "How did you find these?"

"My information broker dug them up."

"I'm impressed."

"Why?"

"There are two here I've never seen before."

"You'd better check them. I have the feeling there's money in them. Or even a golden scepter."

"Maybe you've already earned your fee." She looked at us, as if wanting to give us an embrace, and I kicked myself for not meeting her halfway, because in the next moment she turned abruptly and left. We watched her go, back to the street and the lights of the avenue. The wind blew through her sleek coiffure. She smoothed it down with an impatient move. She was crossing the street now, past a line of cars waiting for the signal to change, their headlights giving her face the cold white cast of a black-and-white photograph. She reached the far corner, where she stood looking back in our direction, as if having second thoughts about ending the evening. She was in front of a building of somber brown steel and dark glass. Its featureless facade framed her momentarily, like a brash commercial graphic. She was the loneliest person I'd ever met, caught within an isolation that seemed impenetrable. She finally turned, and walked on back to an uncle who'd just brutalized her. Why was she so devoted to her cruel family? Henderson and I would have been happy to spend the evening with her, and I knew she liked us. Instead she was returning to Richard Rennseler's house. Was he such a sympathetic person? I asked Henderson what she thought of him.

"He was undressing me the whole time we were there."

"So was I."

"No, you weren't. You look at me with a hangdog expression, which is actually semi-endearing, but Mr. Richard Rennseler is a letch."

"Tell me more."

"A creepy letch. I felt his penile ectoplasm probing me in private places."

I pushed my hat back on my head. This was a new one. "An etheric dick?"

"Sensitive women can feel it."

"I've lived a long time, Henderson. It's the first I've heard of it."

"Well, now you know."

"Henderson, if you ever feel my etheric dick probing you, I want you to tell me about it."

"It wouldn't happen, Jimmy. You're a gentleman."

"Maybe I wouldn't be able to help it."

"Yes, you would, that's just the point. A man is a letch or he isn't. Richard Rennseler is a letch. He enjoys making women feel uncomfortable. He's not evolved enough to know when his penile ectoplasm comes out of him, but he gets a sensation he likes. And he was getting lots of it in his living room tonight. I wanted to scream."

I ordered another sparkling fruit essence. I felt I needed it now. "How about if you're walking down the street, and some guys look at you?"

"If one of them's a letch, I'll feel his ectoplasm poking me in the butt."

"From how far away?"

"Plenty far away."

"No defense against it?"

"Not that I know of. I wish there were." Henderson

looked at me for understanding on this delicate subject between the sexes. Her eye shadow was faintly iridescent, and I was close enough to see the careful gradations of color she'd achieved. That's what I concentrated on, the subtle tint around her eyes, rather than how close her leg was to mine. The last thing I wanted was for my etheric dick to start acting up during a moment of understanding.

"So Richard Rennseler is a letch. Does it make him his brother's murderer?"

"I'm sure he did it. You saw how violent he is."

"Yesterday you thought the wife did it."

"Well, maybe they did it together. Or maybe he's in it with this Rex person. Jimmy, can we get out of here? I want to clean my aura with some summer air."

I laid a couple of bills on the check, made a note in my expense account book, and headed toward the door with her. As we hit the street, a warm breeze blew over us, the heat of the day radiating back out of the island of cement beneath our feet. We walked around a little, past the rose red Georgian townhouses with their bow fronts and iron gates, and then over to Second Avenue, past Boccaccio, the restaurant where Irwin "Fat Man" Schiff was given two in the head by an unknown gunman, following dessert and some bad checks Fat Man laid on the Mafia. At least he got to eat dessert. I didn't mention it to Henderson, as she was cleaning her aura. "So," I asked, "what about Temple?"

"Well, I'd have to examine her tongue."

"Without examining her tongue."

"Her liver is stressed. And not because she drinks too much, but because of pent-up rage. If Uncle Richard shook me the way he shook Temple, I'd have bashed his head in. You were in back of her when he grabbed her, you couldn't see her face. I thought her head was going to explode, there was such a wave of suppressed anger that went through her. Her brow was so compressed the parietal bones actually moved. It was one of the saddest things I've ever seen. People like Temple don't live to old age."

"Do I have to worry about her bumping herself off?"

"Not at the moment. She wants to find out who killed her father." Henderson twirled her small purse on its strap. "Her problem is she's the chameleon type, always changing, trying to blend. Chameleons try to be everything to everyone. Temple's probably happiest when she's exhausted, because then she doesn't have the energy to be a chameleon. Then she's herself, but she'll be almost asleep."

We headed back toward the car. I checked buildings for security system stickers the way kids count license plates—Holmes, TAG, Central Station. Henderson said, "She's the kind of woman who'll do anything to secure a relationship. She's probably been groveling to that family for years. You heard how shocked she was when you suggested she break with her mother. I'm sure they squabble all the time, but I'm also sure they've never told each other the truth." She poked me in the back. "Straighten up."

I straightened. She said, "Sometimes I want to go right over to people on the street and adjust them. I know their lives would be so much better."

We found the car and got in. I took a mint-flavored toothpick from the glove compartment and stuck it in my teeth. Then, by force of habit, I pushed in the cigarette lighter; when it popped I took it out. "Ever try smoking a toothpick?"

"Do you still miss smoking?"

"Only when I breathe." I pulled the Shadow into traffic and headed west.

"What I'd really like," said Henderson, "is for a man to brush my hair for ten minutes every evening while I tell him about my day."

"This doesn't sound like a hard assignment."

"But he really has to listen. He can't just be thinking about sex."

"Give me the hairbrush, I'm ready."

"I'm talking about the man really being present. If he's only pretending to listen while he's waiting for the sex to start, he's not accountable."

"Guys don't like being accountable, Henderson."

"Sorry, those are the ground rules." I could feel her staring at me. She said, "You're rock solid, I know that."

"Thank you."

"And dependable men are scarce."

"More, more."

"But your aggressive liver scares me."

"There's more to life than liver."

"I think you might be addicted to violence."

"If somebody screws around with me, I want to kill them. Is that so violent?"

"When you grabbed Richard Rennseler's wrist, I saw how much rage is in you. That's why we *have* to work on your liver. Because as it is, you're too scary for me to think of in romantic terms. Even if you brushed my hair and listened to me tell about my day, I'd always feel brutality in the background."

"There's brutality everywhere. See that BMW ahead of us? That's a dope dealer's car."

Henderson peered at the car, trying to see the driver through the back window.

"No, you're looking at the wrong place. Look down at the trunk. It's got a bullet hole in it. A bullet hole in a Beamer, that's a dope dealer."

But Henderson had lost interest, in dope dealers, and my liver. She was touching the antique pin of Shu and Tefnut on her collar. "Temple giving me this was such a strange and overly generous gesture." She pulled down the mirror on the visor and looked at the pin. "I think she's the one on the square of Deception. She's deceiving herself in some way. I just wish I knew how. It's strange, but when she gave me this pin I thought—here's the answer. She's giving you the answer." Henderson studied the pin in the mirror. "That's the key to Temple. I'd bet on it."

"**S**HE'S EXPECTING YOU," said Miss Groome from behind her desk. She had the presence of a cuneiform tablet, as if she'd been chiseled out of stone and baked. Tommy Rennseler had probably hired her for just this quality. Miss Groome was perfect for the antiquities trade; you'd never doubt her when it came to authenticating a piece because she looked like she'd been dug up with it, but she was touchy, and I rubbed her the wrong way.

"And how're you today, Miss Groome? The world treating you right?"

"I'm fine, thank you." She dealt with me as she'd deal with a speck of dust in the eye—a momentary irritation to be blinked away. Private investigators, she'd rightly reasoned, come and go, but she was mistress of the pharaoh's chamber. This was going to be her store.

I went down the hallway, past a row of terra-cotta masks on the wall, their faces leering at me out of ancient dreams. It wasn't hard to imagine Miss Groome's face in terra cotta beside them on the wall. I tapped on the office door and entered. Temple was at her desk. She was washed out, with circles under her eyes. She caught my look, and said, "I got sloshed with Uncle Richard last night. He apologized for shaking me and wept some bitter tears about going broke. My family's not so bad when we're all drunk." She opened her desk drawer and took out a datebook. "This is Father's. I found it at Uncle Richard's after he passed out. I was blind myself, but I managed to rifle his office. I thought you'd want me to. That's why I went back. He had several of Father's things, I don't know why."

The datebook was empty, except for days marked with the initials C.B., followed by numerical entries in the thousands. "Who's C.B.?"

"Charles Brand. He was a client of Father's."

"The numbers have to be dollars."

"Yes," she said, her voice indicating that she'd come to this conclusion, reluctantly.

I thumbed through the datebook again. "It adds up to two hundred grand. So, money changed hands. We don't know which way."

"We do. I do." She'd hesitated a moment before saying it, and now her eyes were guarded. She got up from the desk and stepped toward a large jade plant in the corner of the room, its branches spread like a gnarled, many-armed tropical deity. She ran her fingers lightly over the rubbery leaves. A bad hangover hadn't darkened her ensemble. Her summery linen suit, which should have been wrinkled from sitting, was not; she had a kind of control over how she sat, so that nothing creased. Compared to hers, my suit seemed to be made out of used tin foil. Her hair, severely parted, glowed in the beam of the track lighting that shone on the jade plant. She turned back toward me. "I opened the safety deposit boxes you uncovered. They contained two hundred thousand dollars in cash. If I didn't have such a headache I'd give you a happy smile."

"What makes you think it's the two hundred thousand entered here?"

She returned to her seat behind the desk. "Charles Brand probably paid Father for items that never went on our books."

"Tax free."

"Yes." She took another datebook out of the desk and opened it. "My own calendar shows that on the days in question, Father had lunch with Charles Brand."

I glanced over her shoulder at her datebook. Her writing was tiny, precise, almost calligraphic. Every single fifteen-minute slot had an entry, mostly compulsive instructions to herself: 9:15—call for flowers. 9:30—call Newark Museum. 9:45—open boxes from London. The datebook had one other peculiarity. In several places the handwriting slanted to the left instead of the right.

"Does someone else make entries for you?"

She looked startled, until I pointed to the left-slanted writing. Then she smiled, and said, "I can write with both hands. I've always been able to. I was naturally left-handed, but Mother insisted I be right-handed. Wasn't that thoughtful of her? She felt left-handedness was a handicap. So I learned to write both ways. It was one of the reasons I fantasized that I had a twin. My twin's the left-handed one. And he leads a very different life from mine."

"How is it different?"

"He's more adventurous. And he defends himself better than I do. He isn't frightened of Mother."

"And you are?"

"I think Mother's capable of—" She broke off.

"Murder?"

"Mother has no moral sense. That doesn't mean she'd commit murder."

"Let's get back to the two hundred thousand bucks. You figure your father sold things to Charles Brand on the quiet?"

"Yes, but not from our store. I keep our inventory records, and nothing can get lost, or moved, and most definitely nothing could have been sold without my knowing it."

"Could your father have sold Brand items from his private collection?"

"I know the pieces Father owned. I've known them since childhood. I used to play with them, very carefully. I had a statue of Callisto on my bed table when I was five and I still have it because Father would never sell the pieces he loved. They were part of our life, like old friends." She paused, then added, "They've been better friends to me than my friends have been."

"How's that?"

"Statues are patient. They wait."

"What are they waiting for?"

"For us to catch up to them. They want us to be wise the way they are. And even when their heads get knocked off, they never blame anyone."

"Have you knocked any heads off?"

"I dropped Callisto. I was only seven. I had a nightmare, and I did it in my sleep. Mother was furious, but Callisto forgave me. When she came back from being repaired, she never accused me." Temple smiled. "Too crazy for you?"

"I talk to my lizard. He might as well be a statue. So what was the two hundred grand from Brand for?"

She put both datebooks away, faced her computer monitor, and brought up the Brand account. "Here's what Brand bought from us, legitimately: a Roman necklace—strung gold medallions of a child goddess."

Her fingernail touched the glowing screen. "But that was two years ago." She scrolled through a description of the piece to the next purchase. "Here's the only other thing he bought, an important piece, a statue of the same goddess. And that was almost three years ago. Obviously, Father sold him other pieces more recently, but they were never entered on the computer. I have no idea what those pieces were." She swiveled back toward me, and her face showed the disappointment she felt toward her beloved father, who'd worked a deal with Brand that never went into the company records.

I sat down beside her at the desk, in a chair whose arms were shaped like crouching lions, on which I placed my hands. The chair knew Tommy Rennseler's secrets, as did all the statues in the room, but their stony minds were cluttered with secrets, of all their owners; what was one more? Why bother to break the silence of centuries? "So now we know for certain that your father was selling pieces you knew nothing about. I wonder if Rex was a secret partner of his, someone who handled the dirty side of the business."

"It's possible." Her eyes wandered to a Roman player's mask on the wall. The eye sockets were hollow and dark and unrevealing. "When I think about it, this person Rex might have been arranging illegal sales for years. But I'm lost. All I have is what's in the computer." She turned back to it and hit the PRINT button. The printer dispensed the information she had on Brand, and I took it. "Got anything else for me?"

"Nothing really useful."

"Can you tell me more about Akhenaten's scepter?"

"It was created by the same sculptor who made the bust of Nefertiti. That alone makes it incredibly valuable.

The detail on the scepter is supposed to be magnificent. It showed Akhenaten and his child bride. She was also his daughter."

"He married his daughter?"

"To protect the bloodline. It was politically necessary, otherwise the pharaoh could lose his power."

"Now that's a political animal. Or maybe just an animal."

"You have to take these customs within the context of their time."

"They screwed their daughters and worshipped crocodiles. That's some context."

"If you worship crocodiles, you're not going to turn them into handbags and make them extinct. Don't judge the ancients too harshly." She opened her datebook, and I watched her write my name in for the previous fifteen-minute segment.

"Well," I said, "you'll know I was here."

She looked up, and seemed surprised that I was there at all.

Bytes drew a blank on the Community Bank of Ridgefield, Connecticut, where Charles Brand did his banking; she said it might take her twenty-four hours to crack the password. I didn't feel like waiting, so I took a little ride up the Hutchinson River Parkway to Fairfield County, richest per capita county in the United States. On Route 33, I drove past thirteen miles of pseudoclassical mansions, as well as hyper versions of pseudoclassical mansions, one of which had red flags in the yard for guests landing in rented helicopters. I drove my humble Shadow into town and parked alongside a hot dog vendor whose menu was in French. I spent two bucks and had *Le Hot Dog Choucroute Alsacienne Supreme.* Then I walked to the bank, carrying my briefcase, which happened to have video lenses in the hinges. I was wearing a badly made suit I kept for such occasions, when I wanted to look like a low-paid federal auditor. I shuffled through the front door in the manner of a tired, slightly impatient government employee. Someone who's been an air force staff sergeant can look mean without trying. I walked over to the first secretary who looked my way and took out my black leather cop's wallet. "Official business," I said, holding up my three-by-five laminated detective license only long enough for her to see my photo and the words *Department of State* in big letters across the center.

"I've got to look at Charles Brand's account. Tell your boss." I flapped my license and snapped it closed. The secretary blinked sleepily. It was the middle of the afternoon, she was tired, the air in the bank wasn't good, and I was standing over her like the grim reaper.

"Just a moment, please, sir." She walked into the manager's office and announced me as someone connected with the government. The manager glanced out, and I stared back at him with a look that said, Right, I'm a fucking federal auditor. And if you don't cooperate *you'll* be audited next.

In very little time, I had what I'd come for. Brand had withdrawn large amounts of cash on each of the dates in Tommy Rennseler's datebook.

Henderson was seated in my office, after hours, in a short red dress; she said she'd needed to wear red today to strengthen her root chakra. It was strengthening my root chakra too.

The Game of Thirty was on the desk between us, its aged, cracked wood contrasting with the polished veneer of my desktop. Henderson rolled the dice and moved her piece. "So," she asked, "what does that square mean?"

"It's called the Child Is Protected. It's the square of Bes, the god who looks over children."

Ranouka's voice came through the intercom. *"Detective Sergeant Manning for you."*

I picked up. "John, what'd you find?"

"I talked to the Ridgefield PD. Your guy Brand had a complaint made against him by a family there. They said he'd propositioned their seven-year-old daughter."

"Brand's a child molester?"

"The complaint never went anywhere. The Ridgefield PD said Brand looked guilty to them. They think he paid the family off. He's got big bucks."

"Anything else?"

"Did you remember to take your macho serum today?"

"I never forget."

"All right, I'm out of here, somebody just got murdered."

The line went dead and I turned to Henderson. She was staring at the board. She said, "This thing *is* plugged in to us."

"Brand collects artwork depicting children. Now we know why."

"In my clinical psychology class, they said that one out of every ten men is a pedophile. I looked around the room and thought, Him, him, and him." Henderson got up and started to pace in her red flats along the geometrical lines of my 1920s carpet. "If Charles Brand paid Tommy Rennseler large sums of money for unknown somethings—" Henderson spun around, hands on her hips. "—it could have been for *children*."

"Tommy Rennseler would sell him the statue of a child, but he wasn't in the business of selling real ones."

"All right, blackmail."

"But why blackmail?"

She came back to the desk and started playing with the bone dice, rolling them back and forth in her hand. "Maybe Rennseler found out Brand's dirty secret. Maybe Brand had a guilty conscience, and one day he confessed to him. Tommy Rennseler was such a perfect gentleman, so discreet. Brand could have opened up."

"Or slipped up."

"Either way, once Tommy Rennseler had Brand's secret, he was in a position to milk him. My mind is racing too fast, I need to slow down." She peered into the terrarium. "This lizard is not being fed properly."

"He just had a piece of cheeseburger."

"A cheeseburger is not proper food for him."

"If he didn't like it, he wouldn't eat it. You ever try forcing a lizard to eat a cheeseburger?"

"Why doesn't he get any vegetables? Iguanas are strict vegetarians."

"He's not an iguana, he's an agama Harlequin. When he gets mad his throat turns red. Like mine."

"Is it warm enough for him in there?"

"His rock is heated."

Henderson stepped around my chair and angled her head lower, so that she was nose to nose with the Harlequin. "The respiratory and circulatory systems of lizards are imperfect," she said, sorting through the photographic ragbag of her mind. "They have just enough oxygen to supply their tissues and maintain the process of food combustion, which means they can raise their body temperature only a few degrees."

"He's a good lizard."

"They have an eyelike structure, in the roof of their skull. A third eye. Don't you find that interesting?"

I looked at the lizard. The lizard looked at me with one eye and at Henderson with the other. As for where the third eye was looking, it was anybody's guess, and the lizard wasn't talking.

SAUL FELDMAN slipped the diamond and sapphire choker around Henderson's neck, laid it against her blue silk blouse, and fastened it. "The finest piece in the store. It's soft, it fits like a scarf, but it's tremendously understated. This you won't find around the neck of some nouveau riche broad, this is for great ladies only."

Henderson looked at herself in the counter mirror, her fingertips lightly skimming the choker. Saul was nodding. "It's magnificent. Everything I handle is magnificent, only this is more magnificent. Jimmy, what do you think?"

"I wish I could buy it from you."

"Buy, why buy? You need it, you borrow it, and you guard it with your life. Please guard it with your life, Jimmy, if anything happens to it, my children won't go to college and become doctors."

"Don't worry, Saul."

"I'm not worried, I always look this way. All right, we need to give Henderson a bracelet." He reached into his display case. "Here, I sold one like this to the sultan of Brunei."

Henderson drew the bracelet onto her wrist and extended her arm. "I love it."

"Of course you love it, I have only the best, although I have some second best too. I even have some fakes, but we don't call them fakes, we call them the finest Austrian crystal. But this bracelet comes in a sealed box with a certificate on microfilm inside it, no switching with an inferior stone is possible. Do you want the microfilm, Jimmy?"

"Hold the microfilm, Saul."

"She's going as a married woman, she's got to have a wedding ring." Saul held up a wide band bristling with more diamonds. "From Botswana to you." Henderson passed her finger through it. Saul crossed his hands on his little paunch and smiled across the counter at her. "These pieces never looked so good. Be sure to take a photograph, Jimmy. Use a flash. You want to bring out the sparkle. Those are flawless diamonds, pure color, no inclusions."

"Saul, I appreciate this."

"This guy you're going to see—if he knows quality, he'll know this isn't Austrian crystal."

"He's an art collector."

"He'll know. He'll sense." Saul reached back into his case. "Let's throw a Piaget watch on her too. This one has four quietly exquisite diamonds on the band, but the Piaget name stands out nice and big on the face. Slip that on, Henderson, and tell me what time it is."

Henderson wrapped the band on her wrist and closed the inlaid clasp. "Will I be fit to live with after this?"

"I always tell my customers, diamonds make you a better person. Okay, you'd better go if you're driving out to Connecticut. But let me wrap that stuff for you, you don't want to walk out of here wearing it." Saul put the jewelry into boxes and then into a shabby little shopping bag. He handed it to Henderson. "It looks like you're carrying dreck, right? But really, you're carrying Saul Feldman's heart."

We drove into the village of Ridgefield in a rented Mercedes. Henderson wrinkled her nose at the local beauty salon. "Boring. Old money has some of the worst hair styling in America." She was adjusting her necklace, and the sunlight was glancing off the diamonds and sapphires around her throat. In the back seat, wrapped in layers of protective padding, was a porcelain Chinese figure I'd gotten from Temple's shop. It was of a girl around six or seven years old, circa 618 A.D. The glaze was delicate, and the child's skin glowed with a soft whiteness. A blue gown hung in loose folds around her prepubescent body. She was a child molester's dream.

Main Street was tree-lined, peaceful, with wooden benches on the sidewalk and vintage wood-trimmed station wagons parked at the curb, carefully preserved by their conservative masters. There was a park, a library, and the Community Savings Bank. "There's a woman who fell off a horse at an early age." Henderson pointed to an elderly lady walking along the quiet street. "Her C-7 vertebra is locked. See how constrained her arm movements are? I could fix that in a few hours."

We drove to the end of Main Street and turned at the old cemetery onto North Salem Road. Henderson was shaping the crown of her large-brimmed black hat. "Demographics have shown that communities like this are not large purchasers of groin itch powders."

I noted a historical marker that said somebody named Earl David Wooster had been mortally wounded here, and then we drove out into the rolling hills, passing a man and woman walking twenty-five hounds, and every one of those hounds looked at me suspiciously. We peeled off to the right on Ridgebury Road, and now there were little ponds, streams, gazebos, and unmarked, unobtrusive driveways to estates hidden in the woods. I turned the Mercedes into a gravel drive, past a gray wooden gatehouse. The gatehouse was empty, its shingles overgrown with moss. The drive was lined with large oak trees. A rough stone wall appeared, of the kind made by farmers when clearing their fields, and then the field spread into view, transformed into a formal garden of low, flowering hedges and circular paths, and beyond that was the Brand house, a rambling stone building three stories high. To the right of the house was a garage, also in stone, with several cars parked in it, including one antique woodie.

I opened the car door for Henderson, then reached into the back for the porcelain statue, my fingers closing gently on the little figure through its padding. Our visit had been facilitated by a friend of Temple's, a fellow dealer who sometimes sold to Brand and did us the favor of calling him to say that a very special piece had surfaced. I followed Henderson over the crunching gravel, holding the padded figurine as if it were a bomb with a pressure-release fuse in it.

"Stone houses have a very difficult vibration, Jimmy."

"Please don't talk about vibrations to Brand."

The front door of the manor was opened by a young maid in a blue uniform with a *B* sewn on the breast pocket.

"Hello," said Henderson, "I'm Mrs. Breedlove."

"Yes, of course, Mrs. Breedlove. Mr. Brand has been expecting you."

Henderson had chosen the name Breedlove for her mission, as suggestive of old money. I thought it was over the top, but she said there'd been a prominent family of Breedloves at the turn of the century in Manhattan, with a townhouse on Fifth. I could only hope the Breedloves hadn't played polo with the Brands. I noted with satisfaction the fluty tone Henderson had put into her voice when announcing herself.

The maid let us through a wide, oak-paneled hall, whose walls bore portraits of individuals in riding apparel, whom I took to be early Brands. Their expression was sour, and their painted horses eyed me with hostility. The maid showed us into a library lined with leather-bound books. As soon as she left, Henderson pointed to a pair of photographs on the wall, of nude little Victorian girls carrying bows and arrows in the manner of Cupid. The style was tasteful, and the girls' bare asses charmingly innocent. Victorian pedophiles had it made.

"And there," said Henderson, gesturing toward a vase, whose painted figures were naked child-nymphs playing coquettishly with a tamed satyr. At the price of ancient crockery, who's going to call it pornography?

The door opened and Charles Brand entered—tall, tanned, his very slightly graying hair lying negligently across his forehead as if waiting for a hand to push it back. He'd been told a security person would be accompanying Mrs. Breedlove and he brushed past me as if I were a large potted fern. "Mrs. Breedlove," he said effusively, "I gather you've brought me a treasure."

"Please, do call me Ann." Henderson hung her limp hand in the air for Brand to take, but her voice was trembling.

"I'm delighted you could come," said Brand. "It's not often an object such as you've described is sold privately. I feel as if I'm ahead of the pack." He sat down across from her, then nodded my way to indicate that it was time for the base-born to leave the gentlefolk alone. But I wanted to hang in just a little longer, to give Henderson a chance to settle herself; I could see she was still trembling, like an actress on stage without any lines. I said, in my dumbest New York voice, "Don't mind my commenting, Mr. Brand, but you don't have such hot security for a collection this size. That sticker on your door is twenty-five years old. Security has come a long way since you had your system installed."

"Oh?" Brand's expression was the kind used when a pet farts under the dinner table. "It sounds to me," he said with a thin smile, "as if you sell security systems yourself."

"Mrs. Breedlove can tell you how good my work is."

"I'm sure she can." He looked at me with only faint annoyance, for I couldn't be expected to know how to act in elevated company. "I'll talk to her about it later. At the moment we have other things to discuss."

"I didn't mean to interrupt. I just hate to see anybody taking risks on losing things they really love."

"Thanks for your concern," said Brand. His manner was like Helen Rennseler's, expressing a faint weariness with the opportunism of the lower orders. That I'd try and sell him security didn't seem to surprise him, and he was waiting for me to curb my misguided instincts about making filthy money.

"Such a picturesque house," said Henderson, her

voice steadier now. Her glance toward me told me she was okay, and she followed it with a gesture to Brand that seemed to imply that she was used to much larger dwellings. "These cottages are such fun. It's Stanford White, isn't it? My grandmother used to know him quite well, maybe too well, given his reputation. He tried to get her on that swing of his, the one where the ladies swung naked? But Grandmother said, 'Stanny, you're going to get in trouble with that swing,' and then he did get shot in the back of the head, didn't he?" I tried to signal her to tone it down, but Henderson was rolling. "I think your family and mine were friends a very long time ago, Charles. I could swear that I visited this house when I was a little girl."

"What a charming thought," said Brand. His accent was as peculiar as the one Henderson was using, inconsistent from sentence to sentence, an improvised kind of British. When you're rich you can make a fool of yourself in numberless ways, and nobody minds. But his voice had grown more cautious. "You're not from New York now?"

"No," answered Henderson, "we've been at Villa Stefano for years and years. It's the tiniest island, you'd fly right by it if you didn't know it was there but that's the fun of it, don't you think? I actually prefer the London house but Bertie's nurseries are everything to him, and the Italian sun, well, you know what that is for tomatoes."

"I'm afraid I don't have much luck with tomatoes," said Brand. He was now eyeing Henderson more carefully. But I hoped he was simply categorizing her as a society girl with helium in her head, a type he was familiar with.

"Well, of course," she said, "I wouldn't go near a

tomato, you know the Incas fed them to the Spaniards to make them more susceptible to syphilis."

"I didn't know that." Brand's aristocratic eyebrow lifted.

"Or maybe it was the other way around," said Henderson. "Anyway, Porto Ecole is divine, just two hours from Rome, that's really where I spend my time, unless I'm at the mineral baths at Montecatini, which is where I met Ruffle Pietromarchi, and that's how I happen to be traveling with this terribly valuable figurine and a detective to protect it." She nodded toward me.

"Well, I'm very interested," said Brand, with a glance toward the padded parcel on the coffee table.

"I've been worried sick about it," said Henderson, seated primly in her chair, hands in her lap. "Ruff's a wonderful person, really, and I adore her, but she's uncircumspect about men, if you're interested in gossip and who isn't." Henderson leaned forward confidentially. "But first, I'm supposed to tell you that this piece of hers has been through the most careful scrutiny—ultraviolet, X-ray, and thermoluminescence—and there are no repairs, and no restorations. The little girl's robe is blue glaze, which as you know, is very rare for the Tang period, and I carried it *in my purse* through customs, can you imagine, but Ruffle said New York was the only place to sell it, the Romans don't appreciate Chinese art."

She'd hooked Brand now, and I could see he was impatient to unwrap the piece. Henderson's eyes met mine, sparkling with the thrill of the contest. She knew she had him, and I was proud of her, and wished I could see her reel him in, but my part in the plan required I be elsewhere. I gave her a slight nod, and she said, on cue, "Mr. McShane, why don't you stroll in the garden?" She turned back to Brand. "He loves gardens, he can't wait to get outside."

Brand turned and addressed me in the tone used with a household animal. "Can you let yourself out?"

"Certainly, I'll go out through the flap. Thank you, Mrs. Breedlove. You're sure—"

"The piece is perfectly safe with Mr. Brand." She turned to Brand. "These security people are so paranoid, but that's their function, isn't it?"

I backed out of the room and shut the door behind me. The painted Brands glared down at me from the wall. I didn't envy Charles his childhood.

In the hallway, I found the Brand guest book. I ran through its pages for the previous month but found no familiar name. Then, urged on by the imp of the perverse, I signed my name in the guest book.

I entered the living room and noted a few more art objects depicting feminine prepubescence, discreetly placed among more ordinary treasures. No guest would find evidence of jaded tastes, only a bit of whimsy within a broad collection. I supposed Brand enjoyed displaying his secret openly, knowing it was still hidden.

I went through the dining room, whose long table bore a round vase of fresh flowers. The chairs were walnut with red upholstery, and the Oriental rugs were so rare they were threadbare. A sideboard was covered with heavy silver implements, and a gold clock ticked Brand time.

I entered the billiard room. Sunlight came through arched windows segmented into leaded squares. Mission-style chairs sat in the four corners of the room, built high, to afford a good view of the game. Every gleaming object in the room proclaimed that its occupant was secure. As one who installed security systems, I knew otherwise. But if you came in here in your beaver slippers, with nothing more pressing to do than improve your billiard game, and then proceeded to the library to read your gazette by the fire, you might be tempted to believe you were invulnerable—except, of course, for that blackmailing swine, Rennseler.

I exited the billiard room and quietly found my way to the kitchen. It had two stoves to feed one lonesome Brand, and a back staircase for an Irish private eye. The stairs creaked beneath my step, but summer sunlight came through the landing window, just as if I weren't invading forbidden levels. I stepped through the bands of light and continued upward to the second floor.

Other people's houses have eyes when you're in them on the sly. The hallway was emanating hostility, a bamboo chair wishing it could spring at me, and a large Oriental vase hoping to devour me. First stop: the bathroom medicine cabinet, which, after the garbage cans, can tell you the most about a household. As Henderson had predicted, no groin itch powder. But there was a box of 3 cc hypodermic syringes, and beside them a prescription bottle with Brand's name on it. He was shooting himself with adrenal extract, which was nothing too special, but had he also shot Tommy Rennseler with cobra venom?

I checked the hallway again. Someone was moving about downstairs, and I needed to hurry. I slipped from the bathroom into the adjoining master bedroom and started opening bureau drawers. Brand's shirts had been neatly folded for him by the maid, alligators upward. Before my ex-fiancée decorated my apartment, I'd kept my clothes in tea chests from McNulty's, and everything I'd worn smelled of tea; I only needed to dip my sleeve in boiling water for my afternoon caffeine fix.

I opened a writing desk. The blotter was spotless, the stationery untouched. The cubbyholes in the desk yielded envelopes, last year's stamps, and a dried-out French fountain pen. The desk was set between windows to the garden. I could smell the honeysuckle and jasmine. The door to the connecting room was locked, and I took my rake and tension wrench from my wallet and picked it. The room had a plumply cushioned couch, a fireplace, and a locked wooden cabinet. It was old and had a type of lock still used in safe deposit boxes because it's so hard to pick, unless you studied with Willy the Wire. I patiently raked the tumblers from back to front, going slowly, keeping only the slightest tension on the cylinder, until the bolt finally moved. The box opened and I was rewarded by finding copies of a charming publication called *Wonderland*, the quarterly publication of the Lewis Carroll Collector's Guild, which featured the "delights of transgenerational sex," and what were referred to as "pre-teen nudes." It had articles extolling "family fun," in which *Wonderland's* editors maintained that "Incest is a game the whole family can play." Underneath the magazines was an assortment of glossy photographs of men having sex with prepubescent girls. The photos were shot so that the faces of the girls were the focal point, their expression part of the erotic content; without exception they seemed leaden, their eyes dull, their mouths slack; if this was family fun, they weren't having any.

When you force your way into people's secrets, you have to accept the intimacy that it thrusts upon you, but I felt as if I'd touched a snail's back on a wet morning; a thin film of slime seemed to coat my fingers. I returned the magazines and closed the cabinet, resetting the lock. There was a large-screen video system in the room and a collection of video tapes lining several shelves. I scanned the titles. All were wholesome offerings. I checked the record-protect tabs on each tape. The tab on Disney's *The Little Mermaid* had been removed and replaced with a strip of adhesive.

I loaded *The Little Mermaid*, turned off the sound, and pressed PLAY. The video screen showed Disney animation. I ran the tape to the middle, pressed PLAY again, and found Charles Brand in front of a video camera, with a girl who resembled the little Victorian cupids on his library wall—around eight years old and naked. But she wasn't posing in lamblike Victorian innocence, with sunlight in her air. "*My wicked, wicked angel.*" Brand's voice came from the soundtrack. "*What a delight you are.*" The sight of the two of them on a bed together, under the harsh glare of a video spotlight, hit me with such force I found it impossible to look directly at them and looked at their surroundings instead. The room was well furnished. One of its windows was included in the shot, and I saw a jutting angle of the outside of the building. It was log finished, and an overhang was trimmed in twisted branches in the style of a Swiss chalet—clearly not part of Brand's own house, with its imposing stone exterior. Was he in the house of a millionaire friend with the same perverted tastes? But no friend, no matter how rich, could have a child in residence for Brand's use.

I forced myself to look at Brand. His actions had a programmed look, the precise working out of a fantasy that probably changed very little each time he performed it. Suddenly I got the eerie feeling I was looking at a house of child prostitution. Reluctantly, I focused on the little girl. She was fair-skinned, blond, a child caught in a net she could hardly comprehend. *"Are you going to take me home with you?"*

"It's not possible, my darling."

"Why not?"

"Because you don't belong to me."

"You could adopt me."

I'd seen a fair number of ugly episodes in my time, but this one went straight to the pit of my stomach. As I looked at the child's stricken face, I felt something closing around my fingers and glanced down: I'd bent the iron lock-picking wrench in half.

"Your skin is perfect. Do you have any idea what that means? But skin like this never lasts. It coarsens so quickly. In just a few years you'll be lost to me forever."

I straightened the wrench, put it in my pocket, and held back my rage. Much as I wanted to go down and bounce Brand's head off the wall, there was a murder to solve first.

"I could be your little girl."

"You are my little girl."

"Only if you take me away."

"We'll discuss it later"

"When?"

"Later."

"Later, you'll be gone."

"Yes, and later you'll be older. You're growing older every second."

My fury became a kind of nausea and a helpless feeling took me over as I watched Brand bending the spirit of the little girl as I'd bent the iron wrench, but she wasn't iron, she was soft and pliable. And could she ever be straightened again? An eye for an eye isn't my style, but I wanted this rich and powerful man in jail with a child

molestation rap on him, so that he would be the victim—
he would be the one violated every night in the cell block,
by a line of cons who despised sex offenders.

"*Do you know what I'm doing?*" he asked.

"*Yes,*" she answered and then pointed to the wallpaper
beside the bed. "*Do you want to know how many flowers
there are on the wall? I counted them.*"

She was small, with a tiny voice, with a bird's nest
for a heart, and this privileged man was forcing her to deal
with his gross adult energy. Her childhood was dissolving
in his debauchery and I desperately wanted to stop what
was happening but life isn't a videotape you can put into
reverse; these images were history. All I could do was
watch, and try to figure how Brand's pedophilia fit in with
Tommy Rennseler's murder.

"*You're my sweet little girl.'*

"*I'm not your little girl. Only if you take me away.*"

"*You're the best little girl in the world.*"

"*I...hate...you.*"

"*It doesn't matter.*"

"*I'm going to tell on you.*"

"*Who are you going to tell?*"

"*God.*"

"*God doesn't hear wicked little girls.*"

"*You're going to be in trouble.*"

"*Why is that, my darling?*"

"*Just because.*"

"*If you cry, I'll have you removed.*"

"*I don't care.*"

Cruelty has a rotten kind of shine to it, like a Times
Square marquee at midnight, when the neon seems to
get under people's flesh, giving them the sickly hue of
vampires. The light from Brand's video had that hue to

it, a greenish phosphorescence that added to my physical revulsion.

"*I'll buy you a nice present if you stop crying.*"

"*What kind of present?*"

"*A pony. Would you like a pony?*"

She looked at him with undisguised contempt. "*There's no pony.*"

There was a sound on the stairs. I froze, and started constructing my explanation for being where I was, as the advice of Willy the Wire rang in my ears: *Always tell them you're looking for the bathroom.*

The footsteps came to the top of the stairs and continued along the hallway toward me. I quickly ejected the video and put it in my pocket, then replaced the empty box on the shelf beside other Disney features whose center sections probably contained more happy Brand memories. Victorian pedophiles didn't have video; each age makes its improvements.

The footstep in the hallway was a woman's. I prepared myself for extreme embarrassment, which would not be new to me. Then I noticed the open window in the den was adjacent to a rain gutter. It wouldn't be the first time I'd gone down the spout. I slipped out and swung onto it; it was well fastened and in good repair for gathering raindrops in Waspland. I slid down it easily and landed on a cushion of closely trimmed grass at the back of the house. The summer air wrapped itself around me, but its warm smells felt suffocating. *Do you want to know how many flowers are on the wall?*

I was still fighting down my rage. The master of the house was a free man, while the kid he'd molested was a prisoner in some whorehouse of the devil, where other privileged men came to play every day. I wanted to go in and pound on Brand, but he was a prime suspect, and breaking his jutting jaw would jeopardize my investigation. For now, I just needed to breathe. I followed a gravel path into a large, labyrinthine flower garden, where a maid was working. She was black, and carried a basket and scissors. As I walked toward her, she made it clear she wasn't interested in conversation. But you can't stop an Irishman from shooting the breeze. I said, "Our bosses are conducting business. They told me to get lost."

She glanced at me and then turned back to her work. She was cutting the stems of a tall purple flower.

I asked, "Got any false aralia?"

She turned her head. "Say what?"

"False aralia. It's a plant."

"What's false about it?"

"I don't know, maybe it was unfaithful."

She gave me a reappraising glance. We seemed to have said the right thing to each other; a more tolerant look crossed her face. I followed up with, "You must like it here, with all this nature around you."

"You're the security guy came with the lady, right?"

"Right."

She laid each purple flower and stem gently into her basket, her manner unhurried. I watched a butterfly flutter down, fold its black-and-white wings, and disappear in the leaves, like a good detective. I said, "Mr. Brand seems like a decent guy."

She moved from the purple flowers to a cluster of red carnations. "He's better than some I seen."

"How's that?"

"He's got a little give in him." She snipped off a carnation, put it to her nose, and looked at me, the red petals against her skin. I said, "Brand knows how to enjoy himself, does he?"

"All these people—" She gestured with a carnation toward other, unseen estates, with a disdain that their horsey residents might have admired. "—they know how to enjoy. They aren't nothing but enjoy. But Mr. Brand doesn't mind if I enjoy too."

"You know, I felt that about him," I said, playing it as dumb as I sometimes think I am.

"If I want to sit in the garden after work, I can." She added dryly, "Off where nobody sees."

"He ever let you use the pool?"

"Only if I fall in." She moved to a large ball-shaped pink flower. "The bees love this one. I don't like to cut too many of them because the bees need it more than Mr. Brand does." She pointed to a large bee crawling drunkenly over the blossoms. "You know you can hold that bee in your hand and it won't sting you? Bumblebees are very cordial."

"I'll take your word for it."

"Now the little honeybees, you have to watch out for them. They have tight security." She smiled sardonically. "Only thing about Mr. Brand, he sometimes forgets to pay me. Then I have to remind him. Seems like he just loses track once in a while."

"These things happen."

"The person Mr. Brand's been really good to is Miss Garcia. She's the cook. There aren't many houses around here who'll let a single mother live in with her child."

"Why not?"

She wagged the scissors at me. "What do they want with somebody else's kid running around?" She nodded toward the vast, manicured grounds. "This is all about having it your own way." She said it as if the lives of the wealthy amused her. I waited a little, watching the stoned bumblebee, then said, "But Mr. Brand doesn't mind somebody else's kid around."

"He's good to little Natalie. He treats her almost like family. I mean to tell you, that's rare. 'Cause other people's kids are a pain in the butt." She resumed her cutting and the pink flowers fell into the basket, against the bed of carnations. "Mr. Brand buys Natalie gifts. He takes her into town for ice cream. He's even talking about getting her a pony." She tapped a pink flower against her nose. "She sure lucked out with Mr. B."

I brought my nose toward one of the bulbous pink flowers. "How old is Natalie?"

"She just had eighth birthday." She hefted the basket "That's enough flowers for one man." She turned to me "What's your name?"

"McShane"

"I'm Louise, and I don't need any security. You hungry?" She walked ahead of me, her white shoes crunching the gravel. In the kitchen, she laid her flowers on the chopping table beside an empty lineup of vases. She looked at my bulging pocket, where the videotape was stashed. "You carry iron?"

I patted the pocket. "I never use it. But the clients expect it."

"What kind is it?"

"Twenty-five-caliber automatic. It's called a Little Mermaid."

"That's a new one on me." She opened the refrigerator and took out a side of roast beef.

I leaned against the edge of the chopping table. "Where's Miss Garcia?"

"In town, shopping." She laid the slices of beef on French bread, added lettuce, and handed it to me. "That ought to make you feel secure."

I lifted the sandwich and gazed at it fondly. "My employer doesn't approve of my eating red meat."

"These rich ladies get into fads. But a man working security needs blood in his system."

I was leaning against the Mercedes when Henderson came out of the house, with Brand beside her. She was smiling, and he looked pleased with himself. "Come and see us," she was saying. "If you stay at the Hotel Il Pellicano, you're sure meet everyone you know."

I opened the door of the car, and Henderson slipped in. She gave her hand to Brand through the open window. "We have our own polo club, I know you'll like that. Well, goodbye, and enjoy."

I got in and started the car. Brand came around to my side and said, "Be careful of the grass. When you came in you drove on the edge." He pointed to a carefully sculpted line of grass some other vehicle must have squashed.

"Sorry, Mr. Brand, it was real careless of me." And I'll be back to squash more than your grass, pal.

I turned the car and started down the driveway. Henderson gave me the look of an actress waiting for her curtain call. I said, "Nice work. You almost convinced me you knew this Ruffle Pietromarchi person."

"Actually I adjusted her back. So what did you find out?"

I lifted the video out of my pocket. "Brand stars in this, pecker in the air."

"In *The Little Mermaid*?"

"He taped over the center section."

"What's he doing with his pecker in the air?"

"Trying to stick it into a little mermaid."

"How little?"

"Try eight."

Henderson's eyes flashed angrily. "We're going straight to the police."

"We don't want the police in on this until we know everything that was going on between Brand and Rennseler."

"Do you know how easy it is to destroy a human being at that age?" she demanded.

I didn't answer. The child's face was imprinted in my brain.

"What a hateful pig he is." She shuddered. "And I sat there chatting with him."

"You were doing a job, and doing it well." I drove past the Brand gatehouse, onto the road. "He has hypodermic syringes. He's injecting himself with adrenal extract."

"I don't think glandulars are the way to go, frankly."

"We didn't come about his health."

"Yes, but it does show he's feeling an imbalance. Maybe he thinks eight-year-old girls are the fountain of youth. Is there any way of knowing who the girl was?"

"Not a chance. Kids get grabbed for this stuff every afternoon at three. Brand called her his angel. And told her how smooth her skin was."

Henderson looked out the window at the forest, where the dying sun was turning the tree trunks a deep shade of gold, but I could see she wasn't in a mood to appreciate nature; an expression of disgust tightened her features. She said, "I wonder if that's what pedophilia is about—the satin texture of a child's skin. To possess something so fleetingly pure and then to defile it. That's a power move." Her features tightened still more. "Like a little boy tearing the wings off a butterfly."

"Brand's not a little boy." I was thinking about a child I knew, a little girl around the age of the kid Brand had abused. Like Henderson I was filled with disgust, and anger, and that's never a help in an investigation. "You sold him the statue?"

"I sold it."

"Did you get Temple's price?"

"I got ten thousand dollars *more*."

We were reentering the village again. As we passed the park, I saw a familiar blue uniform, worn by a woman on a park bench. Playing on the grass nearby her was a young girl.

"I think that's Brand's cook, Miss Garcia. The little girl is her daughter, Natalie. Brand is very nice to Natalie. He gives her presents. He's going to get her a pony."

"Her posture is awful. See how she's rounded her shoulders, like she's protecting her chest? And her pelvis is terribly misaligned. I'd say she's already been sexually traumatized."

I pulled the car over to the curb and stared at the dash. I could leave things in place, or I could let my Irish impetuosity loose, which usually led to unwanted complications. But I had Brand's smug voice in my head, saying *God doesn't hear wicked little girls.*

"Take off your jewels, it's time for us to become civil servants." We got out of the car and entered the park. The coppery light of the sun was at our back. As the woman glanced toward us, I took out my investigator's license and flashed it. "Miss Garcia, we're from the New York State Child Protection Service."

She froze at the sight of my license, and I knew she didn't have a green card. We sat down on either side of her, and she motioned to her little girl to continue playing. Then she looked back at me, her dark eyes already deported to the plains of poverty. "Miss Garcia, we're conducting a confidential investigation. I'm sorry to tell you that it has to do with Mr. Brand, and that it involves child abuse."

She reached toward Natalie, but then drew her hand back. She was confused, like someone caught trying to cross a rapidly moving stream. Her hand dropped into her lap, with the same woodenness I'd seen in the child on the videotape, as if the same hammer blow had struck them both. Finally she looked at Henderson, and asked, in hesitant English, "What has Mr. Brand done?"

Henderson placed her hand on Miss Garcia's. "It involves sexual intercourse with girls of your daughter's age."

Miss Garcia seemed to want to rise, to grab her daughter and race to another life, but she was held in place by the fear that causes animals to freeze in the hopes of blending with their surroundings; Miss Garcia had blended into the green park of Ridgefield, green as a green card, and she didn't dare move. I said, "Our office is going to seek an indictment against Mr. Brand. Would you be willing to put your daughter on the witness stand?"

"No! We can't—" She looked at Natalie, her eyes scanning the child's body for signs of what Henderson had already perceived, a wounded spirit. Natalie was scattering a ring of bubbles around herself. The coppery light of the setting sun played on the delicate surface of those floating little worlds, which shivered momentarily and then burst on Natalie's hair and shoulders. Miss Garcia turned from Natalie to me, and her eyes were suspicious. Who was I, anyway? A monster with horrible accusations about her employer, about the man who was so kind to Natalie. I said nothing, only stared back sympathetically, and her look changed again, as she reconsidered all those little kindnesses of Brand's, the games, the gifts, and the caresses that accompanied them; their real purpose became clear to her, as they might have all along had she not been so eager for Natalie to have opportunities other little girls of her station didn't enjoy. And certainly Brand had been clever and discreet, for he'd had plenty of practice. But Miss Garcia saw him clearly now. She turned to Henderson, as the tears slowly filled her eyes. "I'll kill him," she said quietly, and I knew she'd be capable of it; the quiet ones usually are.

I said, "You don't want to ruin your life over this. We'll see that Brand gets what's coming to him."

"He's rich. He'll get away." The murderous anger in her eyes was traveling fast, moving right through me on its errand. She was already back at the house, putting a knife in his heart. I said, "The sun is shining. Natalie is alive. If you kill Brand she'll be visiting you in jail on weekends." I took her hand. "Brand isn't worth your freedom. And I promise you, he'll pay for what he did."

She read my eyes, and saw I meant it. She said, "I can't be involved in anything that has to do with the government. You understand?"

"Yes, Miss Garcia, I understand." I took out my wallet. "Our agency works quietly. We're privately funded." I gave her a thousand bucks, in hundreds. "Go home and pack. No explanations to Brand. Just call for a cab and go stay with friends."

She looked at me uncomprehendingly, and then her confusion turned to suspicion. I said, "Don't worry, nobody's trying to entrap you." I wrote out a name and phone number for her. "Once you're settled in, call this man. He's a lawyer who works for our agency. He'll help you."

"Why should he help me?"

"Because he works for us, and you've had bad luck."

She searched my face, and I looked away toward Natalie, thinking again about the little girl I knew, and about the Brands of this world. I felt Miss Garcia's gaze; she was a Latina, a Catholic who believed in saints and their mysterious manifestations; whatever she thought of the situation, she sensed it was best to let herself be guided by these two people who'd come out of nowhere to help her. Her hand closed on the money, and I took a last look at Natalie, spinning in her bubbles. Then I walked away. "Jimmy," said Henderson, striding along beside me, "that was a wonderfully generous act."

"I spend that much a week on bad habits."

"Don't try to be male-aggressive about it. It was lovely." She slipped her arm through mine. "What's your lawyer going to do for her?"

"He's going to give her an American birth certificate with her name on it. Compliments of the McShane identity service."

"Bes," murmured Henderson, "the god who looks over children. The Game of Thirty was right." We got into the car and drove through the quiet village where wooden station wagons went to die.

THE CANOPIED BED was by the open window: Birds were singing outside, flying around in their bird lives while the vague human forms through the window did incomprehensible things.

"*You're amoral. All children are amoral.*" Brand was speaking to the girl. The camera never moved, and at times their figures passed out of the frame, an indication that he'd set the camera up himself and had it on automatic. "*You have a natural decadence, you see. You're entirely to blame.*" Brand was propped up against satin pillows. The girl was looking at a strand of her own hair, intent on it, absorbed in it, as Brand continued: "*You don't care, I know. You have no interest in me. You can sit there, playing with your hair, and I could be cutting my throat. It doesn't matter to you in the slightest. Because you're nature.*" He reached toward her, and I turned away. I wanted to cut his throat myself.

My apartment buzzer rang. I walked to the kitchen and pressed the intercom. "Yeah?"

"*Henderson here.*"

I buzzed her through and waited by the door. Her quick footsteps sounded on the stairs. "You look furious," she said.

I'd left the video running, and Brand's voice was

coming from the living room. *"Amoral—do you know what the word means? Do you understand the concept? No, of course, you don't, why should you."*

Henderson headed straight on in. As I stepped through the doorway, she was already seated, elbows on her knees, staring at the TV screen. "I want to see it. From the beginning."

"The plot is simple." I rewound the tape. Henderson watched the half-hour segment without moving, speaking, or blinking. When it was concluded she looked ill. She said, "He makes her responsible. He just happened to be in a house of child prostitution and there she was, his corrupter."

I gazed out the window, to the roof across the way, where the last rays of evening were casting a slanting shadow on the face of the building. I was thinking about the kid, about the life she'd had somewhere when her childhood was intact. She'd believed in all her fairy tales, and then she'd been grabbed, and reality had been thrust onto her, and into her, giving her the expression she wore in the videotape, of one who knows what people really are, and whose cynical conclusion can never change.

Henderson had taken the remote and was rewinding the film. Brand's gestures were moving in reverse, rapidly, as were the girl's, prisoners in a dream running backward, their tragic interlude now a hurried pantomime. Henderson clicked the PLAY button and Brand's motion changed, back to normal.

"You have an exquisite cruelty about you..."

"He talks to her as if she were an adult. That aids his fantasy of her being the manipulator." Henderson ran a hand through her pleated skirt, smoothing it over her knees, then smoothing it nervously again. Her hand was trembling. "That's the nightmarish part, the way he pulls

her mind along. It's not enough for him to just rape her."
She clicked the video off. "This tape makes me think he
could be our murderer."

"Henderson, you jump pretty fast from suspect to
suspect."

"Well, we have the mysterious payments Brand made
to Rennseler. And now we know just how much Brand
had to hide. He'd have good reason to murder Rennseler."
She picked up a small framed photograph from the end
table. "Who's this?"

"A little girl."

"I can *see* that. Is she a relative?"

"She's my daughter."

"I've been here lots of times and I never saw this
photograph."

"She's about the age of the kid in the film. I've been
thinking about her."

"Where is she?"

"At an air force base in Turkey, with my ex-wife."

"They're in the military?"

"Yes."

"What happened to your marriage?"

"My wife wanted to be married to an officer. When
I decided I didn't want to be one, she walked out. My
daughter was a year old."

"There must have been some other reason she
walked out"

"There are women who want to be the colonel's wife.
My wife was one of them."

"But why?"

"Prestige. A feeling when she walked into a room
that she was being envied by the younger wives. She'd
struggled along with me because she thought she was

going to get the big payoff—the nice house, the good posting, the fancy cocktail parties."

"And now she's a colonel's wife?"

"Roger that."

"I beg your pardon?"

"Yes, she's the colonel's wife."

"And what about your daughter?"

"I get a photograph once a year."

"Do you ever call her?"

"No."

"Jimmy, that's not healthy. She needs to hear from her biological father, and you need to hear her voice."

"I've thought it out and I figure it's better for her if she hasn't got feelings that stretch halfway around the world. I want her to grow up in a family that feels complete just as it is. When she's older, and comes back to America, then we can get to know each other. If she comes back." I strapped my shoulder holster on. Henderson asked, "Why do you have to take a gun to dinner?"

"My suit is cut to fit over a gun. It won't look right if I don't wear one."

"What square of the Game of Thirty are you on?"

"The Executioners of Sakhmet."

"Whom do they execute?"

"People who don't take their gun to dinner." I armed the burglar alarm, and we walked through the twilight to my parking lot on Hudson Street. Henderson slipped into the Shadow beside me, and the silvery pleats of her sheer crepe skirt shifted iridescently around her legs as I backed the Shadow out, but I was thinking about the kid on Brand's tape, and about my own kid, and for the first time in recent history I wasn't imagining what was under Henderson's skirt.

I headed downtown on Seventh Avenue, with cabs careening by me, their frames rattling as they bounced through holes in the pavement. A Buick with two roof antennas and one headlight was behind me, making the same moves I was making on the obstacle course. When we entered Chinatown, the one-eyed Buick was still following us, only it had two eyes now, which meant it had a customized light panel. That way, you don't think you're being followed, you think you've seen two different cars. Except I've got the same light panel.

I parked in the Rickshaw Garage on Bowery and checked the rear end of the Shadow. I was not surprised when I spotted a homing transmitter attached by a magnet onto the crossmember of the frame, with its antenna poking vertically out. I left the homer where it was, as I didn't want to disturb the signal and tip off my followers that I was wise to them.

"What are you looking for, Jimmy?"

"I thought maybe I was getting a flat." I led Henderson out to the street and we passed the painted balconies and pagoda roof of the On Leong tong, whose top floor would never be seen by anyone but tong elders. The power emanating from it was palpable to me, and it spread like a cloud over the streets. We turned onto Mott, past a tea shop where the Ghost Shadows stood in the doorway, young men in black leather jackets and black jeans. They protected the gambling rooms of Chinatown, and no sensible person would want to cross them. Tourists, however, didn't have to worry about them, as tourism was important for the restaurants, which the Ghost Shadows also protected.

"Jimmy, you really should see your daughter," said Henderson.

"I'd get into a fight with her mother and the Colonel. And then the Colonel would be hospitalized."

"That's your disturbed liver speaking."

If it was, I was feeling more disturbed than usual, as the tail that'd been on me for the past few days was now closing in. We strolled the streets, past the gift shops and noodle factories with their tin ceilings and faded Chinese opera posters on the wall. The windows of the illegal garment factories were boarded over, revealing nothing, like most faces on the streets of Chinatown.

"Here's where I get my herbs," said Henderson, pointing to a door with a carved bower of flowers over it. "Doctor Chi can tell what's wrong by just smelling a patient's perspiration. I saw him take one look at a woman and tell her that she'd contracted tuberculosis seven years ago in Hong Kong, and that she'd received treatment for it which was not sufficient. And he was right. And he only charges twenty dollars." She peered in through the window. "Look, that's *ho shou wu*, I take it every day to prevent my hair from ever going gray. And there's some Chinese licorice, which you should take to relieve anxiety."

I was trying to catch a glimpse of the person following us, but all I saw were old Chinese men in baseball caps, and women in knitted vests shopping in the open-air evening bazaar.

We circled back up to Bowery. In the distance, down Division Street, I could see traffic piling up on the Manhattan Bridge. In the mall under the bridge were the lights of a restaurant where you could eat bear paws and the body parts of endangered species. A statue of Confucius graced the intersection, the sage standing upon a large gray block of stone. At his feet flowers had been offered. A breeze was playing with the silvery pleats of Henderson's skirt, making it more transparent. Her jacket was white and thinly woven, and when she put her arm through mine, her breast touched my arm in an intimacy she wanted me to feel, but she'd picked the wrong moment to get playful, as my attention was on the crowded intersection, hoping to spot whoever was following us. A wonton man rolled his dough out on a cardboard box. A vendor selling chicken feet and curried squid pushed his cart toward me. On the fire escape above my head, an elderly woman placed a joss stick in an incense burner, and the thin stream of gray smoke drifted through the iron railings.

We headed back down Pell Street and stepped over rivulets of water dripping out of the fish and vegetable stands onto the sidewalk. As we passed a magazine shop, a movement of gold light caught my eye—Henderson's Egyptian amulet reflected in a spirit mirror placed beside the door to deflect evil energy away from the shop. I scanned the mirror, and made the tail—he was stopped under the awning of a gift shop on the opposite side of the street, and his hand wasn't on the handles of his shopping bag but buried inside it, undoubtedly around the stock of an automatic—an Executioner of Sakhmet. I watched him trying to hang back under the awning, but he was nervous, his feet shifting, and his head turning left and right to check for any potential interference, a sign of his inexperience. A seasoned hit man comes straight on, knowing that a fast hit is the best one. This one was working up the courage.

I was sweating myself, and I didn't need a Chinese doctor to tell me what I was suffering from. We weren't being tailed for information, we were going to get whacked, and an amateur like this clown meant crude action at the first opportunity. I got us away from the crowds and headed down Catherine Street, keeping Henderson on my left, out of range. An import warehouse was ahead, its cavernous interior filled with sacks and crates. An elderly Chinese man sat in the doorway on a wooden folding chair, hands resting on the head of his cane, motionless as the statue of Confucius.

Henderson was talking about a man she'd dated who crushed her illusions by wearing vivid red-and-green plaid trousers. "I could hardly speak to him all night," she said.

I moved her into the warehouse, taking my wallet out at the same time and flashing my tin at the old Chinese man. "Building inspector."

The elderly Chinese man looked at me without expression; Chinatown merchants were always being shaken down by someone with a badge. I had Henderson by the arm and was bearing her deeper into the warehouse. "Jimmy, do you know someone in here?"

The smells were burlap and tea. I pulled Henderson between the stacked-up sacks. "We're being followed."

The hit man was carrying an automatic and we'd have no chance on street level. I caught Henderson at the hips and in one quick lift set her up onto the sacks; I went up behind her, finding footholds where the sacks were wedged against each other, and pulled myself over the top.

The air was close and hot, with a heavy odor of grain. Word would already be flying to the Ghost Shadows that a barbarian had stepped over the boundary. Enormous amounts of pure China White heroin were moved from Hong Kong to warehouses like this one. I felt somebody staring at me from above. I expected a Ghost Shadow with a sawed-off shotgun; I looked up into the menacing eyes of a Chinese parade dragon that'd been roped to the ceiling. I pointed it out to Henderson and whispered a few words in her ear; she scampered across the sacks like a silvery nymph attending the dragon in its seclusion, then desperately reached up to undo the dragon's rope. I lifted a fifty-pound sack of rice onto my shoulder, moving silently with it over the soft surface of the other sacks, to where I could look down.

The wooden folding chair was empty, the elderly Chinese man having departed in a move dictated by solid intuition. The executioner stood below me. He had black hair, shaved above his ears. He wore a khaki fatigue vest, and his bare arms looked as if they'd been tattooed by a backward raccoon. He carried a submachine gun, its wire butt unfolded against the crook of his right elbow: a bargain basement executioner, capable of hosing down the whole street in his nervousness. I nodded to Henderson. She yanked the rope loose, and suddenly the hit man was looking up at a descending red monster, its jaws open and a long red tongue dangling from its mouth. He ducked and fired a wild burst. I threw the sack of rice down with everything I had. It struck the hit man on the shoulders, split open, and flattened him. I jumped down, landed on his wrist with my heel, and twisted. His wristbone cracked like a chopstick, and I pulled the submachine gun from his open hand. He tried to grab my ankle with his other hand, but I gave him the toe of my shoe in the frontal bone of his skull, to jar his cerebral hemispheres and make him wonder if perhaps he should have gotten a high school diploma after all. He made one more feeble attempt to reach me from under his bed of rice, so I interlocked my fingers with his and snapped them backward.

"Stop, you're breaking his fingers!" Henderson appeared at the edge of the sacks, her eyes as bright as the dragon's. She slid down the sacks and landed beside me. "Are you crazy? How could you do that?"

The hit man groaned from under the rice that covered him. I reached down, yanked him to his feet, and thrust him up against the wall of sacks. "Who hired you?" I shook him and rice came out of his hair and sleeves. He was staring at his broken hands. He would not be pulling the trigger of any weapons for some time to come.

Henderson was looking on in horror. That she'd be dead now if I hadn't stopped this character didn't occur to her. I nodded down toward his crudely tattooed arms, and said, "Those are convict tattoos, done with sewing machine needles." I shook him again. "Come on, shitsky, time to sing."

The hit man's eyes slowly cleared, and he looked at me with the hate that had helped him survive in prison, that had kept him scheming, kept his brain and body working, kept him fighting back against nightmarish conditions. He needed a sensitive social worker to bring out the best in him, so I jammed the machine pistol against his forehead. "In Chinatown nobody calls the cops when somebody gets killed. I can waste you and then go have some pork fried rice." I released the safety. "You know any Chinese? You know what *shin sinbin* means? It means crazy, and that's what I am. The lady will tell you."

"Jimmy," said Henderson coldly, "he's got to have those bones set."

The hit man ignored her, his eyes on me, his expression a mixture of obstinacy and pain. "Shoot. I don't give a fuck."

"I'm going for Dr. Chi," said Henderson.

"Stay where you are," I growled, no longer in the mood for alternative healing. I banged the hit man against the sacks again, and a few last grains of rice fell out of his sleeve.

He muttered, "I don't know who called the hit. These things just come down."

I twisted his forearm, turning up a gang tattoo—a noose with the number 96 in it. "You're a Hangman, right?"

"So what?"

"So somebody asked the Hangmen to whack me. How did they know how to do that? You fucks don't advertise in the Yellow Pages."

"I told you, I just got the action handed to me." His manipulative prison eyes were going through their moves, and truth would never be one of them. I swung him around and dumped him into a long empty crate that smelled like it'd held fortune cookies. He hit hard, folding his broken hands on his chest to protect them. "Hey, what the fuck—"

I grabbed two fifty-pound sacks and laid them on top of him, leaving him just enough space to breathe, and then added two more. I figured he bench-pressed that much in prison, so I added a few more, until his cries were muffled in rice.

"You're going to leave him like that?" asked Henderson.

"The Ghost Shadows will find him soon enough. Maybe they'll take him to Dr. Chi. Personally, I hope they turn him into sushi." I tossed the submachine gun onto a tea chest and took Henderson by the elbow. She yanked her arm away from me, and we stepped around the tail of the fallen dragon.

Usually on nights when people try to murder me I drink extra-dry martinis. Now I drank mineral water. This was spiritual progress. I sat at the long, gleaming bar of Shi King's, beneath a dangling paper lantern. Henderson stepped out of the velvet alcove leading from the ladies' room. Her jacket and skirt were luminously pale against the red velvet. I twisted a barstool around and she slid onto it beside me. She said, "I'm disgusted with you."

"I saved your life."

"What you did to that man was horrible."

"Henderson, he was planning to kill us. He *would* have killed us. You want me to give him the Boy Scout handshake? His gang does drug deals and contract killing. I broke his hands for him so he'll think twice before trying to pull a trigger on me again."

"You used excessive force. He was practically unconscious when you crippled him."

"Henderson, guys like that can kill you in their sleep." I knew I'd never convince her. She didn't know what Saul Feldman knew, that another layer of evolution exists, inhabited by creatures without emotions. They had principles, which made them look human, and those principles might include loyalty, honor, and an unholy kind of piety, but the code itself was inhuman. A life meant nothing to them.

She looked toward the dining room. "I don't know how you think we'll be able to eat." She gave me an angry sidelong glance. "Well, you might be able to. You're such a primitive."

"As a matter of fact, I'm starving."

"I can feel your esophagus rippling. It's horrible. Like an animal after the kill."

"They've got great dim sum here."

"You just mutilated another human being. Aren't you sick to your stomach?"

"Henderson, when you let punks interfere with your dinner plans, you're finished."

"Can you imagine the pain that young man is in right now?" She turned and studied me carefully, her eyes taking on a clinical look. "As for you, your meridians are profoundly disturbed."

"That's because I'm worried about the fifty other Hangmen."

"Worry goes straight to the spleen."

"So does a bullet."

"We've got to give up this case."

"An Irishman never surrenders."

"I made a big mistake in getting involved."

"You've been a great help."

"I admit I enjoyed the feeling of solving a puzzle. But the rest of it is ugly."

"Henderson, I always liked working alone. But nothing beats having you along."

"It takes a certain kind of personality to be a p.i. You've got it. I don't." She swiveled around on her barstool, and her skirt clung to the line of her thigh. "I wish I had a cinnamon doughnut to comfort me."

"Have I ever told you that you've got the best legs in New York?"

"Cute legs, Jimmy. But not the best. You have to be tall to have world-class legs. Temple Rennseler has great legs."

The headwaiter showed us to our table, threw our

menus down, and walked away. My foot struck something under the table. I reached down and brought up a neatly tied box. The label said it contained fortune cookies, but it was too heavy for cookies. I opened it. The hit man's submachine gun was neatly laid in wrapping paper. Henderson stared at it. "Is this the hors d'oeuvre?"

"It's a Skorpion 61. Czech security forces used to carry it. This one's got a silencer attached, which cuts the range, but he knew he'd be in close."

"Where did it come from?"

"The Ghost Shadows like you to know they're watching. This is from the Ghost who protects that warehouse. Our little skirmish must have amused him." I lifted a Chinese greeting card from the wrapping paper. I opened the card to find a neatly printed message and read aloud, "He who stands firm in the face of the tiger will succeed."

"Let's hope the Ghost is right," said Henderson.

We stood outside her apartment house on Perry Street, and I was preparing to take her in my arms and press my worried spleen against hers.

"Jimmy, I'm sorry." She was gazing at me in a way I'd never seen before. She was an icy little Henderson. She said, "I almost did something very stupid this evening."

"What was that?"

"You know what. It started when we were standing by Confucius. You looked so nice in the twilight, and I was more attracted to you than I've ever been. But it's impossible now. We're going to remain friends, but we can never be more than that."

"Why not?"

"Because I heal people, I don't cripple them." She smoothed down the lapels of my jacket. "You may have saved my life, but your actions convinced me that our chakras will never ever line up." She studied my face for a moment, then softly said, "Good night, my dear," and went inside.

I was obviously going to have to figure out how to get our chakras aligned, after I found out just what a chakra was and what you fed it. I walked along Bleecker Street to Christopher and turned down it toward my building. Viola was on the stoop in her housecoat, having a smoke. "McShane, you look wired."

"I had a little trouble. It's over. How're you doing?"

"Doing fine." She was clinging to the iron rail, her head hanging forward, her back bent, cigarette smoke curling through the disheveled hair on her forehead. "I'm in the flow."

I went down the steps to my office. When I turned on the lights my lizard was on his rock, staring toward the shadows of the street with his own reptilian interpretation of what was going on there. I put the Skorpion away, dialed New York Homicide, and got through to Manning on the nightshift. "John, who runs the Hangmen?"

"A psychopath named Samuel Stang, the Stinger, as his fans on Ninety-sixth Street call him. Why?"

"I want to talk to him."

"What about?"

"A contract."

"You're going to whack somebody?"

"No, the Hangmen tried to whack me. I want to find out who hired them."

"We're working with the feds on the Hangmen. We get their wiretaps. You want a transcript?"

"I want to hear the tap for the last two weeks."

"All right. I'll bring you in as one of our facilitators."

"Will they buy that?"

"Hey, the fucking feds are just a bunch of bad lawyers and failed accountants. They couldn't get their foreskin out of a zipper. They're no problem."

"Thanks, John. What kind of night are you having?"

"I just came from a guy who got shot in the chest. I asked him who shot him. He said, 'Go fuck yourself' and died. Any other questions?" I was staring at the Game of Thirty on my desk. "That's all, John. Catch you later."

I hung up and continued staring at the game board. My leading piece was no longer on the square of the Executioners, where I'd left it. Someone had moved it back to the beginning of the board, to the square called Crocodile—the Player Is Devoured. I took out my Beretta and checked the back entrance to the office. The shadows from the tree in the garden were like figures from an Egyptian tomb, arms out, walking stiffly. I waited, listening, but the shadows didn't move. I traced the alarm system around the garden windows and door, but it hadn't been touched.

I went back to the front and checked the windows there. A circular scratch was visible on one of the alarm contacts. A thin wire hook had been shimmed between them. It was an old system, which I'd never bothered to update except for the surveillance monitors, because monitors are fun to play with, and electric eye beams aren't. As for the window bars, I saw now that their lock had been picked. I should have had stationary bars instead of hinged ones, but then it would've been hard to keep the windows clean, and as any gentleman will tell you, clean windows are essential for those moments when a miniskirt goes by.

I checked the office computer, but it hadn't been raided, and the locks on the file cabinets and desk drawers were intact. Nothing but the Game of Thirty had been touched.

I went back out to the street. Viola was still on the front stoop. She looked at me through the curling plume of her cigarette. "What's wrong with you?"

"Did you see anybody trying to get into my office window?"

"You got knocked off?" Viola lifted a scraggly strand of hair off her forehead. "Next thing we know I'll be snatched away for unsafe sex." She lit another cigarette. "I'm just an old tub now, but two hundred and fifty years ago I was a real piece."

"You've still got it, Viola."

"If I can find it." She wrapped her housecoat tighter. The frayed ends of her nightgown hung down to the stoop. She looked at her feet and then back up at me. "You think I was always this short?"

"Weren't you?"

"I used to be as tall as you." She peered at me through her small, watery eyes. "Either that or my perspective changed." Her hand was shaking as she tried to light a match. I took it from her and struck it. She leaned toward the yellow flame. "Thanks. An old lady never forgets." She straightened and exhaled with a phlegm-filled sigh. "Maybe I should smoke dope. You got any dope?"

"Not at the moment."

"A little dope might be just what I need." She squinted

toward a pair of men in black leather, who were walking by arm in arm. "When you're in love, you got it made. The only problem is, it don't last." She blew a stream of smoke after their diminishing forms, and it floated toward my office window. "Say, now that you mention it, I did see some guy come up your steps. I thought he must be from the bar. They come out of there plastered and sometimes they stumble down toward your office."

"What did he look like?"

"Had a black suit on, and flashy cuff links. You don't get many housebreakers in French cuffs."

"No, you don't."

"And he was wearing very strong after-shave. I gave him a smoldering glance." Viola exhaled another phlegm-filled sigh. "He missed the kinkiest sex of his life."

"Do you want help up the stairs?"

"Unless you plan on carrying me, McShane, there's not much you can do."

So I stayed with her awhile longer on the stoop, and we watched through the smoke for some kind of solution, to old age, insomnia, and the Game of Thirty.

IT WAS THE END OF THE DAY at the office. Henderson and Ranouka had both gone, and I was alone with my lizard, playing the Game of Thirty against an imaginary opponent. My pieces were spread out on the board like attacking soldiers. I had a clear shot toward the end of the board, and was picking up the dice when the phone rang. "McShane."

"It's Booker. I'm in the van outside Rennseler's. He just got a call shook him up bad. He's been instructed to go to a meet at his boat tonight, Seventy-ninth Street boat basin, eight o'clock."

"Any names?"

"Rex."

"Nice work, Bobby. Are you comfortable?"

"Hey, man, this van is equipped. I've got a stocked refrigerator, a toilet, and I was watching the Mets when the wire went hot." Bobby hung up.

I set the phone down and tapped on the lizard's glass. "Do you see where my lead piece is? The square of the Solar Boat. Pharaoh sails it to his heavenly home."

The lizard stared unblinkingly, a cold observer of the game. I looked back at the board. It had a distinct presence for me now, that of an ancient sage with his knowledge imbedded in these squares; I was interacting with him on the path of chance, and a p.i. will take information wherever he can get it.

I parked on West End Avenue and walked toward the river. The sidewalks of Riverside Park were lit by lamps that glowed down to the water. Near the river was the rotunda, in which the homeless were camped. Beyond them by the toss of an empty dream was the boat basin, ablaze with the lights of the luxury craft anchored there. Saul Feldman was waiting for me at the entrance, which was protected by a chainlink fence topped off by coils of razor wire. He put his hand in his pocket and took out a key to the boat basin gate. We went through it onto the pier. Along with the large power cruisers, rows of houseboats were anchored, and the smell of a barbecue drifted from one of them, where a party was in progress. "Such a romantic way to live," said Saul. "The waves lapping, garbage floating by. When my father was a kid, he swam in this river. You swim in it now, you get a disease you wouldn't believe."

"I appreciate you coming down here."

"No problem. Pinski's boat is at the far end of the pier."

"What does your friend Pinski do in life?"

"Hardware. In Queens. He's got a warehouse as big as Yankee Stadium. Completely filled with nuts and bolts. Pinski himself does not know how many. But it's more than anybody else has." The waves were lapping, and I assumed the garbage was floating by. The river smelled good to me, whatever it carried, and the night was cooler with every step we took along the pier. The Hudson lay dark and wide between us and the lights of the Jersey Shore.

Saul stopped alongside a huge white cabin cruiser. The name on the stern was *Pinski*. "It sleeps twelve. Nice little bunks where you bump your head, but Pinski gives you a Valium and you're comfortable."

"Did you find Rennseler's boat?"

Saul pointed toward a long sleek speedboat of the kind drug smugglers use to outrun the Coast Guard. The name on the stern was *Bullish*. Saul said, "Go ahead, do what you have to. I took care of the harbormaster."

I walked a few yards down the dock to the *Bullish*. The first thing I had to do was disarm the boat's security. It was a Sea Dog dock sensor, which would be hardwired to the boat's battery. I opened the aft cowling on a spotless Mercedes V-8 motor and disconnected the juice. Then I removed the sparkplugs, so the boat wouldn't be going anywhere tonight. I left the cowling open and jumped on board. The sleek interior of Richard Rennseler's boat gleamed with chrome and brass. The dash had a racecar-style wheel, set in black carbon-fiber trim. From the cockpit you looked along a deck shaped like an arrow, to shoot you past anything else that moved on the water. I attached a mike to an air vent near the door of the forward cabin, which would pick up conversation anywhere on board. I reconnected the Sea Dog sensor and closed the cowling. In a moment I was back on the pier with Saul, who gave me an inquiring look. "So what's going on here tonight?"

"Rennseler's meeting someone who threatened Temple."

"Why don't you just grab him?"

"I'm only a private investigator, I can't grab people. Anyway, this guy, whoever he is, would just zipper up. I need information. Temple didn't hire me to protect her. She wants to know who killed her father. So first I listen, and then maybe I grab him."

"You think this guy killed Tommy?"

"I don't know. Richard Rennseler's just as good a suspect. I've got to hear what they say to each other." I looked at my watch. "They're due soon. We'd better get on board Pinski's boat."

We returned to the big cabin cruiser. Saul took out an infrared unit and pointed it at the security control box on board. The unit was disarmed, and Saul put a foot onto the boarding rail, but the *Pinski* shifted under his weight. "Why don't they clamp them to the dock...oy, what a strain...hold it right there...I'm nauseous already..." Saul dropped onto the deck and I followed him. The aft deck was protected by a teak roof, beneath which rattan chairs were placed around a rattan table. Saul opened the door to the main cabin. This was not a floating retirement van with a polyester interior. The joiner work on the walls was hand-rubbed cherry. A round cherry wood pedestal table was at the center of the room, ringed by four suede chairs. Suede banquettes, softly illuminated from below, lined the cabin. Saul went to the bar and poured himself a drink. "Myself, I prefer land. A nice quiet piece of cement to stand on. But everybody's different."

"Does Pinski make long voyages?"

"To the Statue of Liberty. You vomit once and you're back."

From the porthole in the main cabin I could see Rennseler's boat. I took out my receiver and placed it on a table facing the *Bullish*. When I switched it on, I got the sound of creaking decks and lapping water. Saul peered over my shoulder. "A listening device?"

"Yes."

"How much?"

"Two grand."

"This is listening."

"I like to hear voices from a distance. It has to do with my childhood."

"Everybody in my childhood talked at the top of their lungs. They could rupture your eardrums through a metal door." Saul sat down beside a porthole and stared out at the line of boats under the pier lights. "Who's this guy who threatened Temple?"

"Somebody called Rex. I think he might have helped Tommy Rennseler with crooked art deals. There's a ten-million-dollar Egyptian artifact floating around, and nobody seems to know where it is."

"Rex wants it?"

"Richard Rennseler wants it too."

"I met Richard Rennseler once, at Tommy's shop. Just like Tommy, a Wasp and a half. So what's this artifact?"

"A solid gold Egyptian scepter."

Saul got up and made himself another drink. "Ten million dollars is serious money. With ten million I could buy a boat ten times as big as this tub of Pinski's. I could race him to the Statue of Liberty and puke before he does. You want a drink?"

"No."

Saul went to a porthole on the other side and looked out, toward Jersey. "We're born, we have a little heartburn, we die. What's it all about?"

I was watching the pier, across the ranks of boats, to the shore. The voices of the people partying on the houseboat blended with the whispering voice of the current that broke around the pier. Saul's voice came from behind me: "Maybe I should have gone into nuts and bolts with Pinski. He asked me to. He said, 'Saul, the world is held together by nuts and bolts.' Now he's got a yacht and I'm going to Peru in a canoe. I don't know, you can't figure these things at the time."

I saw Rennseler coming through the boat basin gate. He was alone. He walked along the pier to his boat. He reached into the cockpit and punched in the security code on the alarm panel, then climbed on board. His footsteps sounded through my receiver. Saul whispered at my shoulder, "Can he hear us?"

"No."

"That thing is sensitive. I can even hear him breathing. He's out of shape."

"He's nervous. He's going broke."

"He'll have to sell his speedboat. Maybe I'll buy it. I already own a life jacket."

"Saul Feldman, flying down the Hudson."

"And no traffic. That's it, let's go make him an offer."

I saw Rennseler put his hand into his jacket. Then I heard the bolt slide on an automatic. "He's got a gun."

"A gun?" Saul lowered his head below the porthole and cradled his drink between his knees. "We don't want to get any bullet holes in the *Pinski*."

"We'll try not to."

"Pinski would be unhappy."

"So would I." I saw a man coming through the gate. He was tall, lean, in a black suit with sparkling cuff links. Rennseler saw him too and slipped the gun back into his jacket.

"That's the guy. That's Rex." The lights of the dock shone on his face. His dark hair was slicked back from his forehead. He resembled Temple closely enough to be the long-lost twin she fantasized about. He was bigger than she was, his cheekbones were more prominent, his mouth wider and thinner, and the thrust of his jaw more pronounced, but he still had the Rennseler look. I wondered, for one crazy instant, if Temple's fantasy might have some truth in it. Had there been a twin, or an illegitimate brother?

He walked straight to Rennseler's boat and jumped on board with a single powerful leap. Rennseler looked at him, and we got the transmission. *"I don't know how long you think you can get away with this."*

"As long as I have to," said Rex, in a deep, rasping voice.

"What do you want from me?" asked Rennseler.

"The scepter. What else would I want from you?"

"I haven't got it."

Rex grabbed Rennseler by the collar. Rennseler's feet came off the deck. Rex held him there, dangling. *"You sonofabitch, don't lie to me."*

"I haven't got it."

"You and Tommy were in Egypt together when he took it."

"I helped him. But I only saw the scepter for a moment."

"Tommy hid it and you know where."

"I don't. I swear. You know what he was like. He never took anyone into his confidence."

"If you're lying to me, I'll kill you. I may kill you anyway." Rex tightened his grip around Rennseler's throat. Rennseler looked like he might be croaking. I moved toward the cabin door and Saul sprang after me. I motioned him back. "This is dangerous."

"I laugh at danger." Saul crouched in behind me. We ran onto the main deck and jumped off onto the pier. Rennseler had managed to get his gun out, but Rex wrenched it from him as if Rennseler were a child and threw it in the water. Then he picked Rennseler up by the belt and shirt collar and threw him in the water too, with an ease that was impressive. The boat alongside them swung with the current and cracked Rennseler in the head. He rolled over in the water, face down. Rex saw me running toward him and leapt across the bow onto the deck of a boat whose motor was idling. The owner was on the pier, preparing to load a case of booze on board, and just stared as Rex gunned the motor, snapped the line, and streaked out of the boat basin. It was a boat like Rennseler's, made for speed, and it left a huge twin wake behind it. In seconds it was in the middle of the Hudson, a V-shaped shadow on the moonlit river. I looked for Rennseler and saw nothing but a shoe. I dove into the water, snagged his collar, and dragged him to the surface. The filthy river rolled over both of us, and I pushed him toward Saul, who was stretching an arm down off the pier. "I've got him, Jimmy. Lift...by the foreskin...here he comes..."

Rennseler sat on Pinski's deck. He'd changed into some clothes he'd stowed on board his boat, and I was in a pair of Pinski's pants and a sweatshirt with *Pinski* sewn on it. Saul had given us a couple of stiff shots, and I was having a third in the hopes of destroying the wide variety of bacterial life I'd imbibed. Rennseler was toweling his head. "I suppose I have to thank you."

"Just tell me about Rex."

"That's not possible." He reasserted what he perceived to be the social distance between us, even though I'd just pulled him out of the sewer.

I said, "Don't be an idiot. Rex almost killed you. He might've killed your brother. I need to know who he is."

"Your needs don't interest me. I'm not involving myself in any way."

"Rennseler, you're already involved."

"Rex thought I had something he wanted. I don't. He knows it now. He won't bother me anymore." Rennseler stood, handed the towel to Saul. "Thank you for your hospitality."

"Go home," said Saul. "Take a hot shower. Tomorrow get a typhoid shot."

Rennseler turned to me. "Do you want to help Temple?"

"Yes."

"Then let her go to the clinic Helen has found. The events of the last month have brought her dangerously near a collapse."

"Why does everyone want Temple out of the way?"

Rennseler put his foot on the boarding stairs. "You think you're going to solve Tommy's murder. All you'll do is get someone else killed. Maybe yourself." He walked up the pier, past the happy houseboaters, and then on through the gate. Saul said, "How did a sweet girl like Temple come out of a family like that?"

"Rex looked like a Rennseler."

"Yes, and he acted like one, an arrogant prick. You think there's a bastard cousin in there somewhere?"

"And now he wants his share of the family fortune."

"My family already has my fortune. I've got two

daughters ride around on swans." Saul threw the towel into a corner of the deck. "So, shall we say goodbye to the *Pinski*? And go get some penicillin?" We climbed onto the pier, and Saul raised his hands into the air. "A night under the stars. A big moon. Adventure. A ringing in my ears. I'm alive."

"Could Tommy Rennseler have had a son Temple didn't know about?"

"Families are strange. My wife's got relatives I wish I'd never known about."

A rat came out of the stone embankment, nose twitching at the smell of the barbecue. He scurried along the stones, long tail lightly trailing, then crept down toward the edge of the water and disappeared in the shadows, to sniff this barbecue out more closely. You never can tell what might fall a rat's way on a moonlit night.

We walked up the stairs and through the gate. Saul said, "Wait'll I tell Pinski about this. He thinks I lead a humdrum life. But now—a detective, a gun, listening devices." We turned away from the ranks of glittering yachts in the water and headed toward the Rotunda, where the homeless had arranged themselves along the round stone walls. They were somber figures, and their crouching forms were a dark hieroglyphic message at the entrance of an invisible tomb. I felt Anubis, the jackal god of the dead, watching them from the shadows. And he watched me too, with patient, glistening eyes. In the Game of Thirty, everyone comes to the square of Anubis, sooner or later.

RANOUKA OPENED THE OFFICE DOOR. I could tell by her manner as she held it that whoever was outside had impressed her favorably, which meant he was going to be well dressed or rich. "Mr. Hassanein Hamid."

The Egyptian art dealer was both. Ranouka closed the door behind us with an approving little nod to me, as if to say that I might do well to emulate my guest's manners.

"Come in, Mr. Hamid. Have a seat."

His swarthy skin was set off by carefully trimmed gray hair. His suit was impeccably tailored Italian, and he handled himself as one accustomed to power. He extended his hand politely, and I noticed the ring he wore, a large gold oval whose worn-down carvings made me think it must be ancient.

"I'm pleased to make your acquaintance, Mr. McShane."

"The pleasure's all mine, Mr. Hamid. I hadn't expected we'd meet so soon."

"No? But the world is small. As proof of that, you find me here in your office, and I find the Game of Thirty on your desk. May I?" He ran his finger gently along the side of the box, over the carved hieroglyphs. "A fine board. Some of them are much cruder. And of course many of them are fakes." He nodded toward the pieces. "You've learned the rules?"

"Yes."

"With whom do you play?"

"There's someone who comes by."

"How nice." He lifted two of the pieces. "Do you know the significance of this square you're on?"

"Yes, I've been on it before."

"If an ancient Egyptian landed on this square, he'd probably stay home all day. But you have no fear of the Executioners of Sakhmet. Why should you? And this square, where your other piece is, is a happy one."

"The Goddess of Beer."

"Be sure to have a drink today, Mr. McShane. The goddess will smile on you." He smiled and replaced the piece. "If you're studying the game, then perhaps you know its spiritual significance, that the winner gains paradise?"

"I knew that. But tell me—what happens to the loser?"

"The god of the underworld devours his consciousness. His individuality is destroyed." He opened the drawer in the box and brought out the bone dice. "So, learn to play the game well." He rolled the dice, and smiled as they came to a stop. "There—luck is with me. But still, were I playing against you, I'd have to arrange my moves very carefully."

"Are you playing against me?"

"No, Mr. McShane, I'm not. I rather hope we can align our forces."

"And then?"

"Then we share in the spoils. Your share would not be insignificant."

"I'm listening."

Hamid picked up the bone dice again and rubbed them in his fingers. "The scepter of Akhenaten, yes?"

"I haven't got it."

"But you very well might find it. You have the reputation of being persistent."

"Who told you that?"

"Oh, one hears things." Hamid was soft-spoken, suave; I suspected the police departments of Cairo and Luxor had received generous gifts from him, which might account for his coming out of the recent murder investigation untarnished.

"Mr. Hamid, as regards the scepter, my first loyalty is to my client."

"Then perhaps I too should become your client."

"I'd be happy to represent you, but only after any conflict of interest is resolved."

"Mr. McShane, you and Miss Rennseler—excuse me, your client—know what the scepter is worth. What if it is lost to us forever because we don't pool our efforts?"

"A good point, Mr. Hamid. I'll talk to my client and let you know. Where are you staying?"

"At the Carlyle."

"I'll be in touch."

"Good, excellent." He stood and held out his hand again. The energy in his grip was deep-rooted; a sudden tug would not pull him over. He said, "You know, of course, that the Cobra killed Tommy Rennseler, and he wants the scepter."

"Do you suppose the Cobra knows how to play the Game of Thirty?"

"I shouldn't be surprised." Hamid picked up one of the snake pieces from the board.

"You arranged for Tommy Rennseler to meet him."

"An unfortunate introduction. Tommy underestimated the Cobra's will. I hope you and Temple won't underestimate it. I believe I can do business with the Cobra. I don't think you will be able to. So you and I have much to gain from an alliance should you find the scepter." Hamid paused, his eyes locking onto mine, and I felt his gaze taking my measure. "The scepter—such a beautiful object. And yet, from the very first hour it was discovered, it has ruined lives."

"That's the problem with beautiful objects."

"Quite so. Well, let us hope it doesn't ruin us." He said this with something that sounded like sincerity.

"What do you know about Rex?"

"Rex? I never heard the name."

"Well," I said, "enjoy New York. By the way, that's quite the ring you're wearing."

He held his hand up. "Many long ages ago a nobleman wore it to protect against the bite of the cobra. Good day, Mr. McShane."

He left me, and very soon after I left the office too. I had an appointment with a sheik of my own acquaintance.

"Nunzio, did you know there's a naked woman above your head?"

Nunzio "the Sheik" Vito tipped his head back and examined the garishly painted nude above us on the ceiling of the Manhattan Supreme Court Building. The nude was part of a mural commissioned in a less cynical time, when Truth could be depicted as a naked woman. Yet somehow her topless dancer-style still seemed right for New York

City. Nunzio said, "I been in here a hundred fucking times, I never saw her, but Jimmy McShane can sniff out cooz on the ceiling."

We walked through the echoing lobby, where nervous people were placing desperate phone calls, oblivious to Naked Truth above them and the Romanesque architecture that'd been created to help them appreciate the nature of justice.

We stepped through the Corinthian portico and went down the wide granite steps to where Nunzio had left his limo parked illegally. His boss was a Mafia captain named Tony Trombetta. Because of his toupee, Trombetta's enemies called him Twat Rug Tony, and because of his loansharking, drug peddling, pimping, and protection selling, the D.A. had called him on racketeering charges. Nunzio opened the car door and I handed him a video surveillance tape I'd done on one of the D.A.'s key witnesses against Tony. A good district attorney can get a grand jury to indict a ham sandwich, but Tony had big bucks, and with big bucks a lawyer can file enough motion papers to wallpaper the Waldorf Astoria; in addition he can hire an expensive private eye.

Nunzio Vito slipped the tape in his briefcase and looked up at me over lowered sunglasses. He'd become a made man in the Mob when he'd disposed of an informer by smearing him with raw meat and then throwing him into the polar bear cage in Prospect Park. The bear had eaten the informer, including his head. Every time I looked into Nunzio Vito's eyes, I said to myself, *This guy fed another human being to a polar bear.*

"Thanks, Jimmy." He tapped his briefcase. "You got the goods on this canary?"

"His credibility is shot."

"Tony will be very happy." Nunzio opened a copy of the *Wall Street Journal* across his steering wheel. "He told me to tell you—buy as much of this stock as you can." He pointed toward a waste management company the Mob owned; some of the waste they managed probably included the chopped-up bodies of their competition. "It's good for the environment," said Nunzio, "and it'll be good for you."

The luck fairies swiveled my head toward the rearview mirror on Nunzio's door. A black-helmeted rider on a motor scooter was angling toward us out of Foley Square, and I saw a flash of sparkling cuff links. I rolled away, as a soft *pop-pop-pop* sounded, and Nunzio's head snapped forward.

The scooter angled back into traffic and I turned toward Nunzio, who was looking into his *Wall Street Journal* for the last time, head buried in the paper, brains dripping on the mutual fund quotations, and spreading memory traces of ravioli enjoyed on Mulberry Street. The Executioners of Sakhmet had missed me, and gotten him.

I checked the terrain. The quiet hit had gone unnoticed in the bustle of activity around Foley Square. I didn't need the publicity. I was about to become the man who wasn't there. I moved out, past City Hall, and the statue of the founder of the *Herald Tribune*, who sat looking at his iron newspaper. He was solid, and I was shaking.

The fast food stands ahead of me were being patronized by cut-rate lawyers with briefcases, eating Korean chicken that might be ground-up rat. A little farther on, the restaurants and bars were filled with bail bondsmen, clerks, process servers, city councilmen, and labor relations advisors, all of whose faces seemed grotesquely animated because Nunzio Vito's last frozen look still floated in my mind. A New York sparrow gazed at me from over a doorway, then checked the sky for hawks, in a move I could appreciate.

I turned onto Old Nassau Street and made my way through the closed-to-traffic mall, past New Dimension Trophies, where little bronze men threw little bronze bowling balls into infinity. I thought of the pieces in the Game of Thirty and then, remembering the Goddess of Beer I went into a bar and ordered one; for all I knew, it was the goddess who'd swiveled my head at the last minute. I ordered a real beer, not the dealcoholized kind. I figured the goddess probably had contempt for near beer. And I have to say, a beer never tasted so good as it did just then. I drained it down and had another, which I carried to the phone booth at the back of the bar, where I called John Manning at Homicide.

"John, Nunzio the Sheik just got wasted on your turf."

"Where is he?"

"Parked outside the Supreme Court Building."

"Shit. These Mafia hits never get solved. There'll be reprisals and then more hits will go unsolved and my case-closed percentage will go fucking down again."

"John, I don't want you spinning your wheels on this. The hit isn't connected to the Mafia. Nunzio took one that was meant for me."

"Was it the Hangmen again? I'll go up there and wring their goddamn necks for them."

"No, this time it's somebody named Rex. He's connected to the Rennseler case. Tall, thin, wears French cuffs and strong cologne. That's all I know. As soon as I have more, I'll tell you."

"Seems like a lot of people are trying to kill you

these days. Maybe you should go on retreat. I know a monastery in New Jersey. They plant little trees by the roadside. They'd probably let you water the holes."

Temple's house was on Thirty-third off Lexington. An iron gate led to the interior of a cobblestoned court, which had duplexes on either side of it, converted from turn-of-the-century stables. I stepped through the unlocked gate, into the fragile atmosphere of the past. Horse-drawn carriages had pulled in and out here, and ladies in hoop skirts had descended from them, into eternity. There'd been young gentlemen to greet them, and grooms to lead the horses away, and it was unlikely anyone told them that their time would fade into obscurity, from which a private eye would try to rescue them.

Most of the converted stables in the court looked much as they had earlier in the century. I spotted Temple's immediately, for it'd undergone considerable architectural changes, mainly visible through the windows that faced the courtyard, but also reflected in very subtle alterations to the outside of the building. The room I saw had the look of a contemporary gallery—white interior walls for art, and much open space. I lifted the door knocker and brought it down with a few bright, metallic raps. An eye appeared at the peephole. "Temple, it's Jimmy McShane.".

The top half of the Dutch door opened, and Temple appeared, her hair bound up in a kerchief, her shirt tied at the midsection, and her hands in rubber gloves. She stared at me, and for a moment I thought she didn't recognize me.

"Your friendly detective," I said. "I phoned a half hour ago?"

She blinked, smiled, said, "Sorry, I was daydreaming, please forgive me. And—" She removed her rubber gloves. "—on Saturday we houseclean." She swung open the lower half of the double door and showed me in. I expected to find a housekeeper helping her, but there was no one. Temple was wearing a pair of khaki shorts and, as Henderson said, had world-class legs.

"This is a wonderful house. Did you do the remodeling?"

"Father did. He owned the property for years and gave it to me when I got out of graduate school. Can I get you coffee?"

"I'd prefer a beer." I took a seat in the living room. The chairs and couches were upholstered in white, to match the white walls, so that the ancient works of art could float like gods against white clouds.

The ceiling was high, leading to a balcony on two sides, where the old hay loft must have been, and where bedrooms must be now. Temple went down a flight of stairs in the corner of the room, to a basement kitchen. I looked out the window at the courtyard, and again I thought of the young gentlemen on a summer's day, in their top hats, spinning their canes, with everything going their way, but their way had gone right on into the invisible Manhattan that nobody knew, not even a private eye with access codes.

Temple's footsteps came back up the stairs, and she appeared in the doorway with two bottles of beer and some frosted glasses. She'd removed her housecleaning kerchief, and her dark hair lay flat against her head, slightly damp. She took a seat across from me. "So," she said, "I hope you have good news."

My eyes drifted down her long bare legs. A man would have to be a Babylonian statue not to respond to a show like that, but I was hearing the *pop-pop-pop* of the semiautomatic that'd beep fired at me a few hours ago. I said, "Temple, do you have a brother?"

"You know I don't. Why do you ask?"

"Because I got a glimpse of Rex. He looks like a Rennseler."

An astonished expression came across her face. "Where did you see him?"

"On Richard's boat. Then, about an hour ago, he tried to put a bullet in my head."

She came off the couch quickly, nervously. "I'm dropping the investigation."

"You can't drop it now. Even if you do, I'll stay with it, because I've got Akhenaten's scepter under my skin and I want to find it. So let's solve your father's murder. Who could Rex be?"

"I haven't any idea. There are cousins, on both sides of the family. There are resemblances, of course."

"Rex looks a lot like you. Bigger-boned, heavier jaw, maybe a little taller, but the resemblance was striking."

She sat back down now, slowly, a look of deep puzzlement on her face. "Are you sure you weren't imagining it?"

"Saul Feldman saw him too."

"I don't know what to say. It's as if you're telling me my fantasy—about a twin—were true."

"Is it possible that your father had an illegitimate son? One he's kept out of the picture all these years?"

She hesitated before answering, her gaze going to the Game of Thirty on the coffee table. The pieces were out, a game in progress. The leading piece was on the square of Seth, the Evil and Jealous Brother. Finally Temple said, "You've uncovered things about Father I never knew, and never could have imagined him doing. So I can't rule out anything any longer."

"Whoever he is, Rex knows about the scepter. He thought Richard had it. And he wants it. Since he didn't get it from Richard, I imagine you'll be seeing him next. He's violent. Although I guess you know that already."

"How would I know?" She started to get up, as if I'd accused her.

"His note to you."

She sat back down. "Oh...yes. I've been trying to forget that. I'm good at forgetting things, you know."

"Talk to your mother about Rex. She must know something. Now I've got to talk to you about Charles Brand and your father. You're not going to like it."

"Well, I'll just have to accept it." She'd squared her legs and folded her arms across her chest, against what was coming.

"It's very likely your father was blackmailing Brand." This was what I disliked about my line of work, you get too far inside and have to watch people's tender beliefs collapse. People should be allowed to collapse their beliefs in the privacy of their shower, where they can wash them down the drain. She asked, "What did Father know about Brand that was worth money?"

"Brand is a sexual offender."

She flinched as I said this, then asked, "What sort of sexual offender?"

"He likes little girls."

"How little?"

"I've got him on videotape, having intercourse with a child of eight. And he was probably doing the same thing with his cook's daughter, until I got her out of there. Anyway, it's prime blackmail territory."

Her arms remained crossed on her chest, as if protecting her heart. "Father was a rich man. He didn't have to blackmail people."

"I think he couldn't resist the opportunity."

She glanced at a statue, another double-headed male. One face was solemn, but the other was smiling slyly. I said, "It's hard to judge your own father. My old man went to mass every morning, but he was in it up to his ass with the Mob. I learned not to ask questions."

She stood suddenly and crossed to the dining alcove. She opened the bar, poured herself a shot, and knocked it straight back. "How about something stronger than beer?"

"I'll stick with beer. For luck."

"Is beer lucky?"

"Today it was."

She leaned back against the bar, then pointed to the bronze heads surrounding us, and the headless marble torsos. "I used to think I could hear them breathing. I thought they knew my deepest, darkest secrets. Sometimes I wanted to take a hammer to them."

"The Virgin Mary knew my secrets. Now Oprah knows everybody's."

She poured another drink and downed it. "The

statues knew I was deficient in all the things that make a person likable." She tried to pour another drink, but her hand was shaking and she set the bottle down. "The statues knew I was contemptible."

I was amazed to hear her speak of herself like this. I said, "I don't see it that way. You're a giving person."

She made another attempt with the bottle and succeeded, filling her glass and sipping at it. "When Father was killed, I thought it was my weakness that'd made him vulnerable."

"That doesn't add up."

"He was overly solicitous of me. I saw it affect his judgment." She ran the rim of the glass back and forth along her lip. "Mother is right about my not socializing with my clients. It's because I know that once I get to their home, or go on board their boat, I might not be able to cope. I might get drunk to overcome my shyness and act peculiar."

"You're smart, beautiful, and rich. These are important advantages." I looked around at the stone heads. The room felt crowded. I turned back to Temple, with the feeling that the statues were all listening, that I was talking to a dozen people.

"I'm sorry—" She ran a shaking hand through her hair. "I shouldn't be burdening you with this."

I saw the fear coming over her. Her eyes darted nervously toward the window, to the courtyard, but there wasn't anyone there. I said, "Hassanein Hamid is in town, looking for the pharaoh's scepter."

"Yes, I know. He stopped in to see Mother."

"They're friends?"

"More than friends."

"What do you mean?"

"What do you think I mean?"

"They're lovers? For how long?"

"For years. For as long as I can remember. I think they have what's known as a great love."

"Why didn't you tell me earlier?"

"I thought I had. Remember, I have a lousy memory."

"Well, their great love could also be a great motive for murder. Hamid kills your father, Helen gets the business from you, and then she and Hamid join forces. It'd be a very lucrative marriage, the kind she likes."

"Hamid already has a wife."

"In his country you can have several."

"He doesn't want that. He wants the intensity of an impossible situation."

"How do you know so much about what he wants?"

"Because I want the same thing." She was still sipping her drink and looking at me over the top of the glass. "Do you ever make love in the middle of the day?"

"Only on Fridays. I seem to need it more then."

She was walking toward me as if I'd rung a little silver bell and she were trained to perform when it sounded. She was untying her khaki shirt. I stood up. "You're under a strain," I managed to whisper. "I should leave you alone now."

Her long arms came around my neck. Her eyes were glassy, with a luminous blue glaze. Where had I seen that lovely blue glaze before? With the greatest reluctance, I took her by the wrists and lifted her hands off my neck, but she pressed her mouth against mine, and the whiskey taste of her tongue slipped across my lips. With her pelvis pressing against my professional ethics, I sank down on the couch. She sank on top of me, but instead of being excited I felt apprehension and sadness; riding on the waves of our desire was a dead man. His lifeless arm reached through the foam and touched the back of my neck. "Temple, it's not a good idea. We're trying to solve a murder."

I lifted her off me, and she lay back on the couch, staring dully across the room to a shelf on the wall, where Ephialtes and Otus sat, the brother gods who send nightmares to women. She'd moved them from the shop to her apartment, maybe in the hopes of placating them. I felt the reality of her nightmares. Ephialtes and Otus still wandered the world, and the sleep of women is different from men's.

"Oh hell," she said, softly. She looked down, saw the hanging tails of her open shirt, and slowly knotted them, covering her breasts. And that, I thought, is that, I've let the magic moment pass.

She said, "There's a line by Auden. 'Time watches from the shadow, and coughs when you would kiss.'"

"Do you feel someone watching you?"

"Yes. Whenever I make love. He coughs, and ruins it. Always." She let out a long sigh. "I don't blame you for not wanting to get involved."

She repeated the line by Auden, more softly, toward Ephialtes and Otus on their chair of forgetfulness, but she was directing the line at herself, reminding herself of the presence she felt; in the spaces of those white walls something was watching her, and I'd felt it watching me.

"Temple, I never let myself get involved with a client, not even one as beautiful and desirable as you. Things would have gotten confused. I couldn't do the job you hired me for."

She didn't seem to be listening; I couldn't blame her.

Then she looked up suddenly, as if nothing at all had happened, and asked, "Does Hamid think Father stole the scepter?"

"He's sure of it." I stepped around the couch and headed toward the door. "Let me know what you want me to do about Brand."

"Get him." Her voice was what I'd always imagined my lizard would sound like if he could talk.

"For one crime or another, I'll get him. Are you going to be all right?"

"I'll do some drunken housework." She tried to smile. I figured it was best to leave her alone. If I hung around, our edges would blur again, and we'd wind up circling like cupids on a Viennese clock.

I let myself out, into the antique courtyard. The shadows of noon had moved along its far edge, hiding the ghosts of the long dead gentlemen, and the long dead ladies descending from their carriage. I'd be in the shadows with them someday, after chasing my own illusions to the ground. I let myself out through the old iron gate, which creaked its commentary, iron on iron, wearing slowly down.

BYTES JENSEN, Electronic Mole, sat in front of her terminal. A computerized image of Brand's little sex slave was now on the screen—a full-face portrait we'd pulled from Brand's videotape. The computer had analyzed the image, breaking it into distinct geometric planes. Running behind it were hundreds of other faces, of abducted girls the same age, and hair color, their image scaled to ours. The faces pulsed and fluttered, like an angel attempting to incarnate, and Bytes watched the screen as she talked to me: "The files of the International Child Advocacy Committee. Their password is *child*. Original thinkers, right? But this program of theirs is wonderful. We could identify Peter Pan and the Lost Boys with it. It analyzes the features of every kid in its database, based on statistical norms, and calculates the degree of bridge on a nose, for example, or the thickness of the cheekbones, then gives a probable configuration. It matches those configurations against ours. The program thinks I'm the FBI, running a check."

The face of our little abductee trembled, as features of other missing girls came and went, the eyes of each of them seeming to plead that she be the one we select; the scanning from mouth to mouth caused the lips to move, as if in a whispered prayer. "They're talking to us, Bytes."

"I hear them, Jimmy. No charge for this one."

"You're a good woman."

"For an android."

The computer paused at certain faces whose features were close to a match, and our kid's face took on a sudden depth, reinforced by a merged image, the expression deepening but slightly skewed, and the computer moved on, heartlessly. Bytes sat back in her chair and took a swig of the diet cola that fueled her spirit. "The Child Advocates are trying to initiate a government policy to videotape every grammar school kid in America once a year, with voice tracks. Documentation of the entire child population. Wait a second, look at this..."

The face coming up behind our face had locked in, the fluttering gaze suddenly becoming the steady stare of a stubborn child who wasn't going to leave. The eyebrows matched, and the nose, cheeks, and chin. "A slight haloing effect," said Bytes, "but that's probably just a different haircut. Here's the ID."

Beside the girl's head a rectangular block filled with information. Her name was Rebecca Hewitt and she'd been abducted a year ago in Albany while shopping with her foster mother at an outdoor flea market. No suspects, no leads.

"Let's check your Mr. Brand, see if he's ever been in the Albany area." Bytes swiveled to another monitor and had Brand's Visa file up within a few seconds. She scrolled down the charges. "Gasoline. Lake Placid. We're in the ball park." Bytes scrolled through the charges a little further. "Lake Placid again, one month later. And again this month. By the way—" She scrolled back up the account. "Brand bought a video camera earlier this year. A very good one. With lights and tripod."

"Child prostitution is big business," said Manning. I'd caught up to him in a greasy spoon across from the morgue. He was drinking black coffee, the steam rising up past his sea blue Irish eyes. "We've got figures from the feds back at the office. Sex slavery is netting about a million bucks an hour around this fucking world of ours. Half of it involves abducted kids. I come into it when it turns to murder, and it frequently does."

Through the grimy window we had a nice view of the hodgepodge of buildings that form Bellevue Hospital, of which the morgue is a part. There are deserted buildings that lean at weird angles—gutted, vacant, with wrought-iron balconies on which winos sleep. One rubble-strewn yard has truncated concrete columns half buried in the ground and supporting nothing. All of this seems suitable as a gateway to the underworld, and Manning visits it daily. He hunched forward over his coffee cup and stared toward the morgue doorway, at a sign that said PLEASE DO NOT THROW LOOSE CLOTH OR BLOODY SHEETS ON THE DUMPSTERS.

Manning looked back at me. "The kid porn racket is even bigger. Kid porn has larger profits than all of the Hollywood studios combined, something like three billion dollars a year. With money like that, you can buy a lot of protection. So if you're looking to bust a porno ring for some reason, and it seems like you are, you're wasting your fucking time." Manning sat back in his chair, sighed.

"People into kids can even take a child molester's tour. They visit houses of child prostitution in Hong Kong, Thailand, Korea, Cambodia, and the rest of the Asian countries. The package is pricey, but the memories are unforgettable."

I sat in my office, turning the information about Rebecca Hewitt over in my head. Even though I had her name, I was no closer to finding her. If I confronted Brand directly, I'd send him running, and spoil the Rennseler murder investigation, in which he was my prime suspect. I had to let Rebecca Hewitt fade back into the mists of the world I'd stumbled into, the international syndicate of child exploitation, but I felt those mists shrouded the death of Tommy Rennseler. I looked at my lizard. "So let's see what the Game of Thirty says." I rolled my dice, figured my moves, and was able to get my lead piece to the square of the Lovely Ladies, who were, according to the instruction book, temple prostitutes.

Ranouka's voice came over the intercom. *"There is an animated gentleman here to see you. He has no appointment."*

"What do you mean, animated? Is he Bugs Bunny?"

"He's extremely upset. Shall I send him in?"

"Tell him my fee. It starts the moment he comes through my door."

"Don't be pecuniary, Jimmy. It does not befit you."

Ranouka rang off, and a moment later she opened the door, introducing me to Mr. Landless, a middle-aged man with a yellow flower in his buttonhole.

I spoke from behind my desk. "A hundred fifty bucks an hour, Mr. Landless."

Landless was animated all right. He seemed ready to levitate. "Your fee's too high."

"Life's too short. What's your problem?"

"I'm getting married this afternoon."

"Yes, you have got a problem."

Mr. Landless sat down in the client's chair and stared at me through troubled eyes. "Last night some friends threw a stag party for me. For a joke, they rented an X-rated video."

"So?"

"I recognized my fiancée." Landless looked suspiciously at the flower in his buttonhole, as if wondering whether it was bugged. "At least I think it was my fiancée. I'm not absolutely sure. The hair was different, and she was wearing heavy make-up. But the way she groaned when she was—when she was performing the act—"

"Lots of women groan when they're performing the act."

"Not like Dorothy. Dorothy..." Landless hesitated, an embarrassed flush filling his cheeks.

"Come on, Landless, I've done hundreds of matrimony cases. I've had to bust in and photograph people performing the act. I've heard my share of groaning."

Landless unlaced his fingers and ran a hand nervously over his head. He looked down at the floor as he spoke. "Dorothy makes a sort of liquid bubbling sound. Almost like a warbler."

"Like...a...warbler..." I was taking notes.

"And the woman in the film, her posterior was exactly like Dorothy's."

"One posterior is much like another, Landless."

"I felt the resemblance was disturbingly close."

"Okay, so what do you need me for?"

"I've got to know for sure. I don't want to marry a porn star. Can you find out?" He glanced at his watch. "By noon?"

"Dorothy's full name?"

"Dorothy Leon."

"Got a photo?"

"Yes."

It was an eight-by-ten glossy, professionally done, with Dorothy's name at the bottom of it and a theatrical agent's name on back. "An actress?"

"Part-time. She works as a secretary at Chicken Express. That's how I met her. I'm one of their purchasing agents."

"I've had your chicken. It's not bad."

"Yes, we buy a better bird."

I laid the photograph down. "What was the name of the film?"

"*Wet Slut*"

"*Wet...Slut*...name of the company?"

"Banana Productions."

I put down my pen. "Landless, why don't you just ask Dorothy if she was in the film?"

"When? When I'm walking up the aisle? She's with the wedding party already."

"Your fiancée's a struggling actress. Maybe she was desperate. We've all done crazy things. You could work it out together."

He put his head in his hands and his voice cracked. "Her partner sipped champagne from a straw inserted in Dorothy's vagina."

"A theatrical effect."

"We've got two hours. Are you going to help?"

I was flipping through my Rolodex. I found the number I wanted and dialed over the speakerphone, so Landless could hear. We listened to the dial tone, and then a gruff voice answered. *"Yeah?"*

"Joe Banana, is that you?"

"No, it's Mother Fucking Theresa."

"Joe, this is Jimmy McShane."

There was a slight, paranoid pause. Then: *"Jimmy, whattya say."*

"Joe, I've got a client thinks his fiancée was in one of your films."

"Everybody thinks that"

I looked at Landless. "He's getting married in a few hours. He'd like to know. We've got a photo of her. Can we come up and see you?"

"I don't give a fuck. Now?"

"We're on the way." I hung up the phone and led the way out of the office. Then, thinking about Joe Banana and the square of the Lovely Ladies, I went back and grabbed *The Little Mermaid*. Landless and I went out through the iron gate, into the morning sunlight. The street sweeper had just been by, rearranging the filth, and there was a moist smell in the air. "We'll take the Seventh Avenue subway, it'll be faster than a cab."

We walked toward Sheridan Square. The sun was blazing already at ten o'clock. I was reflecting on the daughter I'd never seen, and Akhenaten's golden scepter, and ten million dollars.

"Dorothy is a very conscientious person," said Landless. "She studies hard."

"So give her a break."

"I'd love to. I'd love to be easygoing and youth culture-conscious." Landless stopped on the sidewalk and looked at me. "Only I'm not. I'm forty-five years old. I'm a purchasing agent at Chicken Express. I have old-fashioned values."

"Well, we're not sure yet if it was Dorothy."

"I've got a bad feeling about it."

"I've got bad feelings about everything, but I don't let it bother me." We crossed Bleecker and continued on past St. John's, a church with a nice Federal cupola on it, which I didn't think Landless could appreciate in his present state of mind. We hit Sheridan Square and went down the subway stairs. The train was waiting at the platform. I pulled out two tokens on the run, we pushed through the turnstile, and hopped on the train. The doors closed just behind us, and I hung on to a steel bar and watched the tunnel walls sliding past the window. The air conditioning was broken as usual, and the car felt like something an Egyptian tomb robber had opened.

"She's got a wonderful personality." Landless was shouting in my ear. "The only thing is, she was raised by very strict Catholics. She went to a Catholic school, and every day when she got home she used to dance naked in front of a mirror."

I continued looking at the rushing subway walls, and imagined Dorothy as a Catholic school girl dancing naked in front of her mirror. It was a compelling picture. I'd attended Catholic school myself.

The lights of the tunnel streaked past, like electric serpents in the walls. I saw a worker on an adjacent spur, his jacket glowing with reflective stripes as he felt his way along like a luminous troglodyte. "But even if that's the reason," shouted Landless, "even if she was making a rebellious statement against the Catholic church and her background, I can't deal with it. I know myself. It'd eat me apart."

We were approaching Forty-second Street. The tunnel lights slowed. The station platform, with its waiting passengers, appeared. Their faces moved past me; though we shared this city, we were meshed for this instant only. Since childhood, I'd played the game of disappearing strangers; all their thoughts and schemes were streaming past, never to be known, which, in a subway tunnel, might be just as well. The train stopped and the doors opened. I led the way through the station and up the subway stairs, past a wino curled like an embryo; the smell that came off him was so powerfully filthy it was profound, with a radius of several yards, and he dwelled at its center without fear of intrusion. We stepped through his aromatic existential statement and surfaced on Times Square. Buildings ran row upon row toward the Hudson, and their drab windows reflected the morning light, casting it back to the sky with a leaden glow. On both sides of the street X-rated films were playing. A navy Aqua-Lung was for sale at the army-navy outlet, and a crackhead who looked like he needed an Aqua-Lung moved past us, along with assorted pimps, gangbangers, and hookers patrolling the street. The music was loud, the colors on the marquees garish. I felt comfortable there because nobody was hiding anything beneath a civilized facade; everybody was a threat. It produced a peculiar inner calm in me.

"I don't come here anymore," said Landless. "When I was young I did, but it seemed different then. Your life wasn't on the line."

"Your life's not on the line, relax."

"I can handle that Dorothy's a lot younger than me. I can handle that she's ambitious and wants a career in theater. I can't handle her with champagne in her vagina."

We passed several stores with huge GOING OUT OF BUSINESS signs draped over a glittering array of bogus brand-name cameras and tape recorders, and characters you wouldn't want to have anything to do with were waiting to serve you.

"How could Dorothy have connected to anybody with a business on this street?"

"She probably didn't," I said. "And in an hour you'll be married to her."

"People in these films are at terrible risk for AIDS." Landless had his nose in his flower, possibly to block out the faint smell of urine that bloomed in the doorways. "Dorothy made us both get blood tests. Now it makes more sense."

"She tested negative?"

"Yes."

I stopped on the street. "Look, you're both healthy. Why don't you just forget about the champagne in her vagina?"

"I've got to know."

"She's a beautiful young girl. You're a lucky guy."

"I can't marry a girl who performed sex for money."

"Landless, you're forty-five years old. You buy chickens for a living."

"I know, I'm no prize. But I have my pride."

I resumed walking. Landless was rearranging the silk handkerchief in his lapel. "Dorothy thinks she has a future in show business."

"Does she?"

"I've seen her in workshops. She's not all that talented, to tell you the truth. Neither was the girl in the film."

I led him through the doorway of Acropolis Books and Magazines. A swarthy kid in sleeveless T-shirt and floral pants looked down from a stool behind the front counter. I said, "Banana's expecting me. Tell him it's Jimmy."

The kid picked up a phone and dialed. "Somebody named Jimmy for you." He hung up and nodded to me. "Door at the back of the store."

The aisles were filled with customers quietly leafing through the merchandise, horny men from every walk of life. Any one of them would probably have been happy to marry the star of *Wet Slut*.

When we reached the door, the kid at the front pushed a button and released the solenoid lock. I opened the door and went into the back office. Joe Banana sat behind a large desk. Autographed photos of X-rated actresses hung around him on the wall. A fan was blowing warm air over him.

"Jimmy," he said, making a gesture of rising to greet me, which he didn't complete; the heat was too much for him, and he sank back into his chair. He was a small, soft-looking man with a gray zipperhead haircut, and he wore a monogrammed shirt with a hand-painted tie. He'd produced hundreds of bargain basement porno films, and the stars on his wall were unknown to anyone but him.

"Joe, this is Mr. Landless, my client. As you can see from his flower, he's on the way to his wedding."

"Congratulations," said Banana, flashing his expensive dental work. "It's a nice day to get married."

Landless mumbled something, and I took out the photograph. "Joe, take a look. Did you ever hire this girl?"

Banana studied the photo; "Never saw her before in my life." He handed it back to me.

"You're sure?"

Banana gestured to the stars on his wall. "I know these girls. We get close. You get in a creative situation, you get close."

"We can bet the farm on that?"

"Absolutely." Banana's smile to Landless widened, showing more polished porcelain. "I know every broad in the business. That girl never made a film with me or anybody else."

Landless's eyes were brimming with tears. He looked like a man who'd just passed his cardiac stress test. "Thank you." He took Banana's manicured hand. "Thank you very much."

"Don't mention it."

Landless turned to me, as one hand went to his wallet. "Mr. McShane—"

"Forget it, Landless. It's a wedding present. Go get married."

Landless grabbed my hand. "I'll send a bird to your office."

"Fine."

Landless turned to Banana. "I'll send over a bird to you too."

Joe Banana shot me a questioning glance. I said, "Mr. Landless works for Chicken Express."

Banana leaned back into the breeze from his fan. "A plump chicken. I buy one sometimes."

"Well," said Landless, "I'd better run. You're both invited to the wedding. Little Church Around the Corner. There's a reception afterward. Plenty of chicken." Landless backed out of the office and closed the door behind him.

"A happy man," said Joe Banana.

"You did the right thing, Joe."

"Sure. Why wreck some guy's dream?"

"It was her, right?"

"Not a great star, but she had an innocent look. That's always tasty."

"She was educated by Catholic nuns."

"The perfect start for this business." Banana turned to face his fan.

"How many films was Dorothy in?"

"Just *Wet Slut*. She needed some dough, she got it, she split." Banana swiveled in his chair to look at the gallery of actresses on his wall. "Lots of them are like that, we pass in the night." He swiveled back toward me. "I'll tell you this, that guy's got himself a lovely girl. Very quiet and sensitive, but she practically sings while she's getting pronged. It's very cinematic."

"Landless didn't think she had much talent."

"She was new, she needed time to develop. I think she would have blossomed under my direction."

"I'm sure she would have, Joe." I ran my finger along the edge of his desk. "Anybody you know making child pornography?"

Banana drew himself up stiffly. "I have nothing to do with kid porn, Jimmy."

"No offense meant, Joe."

"The money's there, but I got my principles. X-rated films, sure, who gives a fuck, it's consenting adults and nobody gets hurt. Do you know it's been proven that X-rated films keep Peeping Toms off the street?"

"You're performing a public service, Joe."

"But a kid deserves a life. Besides, you get nailed making a kiddie flick in the present climate, a lady judge will give you two life sentences." Banana looked at me through a paranoid veil. "Somebody tell you I'm making kiddie flicks?"

"No, I'm tracking a child molester. He stars in his own reel." I took Brand's video out of my pocket. "Got time to take-a look at this?"

"At *The Little Fucking Mermaid*?"

"It's the X-rated version."

Banana shrugged, and put the tape into the big screen video behind his desk. He pressed PLAY and Brand came on screen with the eight-year-old girl.

"Amateur videos are ruining this business." Banana opened his cigar case, a look of disgust on his face. "Any jackoff can make a film. It hurts the real directors like myself."

"I'm sorry to hear that."

"Hey, *c'est la vie*." Banana lit the cigar with a two-inch flame from his butane. "I suffer for my art."

"Look at the room the kid's in, Joe. I'm betting it's in the Adirondacks around Lake Placid. Do you recognize it?"

"Let's say it rings a bell."

"How do I find it?"

Banana blew a puff of smoke toward the screen and ducked my question. "The room's tilted. It looks like a fucking chimpanzee is holding the camera."

"Come on, Joe, the kid's a prisoner. What if she was your daughter?"

He gazed at me through the pungent smoke of his cigar. "He should've kept the window out of the shot. See those logs? That's how you can tell where it was made."

"You've been there?"

"I've heard about it." He tapped the ash from his cigar. "He wanted the window in the shot. Thought it was good composition. What a schmuck."

"Where, Joe?"

"I hear things. I'm in the loop. But I never had anything to do with the place, okay?"

"Okay."

Banana placed his cigar carefully on the rim of the ashtray and looked back up at me. "How'd you know it was Lake Placid?"

"Credit card check."

"Plastic. It's convenient, but oh boy." He turned the ashtray slowly, until the tip of the cigar was pointing at me. "Little town called Pertshire. Look for the name ETL." Banana swiveled away from me, his chair tilting backward as he gazed at the photos of the porno starlets who smiled down at him from their place on the wall. Cigar smoke wreathed his head, as he said, "The little birds fly up and you live forever, right?"

"THE PROPERTY used to be called Blue Wood. It belonged to the people who owned the Adirondack Railroad. Now it belongs to a human potential group, an outfit called Executive Training Lab. They hold training retreats for bigshot business executives." Sheriff George Dillahunt of Perthshire was a thickset, weather-beaten man who'd spent the early part of his life as an Adirondack hunting and fishing guide, and then as a game warden, and his eyes were those of a tracker, scanning for details; I doubt if much escaped him in the town he served. Manning had established my bona fides with the sheriff, and we were getting along pretty well, seated across from each other in his office, but those dark eyes of his had a current in them that came from the deep forest. There was a disquieting energy in his gaze, which shot out every so often, as if he were looking at the trail on which we were both walking and he saw things I didn't. "I've been suspicious of the Lab for months, but the County Board of Supervisors loves them because they've been very charitable to the county." Dillahunt rocked back in his chair, his leather boots and holster creaking. "They offer something called modern management. They're supposed to be taking mid- and upper-level

managers and filling them full of teamwork skills."
He nodded toward his office window, and Stoddard
Mountain, which looked down onto his little town.
"Clients arrive on private planes, they're met by a
limo, stay a few days, and fly away. But it doesn't
look right to me. For one thing, it's always men, never
women. And none of them ever come into town for
anything. You'd think they'd be curious about the
town, wouldn't you?"

"They don't want to be seen."

"Tell that to the board. After I expressed concern
about the Lab, the board president called me paranoid. So
I'll be interested in whatever you can tell me about these
people at ETL."

"Executive Training Lab is a front for a child
prostitution ring."

The sheriff leaned forward in his swivel chair. "Child
prostitution? In this county?"

"Third World kids are nabbed and smuggled into
Canada and the U.S. And sometimes American kids
get caught too. It's an international business. ETL's
assets are probably in a corporation in the Bahamas
or the Cayman Islands, with government protection
against law enforcement agencies. And some night
they'll just disappear from here, and you'll never see
them again."

"Well, I can't just bust in there. We have to write up
an affidavit, and you've got to provide adequate evidence
for the judge issuing a search warrant. What've you got?"

"A videotape. It shows a girl being molested."

"On the Lab property?"

"That's what my informant says."

"Your informant will have to sign the affidavit too."

"That's not possible. And I have to keep the video out of it, because it's part of another case."

"Then how do we get a search warrant?"

"We don't. I just want you to keep your patrol cars out of the area while I go in." The sound of the dispatcher's radio came from the other room, with updates from the two vehicles out attending to the local situation—a dog running loose, a loon in the doughnut shop. I said, "I'll get you hard evidence and then you can make the bust."

"It'll be an illegal entry, and it won't be admissible. A monster lawyer will come in and chew my nuts off. We need probable cause to enter."

"I'd like to show you the tape."

"Other room." Dillahunt led the way and closed the door behind us. He put in the tape, pressed PLAY, and watched. In less than a minute he was squirming uncomfortably. "This makes me sick," he said, getting up and pacing with frustration, his boot heels thudding on the floor. "Who is that sonofabitch anyway?"

"A Connecticut millionaire."

He shook his head, sat back down, and continued watching, his rage building, until he looked ready to pull out his .45 and fire it at the screen. "Whoa!" He came forward, pressed the PAUSE button, and pointed to the screen. "That chair in the corner?"

"Yes?"

"Built by Fred Wiggins. The Lab wanted to shop local and they got Fred to build them some furniture. I have one of his chairs myself. Fred always puts that flower design in the backs." Dillahunt turned toward me. "So the Lab fucked up. This tape was made on their premises." He hit the EJECT button, went to the window, and stared out, hands on his hips. Finally he turned back to me. "We've got to take them down right, or they'll wriggle out of this. You know what I'm afraid of? We try for a warrant and somebody tips the Lab off. First thing they'll do is kill that kid and drop her in a lake. Because without the kid, there's no case. Does the Lab know you're onto them?"

"No."

"All right, so we've got surprise going for us."

"Sheriff, I'd like to show you my van."

I knocked on the back door of the van, and Henderson answered. I wasn't back in her good graces yet and she was still unhappy about my chakras, but she wanted to help free the little girl she'd seen on the videotape. "Come in," she said, "we're just making some litchi berry tea to improve our night vision."

Bobby Booker put out his hand to Dillahunt. Bobby was bald, black, and bearded, had graduated from the FBI Academy and worked as an agent for a while, then headed out on his own into the more lucrative free-lance surveillance world. Now he gave Sheriff Dillahunt the guided tour. "...the roof vent houses a periscope. It's got a Javelin Night Vision System, hundred thirty-five-millimeter lens, automatic brightness control, forty-millimeter intensifier for maximum resolution."

Dillahunt sighed, probably thinking about the budget his office had. He said, "That scope costs around eight grand, doesn't it?"

"We'll see their nose hairs," answered Bobby. "We've also got a Gibson parabolic listening dish, hear a quarterback say *shit* in the huddle a thousand feet away." He stepped over to the desk, which held a large instrument panel and a color monitor. "Everything works on a joystick controlled from here."

Dillahunt looked at me. "You folks came prepared."

Bobby continued: "Here we have goggles for night driving. They'll turn a dark road into daylight and let us drive in without anybody seeing headlights. Also a thermal viewer that'll display body heat. These units all come with weapon mounts."

The sheriff was looking at the kind of surveillance equipment lawmen dream about owning. "You could get me names of Lab clients with this stuff, right? Who they are, where they come from?"

Bobby nodded. He was deeply attached to the dream devices that turned him into a night-hunting owl, capable of seeing and hearing the human rodents of this world as they creep in and out of their holes.

The sheriff unrolled a county map onto our desk and pointed to a large piece of rural property outlined in blue. "Here's where the Lab is."

Bobby said, "I was up there this morning."

"You don't waste any time."

"I tried a phone tap. They're jamming the line with white noise. There's no way we can hear who's calling them, but we'll get the Lab's side of the conversation with the Gibson dish."

Dillahunt ran his finger along the map. "This is an old logging road. It's grown over, but you'll get in. It'll put you just below the ridge that looks down onto the Lab."

"You coming with us, Sheriff?"

"I'd love to watch you work all this shit, but if I'm in the van with you it could spoil our warrant. I'll be out at the highway. We'll set up a secure channel."

Henderson was wearing an oversized tee and ribbed brown leggings. Bobby was wearing his eleven-thousand-dollar night vision goggles, and we were driving like a submarine in pitch-black darkness along the old logging road, which wound through the woods. I was in the front captain's chair beside Bobby. Henderson was leaning forward between us, the bare shape of her arms faintly visible in the subdued light of the dashboard. I leaned over and put my lips on the delicately scented flesh of her arm; one of her eyebrows arched up radically, but she said nothing. I nibbled blindly up her arm, as the van bounced over the uneven ground; one of the bounces took me from her arm onto the soft fabric covering her breast, and my nose sank into it. She lifted my head by the ears. "You've had enough."

"Impossible."

"We're here," said Bobby, and I saw the ragged outline of spruce and pine forming the top of the ridge. Bobby brought the van to a stop just below the ridge. We were like a huge silent boulder in the darkness.

"Can we speak?" whispered Henderson.

"Van's soundproof," said Bobby. He threw a switch on the dash. "The springs are locked. We can move around." He climbed out of his captain's chair. I followed him into the back of the van and closed a thick curtain behind me. Bobby turned on the interior lights and went to his workstation.

"Periscope up."

The roof vent opened and the periscope slid silently upward over the top of the ridge. The slight bit of available light from the stars and the moon was amplified in the scope, and the estate appeared in faint outline on our monitor. Bobby adjusted the gain on the night vision lens, and the image grew clear and sharp. The lodge was a large old building that was a mix of logs, stone, and decorative branches worked into porch rails and door-frames, all of it supposed to give the idea of roughing it, but in luxury. "It's a no-shit house, all right, heavily protected." He pointed at three figures outside the house. "One fixed and two floaters."

The fixed guard was on the front steps. The two floaters moved over the grounds, from the lodge out to the wall, and then around its perimeter, their forms shimmering like ghosts. I motioned Henderson closer to the monitor. "Seem like an executive training lab to you?"

Bobby flipped a switch and started his reel-to-reel tape recorder going. "Mike's hot." He put his headphones on and began working the joystick that controlled the mike. The needles on the vu-meter jumped. "Lots of ambient stuff," he said. "The unwanted sound of nature. I'll take the first shift. You guys relax."

Henderson and I sat at the fold-down table. She asked, "Why can't the sheriff just march right in?"

"The Lab would walk on a technicality. People's rights of privacy are stronger than they've ever been."

"What are we listening for?"

"For the weak spot."

"What if there isn't one?"

I reached under the table to a drawer, where I'd stowed the Game of Thirty to help pass the time. I brought it out and placed it between us. "Somebody always makes a wrong move."

It was the middle of the night. The van was dark except for the glow of the monitor and a small desk light. It was my shift, but the activity in the lodge seemed to have shut down. The only sounds were crickets, and a whippoorwill who'd been sounding off every hour or so. Bobby was sitting in a chair, asleep or meditating, I couldn't tell which, but he hadn't spoken for a while. Henderson was stretched out on the bed, but I knew she wasn't asleep, as she'd been turning restlessly, and now she spoke from the shadows. "I've started to think that the human race is going through a horrible pedophilia phase. Thirty percent of the women in America claim to have been sexually abused as children. With that many people involved, it starts to look like normal behavior."

I said, "Let's hope it's a distorted statistic. These days if a father makes his daughter wash the dishes she calls it abuse."

Bobby spoke from his chair, his head coming forward into the glow from the monitor. "I've been remembering something I haven't thought about in years. Want to hear?"

"The night is long."

"Well, the apartment I grew up in didn't have too much space. Me and my brothers and sisters all slept in the same room. My older sister and I slept in the same bed." Bobby's voice was gentle, almost feminine, in sharp contrast to his rugged exterior. "Thing is, she initiated me into sex. And I was grateful to her. I still am. Maybe it's because we were both children and there was so much love between us that there was no feeling of exploitation."

"And how did she turn out?" asked Henderson softly.

"Fine."

The cellular phone rang. "McShane."

My important calls were being forwarded to the van. There was a brief undersea cable pause and then: "Rafeek Shaddi here, Mr. McShane. I am uncovering some correspondence. Are you buying?"

"You bet, Rafeek. What have you got?"

"I have ingratiated myself with a corrupt assistant of the art dealer Hassanein Hamid, by numerous costly little gifts, but it has paid off handsomely I am thinking. The entire matter of the golden scepter of Akhenaten is clarified."

"My colleague is here and I'd like her to hear this. Okay by you?"

"Okay."

I hit the speaker button, and the Egyptian investigator's amplified voice filled the van. "Your dead man Tommy Rennseler had a buyer for the delightful scepter. He wrote this to Hamid some time ago, when the existence of the scepter was only a rumor In his letter Rennseler asks Hamid, and I am now quoting directly from the correspondence, 'Does the scepter actually show Akhenaten 's child bride? My client will purchase it at the price you mentioned, if this detail is preserved.' Are you being with me, Mr. McShane?"

"I'm being with you, Rafeek."

"The buyer is an American named Brand. B-R-A—"

"I've got the spelling."

"Fine, fine. Hamid's corrupt assistant told me that Tommy Rennseler had arranged other purchases through Hamid for Brand. There are a few more details here that could be significant." There was another intercontinental pause.

"I'm buying it all, Rafeek."

"You are like me, Mr. McShane, you are wanting every scrap because who knows, eh?"

"That's it, Rafeek, who knows."

"Number one: Your dead man Tommy has a brother, Richard, whom you undoubtedly know of. Richard was here at the time the scepter went missing. I am thinking he is up to his giggy in this affair"

"Right on, Rafeek."

"Now item number two: The ancient art works this Brand fellow purchased were all of female children. I have noted several in Hamid's correspondence: 'a serving girl wearing the sidelock of youth.' Here is another: 'Amarna princess, aged six, in ceremonial wig.' And one more: 'Theban girl, nine, studying the art of the dance.' It is sounding like he is liking the charms of children, so touching, eh?"

"Very touching."

"Well, I am getting a picture of Mr. Brand. He's a wealthy collector who, it may well be, is now in possession of the golden scepter of Akhenaten. So you'll be sending my check double-quick to the Riggs Bank?"

"First thing in the morning, Rafeek."

"I am being most grateful, Mr. McShane. You are an upstanding dick." Shaddi hung up and I punched the speaker button off. Henderson was already pacing the van. "The money that Brand paid Tommy Rennseler—"

"Not blackmail. He was giving Rennseler a payment on the scepter."

"And Brand has it now?"

"Roger that. And we're in the goddamn Adirondacks."

"You know you had to come here."

"I should've just rushed this place on my own."

"Yes, and gotten people killed." Henderson yanked my jacket open and jammed her fingers into my stomach, just below my rib cage. "We've got to soften your liver." She pressed in under my ribs and poked what I supposed was the offending organ.

"Ouch."

"Of course it hurts. You've stored enormous heat there. But massaging it will help."

"Henderson, I want you to know—you're the first woman to ever massage my liver."

"Just try to learn patience." She nodded toward the image of the mansion on the monitor. "Remember—Brand visited this place. It could be the key to everything. For all we know, the scepter could be down there. All right." She removed her fingers from under my rib cage. "I think I released some of the heat in you."

"Now do I massage yours?"

"I don't need it." Henderson picked up the knucklebone dice, rolled them, and moved her piece. "What's the meaning of this square?"

I looked at the rules. "It's the square of the Mansion." I glanced over at the Adirondack mansion on our surveillance screen. "It's the place where divine justice is dispensed."

We worked two-hour shifts through the night, and when morning came Bobby cooked us a heart-attack breakfast of bacon and eggs which Henderson ate without comments about nitrites, cholesterol, or the antibiotics given to the chickens who laid the eggs;

presumably she felt the surveillance situation gave us a dispensation to eat something other than seaweed and tofu. A limo had left the estate at eight A.M. Now it was in our monitor again, on the way back, coming through the gates of the estate. As it approached the house, a woman came out of the lodge and stood at the head of the driveway. This was Dr. Cheryl Whittiker, whose credentials were seemingly impeccable. The sheriff had given me a glossy publicity handout from the Lab, which touted her doctorate in psychology, her M.A. in business, and her years as a management guru who'd helped a wide variety of American companies in their executive training programs. Impeccable credentials are reassuring, but in twenty-four hours I could have provided credentials that would turn Mickey Mouse into a noise-technology expert from Brazil with a government contract to soundproof all the public lavatories in the state of New York.

Now, as the limo parked in front of her, Dr. Whittiker was there to open its back door. A middle-aged man in a sport coat got out, carrying a briefcase. The mike was picking up birds and a little bit of breeze activity through the leaves, but the human voices were clear enough.

"Hello, Mr. Thurmond So nice to see you again. Did you have a good flight?"

I tracked them on the mike into the house. In twenty minutes time I had his full name, Donald Thurmond, and the city he'd come from, because people like to make small talk. By the middle of the afternoon, four guests in all had arrived, and we had their names and the towns they lived in. I called Sheriff Dillahunt. "I've got some customers for you."

I gave him the names, and Dillahunt ran them through the National Crime Information Center. He was back to me in a half hour: "Nothing on any of them. They're clean."

"Let me try something else." I dialed Manhattan. "Electronic Mole, I dig for you."

"Bytes, it's Jimmy. I've got four individuals. I'm looking for criminal activity. Something. Anything. I need an SPH on each of them immediately. I'm in Booker's van. You've got the number. The names are coming over your fax, *now*."

It was Henderson's shift at the desk, and she spoke with her eyes on the monitor. "SPH?"

"Statement of personal history. We're going after these suckers from the day they drew their first breath."

Bobby hit the SEND button on our portable fax, and the information started on its way to Bytes. I could feel Bytes's mind firing up, preparing to trace the labyrinths these men had traveled so far in their lives.

During Henderson's shift, she yelled for us and turned the speaker up. I heard a familiar child's voice: *"Do you know how many flowers are in this wallpaper?"*

Henderson swiveled toward me. "She's there."

Bobby looked at us. "That's the little lady we're here for?"

I had my ear against the speaker, but the girl's voice was muffled beneath other sounds, and then it was gone altogether, as a closing window took her beyond the sensitivity of our mike. Bobby relieved Henderson at the desk, and she joined me at the table. She had a triumphant look in her eyes. I said, "She's not out yet."

"Yes, but we're going to get her out." She handed me the knucklebones. "Let's see what the Game of Thirty says."

The board was between us on the table. I rolled the knucklebones and moved to the Unwearying Stars. Henderson smiled. "That's you," she said. "Unwearying. You found her."

I didn't tell Henderson what was going through my mind, that if we didn't get a warrant, I was going to mount an attack on the lodge with a bomb I could make from chemicals available at the Perthshire hardware store: The bomb explodes at the back wall of the estate, the guards go toward it, and I go in over another part of the wall. I had to keep myself from imagining what was going on in the lodge at this moment, with Rebecca Hewitt and Mr. Donald Thurmond, or whichever of the men was in the room with her. She'd have to endure one final afternoon, but I was taking her out by nightfall.

The phone rang.

"McShane."

"The evil that men do lives after them."

"Bytes, I love you."

"On a college weekend twenty years ago, Mr. Donald Thurmond went to Daytona, Florida, where he skipped out of a restaurant without paying the bill. He was arrested, made bail, and was ordered to appear in court. He seems to have said to himself screw it, I'll never be back there again, because he didn't bother to show in court. A warrant was issued for his arrest."

"And they never got him?"

"No record of it. I'm faxing his file, now."

The fax machine rang, and Bytes's transmission started. I dialed the sheriff. "We may have an active warrant. I'm coming through the woods. Meet me at the road."

"Ten–four."

Sheriff Dillahunt sat behind his desk, on the line to the Daytona chief of police.

"...appreciate it if you'd check and see if the warrant is still active...much obliged, I'll hold." He looked across the desk at me. His eyes were knucklebone bright. He snapped back to attention, phone shoved hard against his ear. "Still active? Will you extradite? ...I know it's a piss-ant charge, but the man is involved in a child prostitution ring and I'm trying to break...that's right, there's an eight-year-old kid in there getting hammered at this very moment by Mr. Donald Thurmond." Dillahunt looked at me, and smile lines spread from the corners of his eyes. "Thank you very much, Chief. You come up this way and I'll show you the best trout fishing you ever had." He slammed the phone down. "Let's ride, cowboy."

Judge Matthew Peers had recessed his court for us and was entering his chambers now, an irritated look on his face. "This better be good."

"Judge, this is Mr. McShane, a private investigator I'm working with. We've got an active arrest warrant, we know where the individual is, I want to search, and we don't have much time."

"All right, George, hand it over." Judge Peers took a seat behind his desk, put on his reading glasses, and picked up his pen. As his eyes ran down the warrant, he placed his pen back on the desk and looked up at Dillahunt. "You want to search the Lab?"

"That's right, Judge. We believe Thurmond is there at this moment."

The judge looked back down at the warrant. On the way over to the courthouse, Dillahunt had told me how easy it was going to be to get the warrant, how the judge wouldn't mind being pulled out of court because he was a stickler for points of law like the one Thurmond had broken—a defiance of the court by failure to appear. But he was lingering over the warrant, his brow creased by a frown.

Dillahunt asked, "Is there something wrong?"

"I have a hard time following this."

"Following what, Judge?"

Judge Peers looked up over the edge of his reading glasses. His gaze showed no feeling, only an acute attention, the mask of the judicial bench. But something was moving in back of that gaze, and it was moving fast.

Dillahunt said, "You're hesitating. I don't understand why."

"Are you sure you want to do this? To disrupt a seminar for this man?"

"Absolutely. And as I said, time's crucial."

The judge picked up his pen again, but made no move to use it. Dillahunt placed the tips of his fingers on the desk. "Judge, the man failed to appear in court."

"It was twenty years ago."

"That may be. But I know how you feel about people who don't show up for appearances in your court."

Judge Peers stared at the sheriff. His reluctance was getting to Dillahunt. "Judge, the four corners of the warrant are good. If you can't sign it, I'll go to the justice of the peace, and he'll sign it. But I can't lose any more time."

The judge nodded his head slowly, signed the warrant, and shoved it across the desk.

"Much obliged, Judge. We're out of here."

I followed Dillahunt from the judge's chambers. He put his trooper's hat on and started moving down the wide marble steps, fast. By the time we reached the front door we were running, and it was only a few steps to the patrol car. It was moving before I'd closed my door. The tires squealed as we peeled out of the courthouse parking lot. I asked Dillahunt, "What was he hesitating for?"

"He's a crusty old buzzard. He wanted to be sure we didn't go off with a flawed warrant."

My pocket cellular rang. I answered it on the speaker. "McShane."

"Jimmy, it's Henderson. The Lab just got a phone call that's upset them. They know you're on the way."

I looked at Dillahunt. "He called them."

Dillahunt switched on the bubble light. "We're five minutes from their front gate." He put the pedal to the floor and we sailed through Perthshire, bubble light flashing, as he got on the radio to his deputies. "The Lab out at Blue Wood. Move." He put down his mike and turned to me. "Peers has been on the bench for thirty years." He cut the wheel smoothly as we hit the first curve out of town. "He's never made an improper move."

"Well, he's made one now."

"The Lab must have paid off some people around here. But to turn a judge?"

"They found his price."

"He'd never risk his prestige for money."

"So what would he risk it for?"

"I'm goddamned if I know."

"Try the unthinkable."

"He's a child-molester?" Dillahunt continued working the wheel smoothly as we sped along the winding mountain road. "But how could he have found out what the Lab is really selling? Nobody around here had any suspicion. You saw how strong their cover is."

"There's a pedophile network. If children are your thing, you find the network, or it finds you. They've got newsletters, mail drops. Word gets around. It got to the judge."

"But why did he risk using a place so close to home?"

"All his life he's had an itch that was hard to scratch. When he found he could scratch it in his own backyard, he couldn't resist."

"He's the stuffiest prick you ever saw on the bench."

"How is he on sex offenders?"

"He throws the book at them." Dillahunt fell silent then, as the pines and firs of the Adirondacks went by us. The sun was behind the trees now, strobing through their blurred forms. "I'll nail him. He's obstructed justice."

"You'll never prove it."

"You figure his ass is covered?"

"Completely. He'll never see the inside of a prison."

"I can force his retirement."

"Don't count on it."

We rolled up to the Lab gate and a security guard was waiting for us. He was in a three-piece suit, but I saw the bulge of a waist-level holster under his jacket. "Sheriff, how can I be of service?" He was on the other side of the closed iron gate, as Dillahunt leaned out the window of his patrol car.

"I've got a search warrant. Open the gate."

The guard pulled out his two-way radio, called the house, and relayed the message. He nodded, then looked back at us. "No problem." The gate opened and Dillahunt drove through. My own radio came on, and I heard Henderson say, "They've told Thurmond there's someone to see him on the porch."

Dillahunt growled, "They're feeding him to us. They want the arrest to take place outside the building. We won't be able to search inside."

We looped into the circular parking area and jumped out. The front door of the lodge opened and Donald Thurmond stepped onto the porch, accompanied by Dr. Whittiker and a security guard. The moment she had him on the porch, Dr. Whittiker faded back into the house. When Thurmond saw the sheriff's uniform, and the patrol car parked behind him, he froze, and I saw the fear shoot through him. He'd long ago forgotten the restaurant he'd skipped out of as a kid, and the court appearance he'd failed to meet. All he could think now was that he was going to be arrested in a house of child prostitution. His desperation surfaced a second later, as he yanked the gun from the security guard's holster and shot Sheriff Dillahunt.

Dillahunt spun around, holding his thigh. Thurmond

shoved the security guard aside and ran into the house. Dillahunt yelled to me, "There's our probable cause, McShane..." and slumped down to the ground, as his deputies appeared at the entrance to the estate, their bubble lights flashing. I ran to the porch, my Beretta out, and flattened myself against the log exterior of the house, just beside the door. I could smell the faint odor of oakum with which the logs were chinked. I dove through the door and struck a hallstand, which tumbled over at my feet. A moment later, one of the deputies came in behind me. I nodded to the main office door, and we entered it, carefully. Dr. Whittiker was picking up the phone. She was in her mid-thirties and was dressed in a wine-colored business suit. How this attractive woman came to be the hostess in a kiddie whorehouse was a question I didn't have time to pursue at the moment, but when in doubt consider the profit motive. She said, "I'm not saying anything until my lawyers get here."

"Lawyers, plural," I said to the deputy.

"She's going to need them."

I left him and moved slowly to the doorway of a sitting room, where a fire burned in the fireplace and stuffed deer heads stared down from the wall. Sitting in a pair of horn and antler chairs were two security guards. Their guns were on the table. They were exercising a shrewdness gained from long and unpleasant experience with the law. If they offered no resistance, only small amounts of their shit were going to stick to the sheriff's shovel when this day's digging was done. "We just take people to the airport and back," said one of them.

Through the window behind them, I saw the other deputy helping Dillahunt. That left the next move in my hands. I went to the stairs and took them quickly, through the scent of Thurmond's cologne. He'd been all freshened, ready for the limo back to the airport and a cozy private flight back to his home, and now he was hiding on this floor somewhere, with a weapon he knew how to use.

I spoke to the empty hallway. "Thurmond, you can call your lawyer." There was no response. "Don't get yourself in any deeper."

The only sound was the voice of the deputy downstairs, handling Dr. Whittiker. I opened the first door in the hall and stepped into the smell of frankincense. The room was decorated as a chapel, with an arched window in stained glass; candles burned on either side of it before a small altar. Beside the altar was a bed, and on it, immaculately white, lay a little girl's first Holy Communion gown.

I opened the next door and found a miniature gym, with a balance beam, on which a little girl's leotards hung. I had the picture of the place now, and of a level of human desire where gratification was molded to forms that were both horrifying and pathetic. I stepped back into the hallway.

"Thurmond, I'm not a cop, I'm a private investigator. I can help you. We just want to shut things down quietly, okay?"

The hall remained silent. He was in one of the rooms, possibly with a little girl whom he could take as a hostage in order to escape. I had to flush him out without harm coming to any of the children. "Thurmond, listen to me. You've got a problem, but it's not the end of the world."

I pushed open the next door. It was decorated as a Victorian nursery. There were antique toys, a brightly painted rocking horse, and four little girls huddled on a canopied bed beside a window. Standing beside them was

Thurmond, the gun in his hand. He had it pointed at them.
I tried to keep my voice calm.

"Don't hurt them, Donald. They're just kids. They're
innocent, they've got nothing to do with any of this."

The window was open and I could hear the crickets
chirping their evensong, but the sound was muffled by the
beating of my heart, which felt like it was coming through
my ribs. The little girls were like broken dolls, their eyes
having a painted, glassy stare, as if their souls had flown
away. Thurmond stood in the light of the setting sun,
with the realization in his face that all the steps of his life
led to precisely this place, with these figures surrounding
him, and the long shadows of the day falling just so. What
he didn't realize was that the crucial step was taken on
the day he'd walked out of a restaurant without paying.
He looked down at the little girls who had given him
forbidden pleasure; outside the window the birds were
singing. It was their last song. He put the gun to his head
and fired. A spray of blood splattered the canopy curtains,
and the crickets stopped chirping.

The little girls hardly reacted. Maybe they thought it
was another kind of game that men came here to play, and
that Thurmond would get up in a while. But he was very
dead, and I covered him with a blanket. Then I knelt down
in front of the girls. I wanted to be on the same level as
them, no taller, and with their perspective, so I could ease
them out of this stage of their nightmare. The State would
soon take over, and their parents would be found, but this
transition, right now, was an important one, for they were
still wrapped in an atmosphere of gross sexual fantasy;
they were coated with its emotional substance, and they
had to slip out of it cleanly and quickly.

The oldest one was Rebecca Hewitt. I recognized

her, even though her hair was tucked up inside a Yankees baseball cap. She must have represented the wholesome American kid in pedophile fantasy because her outfit was completed by blue jeans and a sweatshirt. The next oldest was in a long white cotton nightgown and held an antique teddy bear. She stared at me mutely, her thumb in her mouth; she'd lost the exuberance of her age. She'd been made into a rubbery puppet who'd danced with jerky movements through acts and actions she'd been unable to comprehend, her world a theater of adult male dreaming, desperate and ritualistic. She'd been too young to deal with its intensity and had chosen to remove herself, leaving a puppet to dangle in these dreams. I said to her quietly, "The bad men are gone." The vacancy remained in her eyes.

Beside her cowered the youngest girls, who couldn't have been more than four. They were dressed in sailor suits, like Shirley Temple in a Hollywood cuteness fantasy. They might have been sisters. One of them looked at me, and said, "Are you my Daddy?"

"No, honey, I'm not, but I'm going to take you back to your daddy." I didn't touch her, or the other one. I didn't think my touch would get through to them, and the touch of any man was questionable at this point. These two little sailors had been drifting on a sea of uncertainty, their horizon continually ominous, from which the monsters of the deep appeared periodically to ravish them, wrapping them in erotic tentacles which, for all they knew, might easily strangle them. A shipwrecked man, adrift for weeks or months alone, could not have looked more alienated from humanity than they did. For all the cuteness of their outfits, they weren't cute; their eyes were wild with speculation and anxiety. On some level they must have framed the question—what world is this? I felt incompetent to comfort them. They'd met a monster I'd never grappled with.

I looked at Rebecca. She was staring at me from under the brim of her baseball cap, her weary gaze guarded. But in it I saw a knowledge far beyond her years. She'd been forced out of the cocoon of childhood. I hoped we could get her back into it again, but I didn't know if that fragile envelope could be repaired, or even if she'd fit into it now. I said, "Rebecca, you're going home. Everything's okay."

She turned away from me, not ready to believe. She was looking at the flowers in the wallpaper, and I saw her lips moving as she counted them.

Sheriff Dillahunt limped through the door behind me, accompanied by Henderson. I said to her, "Maybe you should take over here."

She said, softly, "You're doing fine."

HENDERSON, RANOUKA, AND I were eating in the back garden of the office. I'd beefed up the security system; if an intruder's footstep were any heavier than a tomcat's, an unforgettable jolt of electricity would run up his legs, spiral his nuts, and proceed to his skull, where it would exit with a wonderful display of raised hair.

Ranouka spooned saffron rice onto our plates, along with eggplant cooked with coconut. I was sitting in a wrought-iron chair I rated as among the most uncomfortable of my life. Henderson had purchased four such chairs, and the NYPD could have used them to advantage in their interrogation rooms. They were worked through with decorative designs in the shape of roses, which were imbedding themselves in me; the chairs were painted white, as was the iron table on which lunch was being served. Ranouka and Henderson sat beneath the shade of the tree. They did not seem to mind the iron chairs, either because their bottoms were more padded than mine, or because they could tolerate a little discomfort if the furniture was picturesque.

Viola leaned out her window, banged a broom handle on the fire escape, and shouted down at the kitchen of the restaurant next door. "Turn off that fan!" She tried to throw a pan of water toward the restaurant, but

it splashed into our garden, just as my cordless telephone
rang. Ranouka answered it. "McShane Detective Agency.
Yes...yes, he's here..." She pushed the MUTE button.
"NYPD. Detective Manning."

I took the phone. "John, what's up?"

"A Connecticut millionaire was found murdered this
morning. Why is your name in his guest book?"

"Brand's dead?"

"From an injection of cobra venom."

I stood across the street from Antiquity International,
waiting for Temple to show. While I waited, I monitored
Miss Groome through my pocket receiver, whose
earphones look like those for a Walkman. Just another
music lover, keeping time on the corner. But the tune was
Miss Groome's, and it was double time. She was on the
phone, to Helen Rennseler.

*"Yes, Mrs. Rennseler, I know you and I can do a
better job. And I quite agree—Temple needs a long rest.
She's been distracted and, if I may say so, very difficult to
work with."*

The dry, flat tone of Miss Groome's voice was the
sort the pharaoh's attendants probably heard when they
were being sealed up alive with him in his tomb. Very
efficient and final, and please don't anyone make a fuss. *"I
think your plan is excellent. I'm prepared to take over any
time you say...thank you for your confidence..."*

I put the headphones away and crossed the street to
the shop. Miss Groome looked up and buzzed me through.
"Miss Rennseler isn't here."

"I know. I'll wait." I moved toward Temple's office.

"I'm afraid I can't permit you back there."

"I'm not asking your permission." I opened Temple's door and entered. Miss Groome followed me in.

"This is a private office."

And soon to be all yours, I thought.

Seeing that she wasn't going to be able to remove me bodily, she gave ground, but the look in her eyes said that our contest wasn't over, and that soon she'd be the one in charge. "Close the door behind you, Miss Groome."

Her protruding eyes bulged a little more, and then she closed the door with a resounding slam, sealing the attendants in beside the sacrificial goat and the pharaoh's pet monkey.

I sat down in Temple's chair and slowly rotated in it. On the wall just behind me was an ancient piece of Hindu sculpture, of a goddess with a dozen heads radiating out from the central head, which smiled benevolently; the other heads expressed increasing degrees of ferocity, until, at each end, was the head of a snarling tigress.

On the wall opposite me was an illuminated niche. It held a bronze, armor-clad Amazon, with a small shapeless something in her hand. I got up from the chair and read the brass plate beneath the piece, which explained that the Amazon had cut out the liver of a prisoner and was examining it for portents. Well, a girl has to look somewhere for help, and this was before the astrology column in *Vogue*.

The entrance bell jingled at the front of the shop, and I heard Temple's voice. A moment later she appeared in the office doorway. She entered and closed the door behind her. I said, "Brand has been murdered. A fatal injection."

She sagged back against the wall, her eyelids closing.

She was a real 1920s collectible, with her half-moon eyebrows, her high cheekbones, and slicked-down, track-lit hair. I said, "You'll be getting another visit from the police. Tell them everything you know about Brand, and that we suspected him in your father's death. Tell them that's why you directed me to visit him. Otherwise, I could have a lot of explaining to do."

She opened her eyes, and asked, softly, "Am I to blame?"

"What do you mean?"

"If I hadn't gotten you on everyone's trail, stirred things up…" She closed her eyes again and swayed slightly; her lips moved, but I couldn't hear what she was saying. I felt the cow goddess of love nudging me again. I was wrapped up in Temple, but the voice of Willy the Wire kept saying that I didn't have the right pick to the lock around her heart. I had a picture in my mind, of Temple as a young girl, wandering the streets of Manhattan alone, lost in her dream of ancient kingdoms. The young men of her acquaintance probably thought she was whacky, and she probably thought they were shallow. Dead kings held her imagination, and now her dead father was holding it.

She was standing in front of the Hindu sculpture. The dozen heads of the goddess seemed to radiate out of her own. She said, "I found an old diary of Father's at the house on Fire Island. It's nearly ten years old, so I didn't think it could have much relevance, but I went through it anyway." She opened the diary, and read: "*Rex appeared last night at the shop. He said he was going to kill me. How could this awful situation have ever developed? But of course I'm to blame.*" She closed the diary, and looked at me, her eyes filling with tears, and I felt the pull between us. She was finding things out because of me, and

I was there each time her feelings were exposed. It made her vulnerable, and a woman's vulnerability is a warmth into which a man can step, but I knew it wouldn't be fair to take advantage of it. It was murder haunting us again, murder that was our aphrodisiac.

Manning got out of an unmarked patrol car, and we walked through Washington Square, where a pair of citizens were threatening each other. One had a broken brick in his hand; the other had reached into a litter basket and taken out an empty bottle, with which he held up his end of the encounter.

I looked at Manning.

"Fuck 'em," said Manning, and we continued through the square to MacDougal Street. I pointed out a pair of turn-of-the-century pineapple gateposts at number 129. "You don't see many like that anymore."

"I don't give a fuck if I ever see one," said Manning. We walked over to the Café Reggio. The coffeehouse was empty. We went to the rear of the somber little place, whose walls were dark from decades of cigarette smoke. Manning settled himself, his big frame like mine, a little too much for tiny café tables. He gave the pretty young waitress his cupid's smile, and I saw her resist the impulse to reach out and run her hand through his curls. "Bring us two double espressos and a couple of cannolis," said Manning, with a double espresso's worth of charm in his voice. He had sources all over town, but he was always collecting more. I brought him up to speed with what I knew about the Cobra and Rex, and the waitress brought our cannolis. Manning bit into one, and powdered sugar coated his upper lip in a scraggly white mustache. "Are you providing security for the whole Rennseler family?"

"I'm watching Temple and her uncle."

Manning turned the pastry in his fingers as if trying to find which way to attack what remained of it, then swallowed it whole. "I'm leaving the case on inactive status. We can't expect any cooperation from the Egyptians because the fundamentalists are blowing up tour buses every day at the pyramids, and the police there are out flat just trying to keep the country from coming apart. They don't have time to solve a New York City murder. I told that to the Fairfield County D.A. I got you off the hook with him, by the way."

Manning brushed the powdered sugar mustache off his lip. The espresso machine was wheezing steam. A bronze bust of Shakespeare stared out the window at a boom box floating by on rap pentameter. Manning sighed, looked around the empty café, as if hoping to find a clue to something, anything. "Fuck. Or did I say that already?" He sighed again, gulped down his espresso, and stood. "I gotta go, I'm due at the morgue."

We walked back up MacDougal Street, through the smell of incense from an Indian shop, and frying onions from a sausage and pepper joint, into the sound of chess pieces clicking on the cement tables in the park. The two disputatious citizens had moved their shouting match alongside the chess tables, but the chess players didn't even bother to look up. The citizen holding the bottle threw it at the other citizen's head, where it struck a direct hit and exploded. Manning and I walked on by him. I said to Manning, "In old New York, this used to be the hanging field. That big tree over there was the gallows."

Manning looked at the collection of dope dealers, drunks, and crackheads gathered in the park. "It was a great loss to the city."

"All Arabs fear the desert, Miss Henderson. They are afraid of the djinns who live there." Hassanein Hamid had noticed the Egyptian amulet Henderson was wearing. We were in the Rennseler apartment, and Helen's maid, Angela, had just placed a tea tray in front of Henderson and me. Hamid smiled toward Henderson and passed her a cup. "I trust your little pin will keep you safe."

I glanced at Helen. She was wearing a sleeveless shirt and skirt in a shade of yellow I had in my crayon box as a kid; she was the color of the misshapen suns I used to scribble, but there was nothing scribbled or misshapen about Helen; her slender legs and bare arms were the products of daily workouts. She'd called me here for a reason that would have to wait until Hamid's elliptic Egyptian style had brought us to the point. While he talked I looked at the Game of Thirty on the table in front of us. It looked as if Hamid had been playing with Helen. The lead piece was on the square of Mafdet, a friendly goddess in the shape of a leopard, who protects against snakes.

"In southern Egypt we have people who can trace their lineage back to the eighteenth dynasty, to Akhenaten's reign. Can you imagine? They carry family memories of the ancient Theban rites. So, in a very real way, the gods of ancient Egypt live. Your amulet may still contain a special power."

"Oh, I think so," said Henderson, touching the pin on her dress. "Last night I dreamt I was inside an

Egyptian tomb. A door opened and I saw the scepter of Akhenaten."

"Did you indeed?"

"It was beautiful. It lit up the entire tomb. And I said to myself, *This is why everyone wants it.*"

"Let us hope it is a precognitive dream," said Hamid, dropping his mask of urbanity for a moment and leaning forward with genuine interest.

"Would anyone like more tea?" Helen intervened nervously, teapot in hand, even though Hamid had just filled our cups. She gave Hamid a look that said it was time, and he, apparently, was delegated to do the manipulating. "Mr. McShane, you are a patient man, sitting here with us as we talk about dreams. Well, then—" He set his teacup down. "You know Charles Brand wanted the scepter. But do you know why?"

"Because he lived in Wonderland."

"Excuse me?"

"He was a child molester."

"Yes, exactly. Brand wanted the scepter because it depicted his aberration, royally sanctioned if you will, one of the privileges of the pharaoh. People like Brand are always looking for historical approval, a sort of wink from the past that says, *It's permitted.* I suppose it eases their conscience."

"Brand's dead, Mr. Hamid. It's Temple's safety I'm concerned about now."

"Naturally. So are we. But first you must understand about Akhenaten's scepter—"

My beeper went off. Bobby Booker was on the other end, outside Richard Rennseler's house, and his words sounded in Helen's living room. *"Jimmy, I'm not the only one watching Rennseler. There's somebody in back of the place, and I'm going to check it out."*

Before his message ended, I was already on my feet. So was Helen. "No!" she cried. She had lost the color in her stretched-tight, sculpted cheeks, and her eyes showed an anxiety I hadn't thought she was capable of feeling. "You mustn't intervene."

I was already turning toward the elevator, with Henderson beside me. Over my shoulder, I said, "You people are too discreet for your own good. You're all going to wind up dead."

"Wait," said Helen. "The situation isn't what you think."

I stepped past the porcelain temple dogs and pressed the elevator button. "Helen, there are two people after the scepter—the Cobra and a man named Rex. One of them killed your husband for it, and he probably killed Charles Brand for the same reason. But he still hasn't got it, and the list gets shorter. Your brother-in-law is next."

The elevator rose up and came to a stop, the door sliding open. Helen grabbed me by the sleeve. "Mr. McShane, Rex is my son."

I rested my hand on the head of a temple dog, its baked finish smooth and cool beneath my fingertips. "Give me that again?"

"Please," she said, "don't harm him."

Bobby's van was empty, and I saw where he'd gone— a corridor between the townhouses, leading to the rear of the building. I ran through it and found him unconscious on the pavement beneath the fire escape. Henderson ran up behind me and knelt over him. She lifted his head and examined the bruise that had flattened him. "I'd better stay with him."

The back door opened and Brigid looked out. I ran toward her. She tried to slam the door, but I jammed my foot in it. "Brigid, I know we've never been really close, but somebody is about to kill your employer."

I pushed the door open as a cry came from the second floor. I raced to the stairs and went up them two at a time, to an office at the end of the hall where I found Rennseler on the floor, a hypodermic syringe dangling from his neck. He was very carefully trying to remove it. The room was flooded with the brassy light of dusk. It was a second before I realized there was a skylight overhead, and it was open. Looking up, I saw Rex coiling a rope around his shoulder. He disappeared from view, and I heard his steps on the roof overhead.

Brigid hurried in behind me. I was moving toward the windows. "Call an ambulance and tell them he's been poisoned." I ripped aside the curtains, but the windows were gated and padlocked. I ran into the hall and up a flight of steps to the roof door. It had a police bar across it. By the time I got outside, Rex was on the roof of the next building, headed toward his goal—the third townhouse in the row, a nice example of neoclassical, whose face was undergoing renovation and was covered with scaffolding.

He turned and saw me. I hit the deck as a burst of automatic fire chewed up the roof. I got off a few rounds from my Beretta, but he was already dropping onto the scaffolding, and in another moment he had vanished.

When I went back into the house, Rennseler was the color of bacon fat, but the needle was out of his neck. I picked it up and held it to the light. "Three-quarters full. You're lucky."

His hand was shaking as he pointed to his desk drawer. "In there, quick…"

I opened it and found what he was after, an antivenin kit, marked with the symbol of a snake. It contained a syringe and a small vial of serum. I put the needle into the vial and filled it. "Let's have your arm."

I searched for a vein, as he spoke. "After Tommy was murdered…I figured I could be next… I knew no hospital in New York would have it."

I injected him. "Saving your life is getting to be a habit." He looked at me, his lips bloodless, and passed out before I had a chance to tell him that he couldn't have died tonight, that the leopard goddess who protects against snakes was watching out for him.

"He's probably having convulsions by now," said Henderson.

"A few convulsions will do him good." We'd dropped Rennseler off at Lenox Hill Hospital, along with Bobby. Bobby's wound was superficial, but they wanted to X-ray him anyway. I rang Temple from a phone in the lobby, but got no answer, so Henderson and I grabbed a cab downtown. As we rode, she said, "Anxious situations like this always happen when Mars transits my seventh house."

I didn't know about Mars, but Henderson's leg was against mine, and I wasn't having convulsions. What more could a private detective ask for on a summer's night?

HENDERSON AND I went down the steps to the office. "I can't understand," she said. "Why was Rex kicked out of the Rennseler family in the first place?"

"Temple never even knew him, so he probably wasn't a Rennseler. My guess is that he's Helen and Hamid's son. Hamid didn't want him in Egypt with him, he'd have been an embarrassment, a Son of Satan. So Helen farmed him out. And then I suppose he came looking for a payoff. Things got nasty, and Tommy got killed." I disarmed the entrance to our offices, and Henderson and I stepped into the outer hail. I switched on the lights and opened my office. "Rex knew about the scepter and wanted it. Once he had it he could tell them all to go piss up a rope."

I hit the answering machine. The voice of John Manning came out. *"The feds played me their Hangmen tapes. The person who took out the hit on you was this guy Rex. If you want to hear the tape yourself come by Midtown North tomorrow morning."*

Manning signed off, and the voice of Bytes Jensen came on. *"Jimmy, I ran through Tommy Rennseler's old credit statements just for kicks. He flew to Lake Placid seven times this past year. Two of the dates coincide with visits Charles Brand made there. I have exact dollars, dates, et cetera. This is the Electronic Mole, signing off."*

Henderson's eyebrows had shot up. "Brand and Rennseler were both child molesters?"

I sank down in the client's chair and rubbed my forehead. "I've been thinking too much. I'm getting a headache."

"We both need spruce oil to steady our focus." She darted out to her own office and returned with a small bottle, then laid a drop of oil on each of our brows. "My mind is still racing much too quickly," she said. "We have to play the Game of Thirty."

"Not now, Henderson."

"Yes, now. That's the kind of mind I have. I think better when I'm concentrating on something other than what I'm thinking about." She opened the drawer, took out the bone dice, and threw them. She moved her lead piece to the square of the Royal Twins, then opened the leather-bound book of rules and looked up the entry on the twins. "They're still in the egg of the Great Cackler. They've never been separated. They're bound in the embrace of eternal love." She laid the book down and stared at me. Her eyes were wide and bright. I could see the bells going off in her mind. "Do you know what a cranial adjustment is?"

"I don't think I want one."

"You don't need one. But people who've suffered severe trauma, physically or emotionally, can get cranial misalignments. The cranial bones compress. I work on their heads with my fingers and move those bones back into place."

"Now I'm positive I don't want one."

"The point is, those bones move, with only the slightest amount of pressure from my fingers. Here..." She touched at the bones behind my eyebrows. "...and here..." She ran her fingers along my jaw. "...and here..." She touched my cheekbones. "All those bones can move. Do you understand what I'm saying?"

The burglar alarm went off. "Back door!" I ran down the hall, my Beretta out. The window to the backyard exploded inward with the shattering sound of glass and the soft *pop-pop-pop* of a silenced semiautomatic

Another round of fire took out the other window, as the phone rang and I heard my answering machine go on again. *"Jimmy, this is Saul. I just remembered what it was I didn't like about Tommy Rennseler. One day he came into my shop when my nine-year-old daughter was there, and the way he looked at her gave me a frosk in the pisk. Do you know what I'm saying? I wanted to tell you before I went down the Colorado River in a rubber raft, which I'll be doing three days from now, Rita has already purchased the tickets. It's been nice knowing you, Jimmy, goodbye."*

I was crawling toward the back door. I knew Rex had to be in the backyard tree, as it was the only thing in the garden that wouldn't produce an electric shock. Henderson had forbidden me to wire it because the electromagnetic current might impede the flow of the tree's rhizome. Now Rex was trying to impede mine. He had to have come down the fire escape and swung over into the tree's high, heavy branches.

I angled toward the shattered window. I could see the outline of the tree against the sky, and then a burst of little *pops* took out what was left of the window.

I felt Henderson tugging at my sleeve. She was flattened out beside me. "Don't shoot!"

I yanked my arm away from her, kicked the door open, and dove through, firing.

The hard surface of the yard came up to meet me. I rolled over and fired again, then rolled underneath Henderson's round iron picnic table. Bullets pinged off the top of it. I wrapped my hand around the center pedestal of the table and lifted it. Using the table as a shield, I charged the tree. Rex swung out of the tree, onto the fire escape, which gave a creaking groan as he landed on it.

I couldn't fire, as there were windows all along the fire escape, with faces in them. The last section of the fire escape had been drawn up. I caught the bottom rung and yanked. Rusty bits of iron fell in my eyes as the ladder slid down. I started climbing. More heads were popping out of the windows above me, directly in my line of fire.

Rex turned onto the uppermost landing of the fire escape. He was scrambling past the last window. The window shot open and Viola rammed a broom handle out. "Sons of bitches! Turn off that fan!"

Rex stumbled over the broom handle and went down. I rounded on the landing below him, as he came upright and climbed over the edge of the roof. Just as I reached Viola's window, she shouted, "My ovaries are vibrating!" and hit me with a pail of soapy water.

Blowing soap suds, I went up and over the edge and rolled down onto the tarred surface of the roof. Henderson was coming up the fire escape, yelling at me not to shoot.

Rex ran to the other end of the roof and leapt easily to the next building. The long jump was one of my events, and I charged the edge, got good liftoff, and fanned with both hands, through the scent of *Spellbound* left in the air. I hit the next roof and fell forward.

We sprawled on the roof together like a fallen trapeze act. Rex looked up at me, eyes burning with fury. As we struggled to get our breath, I saw his expression changing, and then his whole face altered, his cheekbones sinking and his jawline softening. It was as if a mask were collapsing inward on itself, and as it collapsed I realized that it was Temple I was holding down. A wisp of hair had fallen across her forehead, where it clung, damp and curling. Her gaze was confused, and her voice was frightened. "Jimmy, why are you sitting on me?"

Washington Square Park was crowded, its denizens gathered to buy dope, beat drums, look at the moon through the pollution. It was a warm summer night, the kind that brings people out to party, or to circle alone, but to be there when the parachute opens with a soft, sensuous ripple and our dreams descend to us through the Manhattan sky. Henderson, Temple, and I were on a bench under a big tree, in the dappled shadows of its leaves, and yellow light from the park lamps played on Temple's face, which changed with the appearance of her many selves, out of the bottle at last. "Daddy was bad with me," whispered Temple. Her feet had come off the sidewalk, her legs seeming to shorten; her voice was tiny, with a chime-like purity. "Daddy made me do naughty things."

"And did anybody else know about it?" asked Henderson gently.

"I'm not allowed to tell," said the small voice, and then it faded, like a fairy disappearing into the shadows of the leaves, and Temple's legs seemed to lengthen again to normal.

Henderson said to me softly, "The body of a

multiple can change significantly. The way I manipulate cranial bones with my fingers, she manipulates them with her musculature." And Temple's face did change, the planes shifting to create a more rounded shape, as another personality surfaced. I've seen plenty of strange things in my life, but this made the hair on the back of my neck stand up. Her eyes seemed to sink into her head, the sunken eyes of someone very old, old as a statue from Ur. The lips hardly moved. I heard a rushing sound of breath, like wind moving through a newly opened tomb, and then the voice followed: "Whenever her father raped her, Temple looked at the statue that was on the night table beside her bed. It was a statue of Callisto, who was seduced by Zeus the father. And I, Callisto, was born."

Henderson and I sat in silence, waiting. I'd seen this face of Callisto in Temple before, but fleetingly, as an expression that would flicker across her eyes. Now it had surfaced with authority and control, sustained by an inner alchemy I couldn't begin to understand. It was as if one of the world's greatest actors were running through her repertoire, and the characterizations were created without make-up or latex layers to alter the shape of the face, but by a precise control of the appropriate muscles. Such control had to have begun in early childhood, when the personality as well as the body wasn't fixed in its boundaries. Those boundaries, which solidify in the rest of us, were still porous to Temple; she passed through them effortlessly. Or rather, the broken pieces of her personality passed through them. Finally Henderson said, "When did it first happen...Callisto?"

The rush of breath came again, as the stony lips

moved. "Temple was eight. I watched from the night table. Her father raped her and we changed places. She became a statue. And I was made real. Stone feels very little, and that was what was needed; the raped child must not feel."

The carnival of faces that passed through the square, the wild punkers, the exotic Rastamen, the kids with their clothes on backward, were just a feeble attempt to stretch and contort identity. A master of the contortionist's art sat on the bench with us, but it was a tortured mastery, and ultimately an unconscious one, for Temple herself was gone. The rushing sound of breath continued from the living statue called Callisto: "Rex killed Tommy. Rex is the brave one. I did not want him to kill you, but he was afraid you would finally track us down and we would be extinguished."

Callisto's round countenance dissolved, and the cheekbones and jaw became more prominent, the lips setting into a hard line. A masculine force tippled through Temple's arms and legs, and it seemed as if her finger joints were expanding as a lithe gesture ran through her hands, like the secret seal of an inner society. Rex's eyes gazed out.

It wasn't the impersonation of man, it was a man. The transition affected me like the step off a carousel, when the ground seems to be moving; I felt all of Washington Square shifting under my feet. I'd been more than a little in love with this woman who had just switched sexual polarities.

As with Callisto, I realized that I'd seen Rex's fleeting presence in Temple's eyes before, a slippery movement in back of the gaze, the bodyguard checking in. He'd been there, buried in the depths, and watching. Now

I looked fully into his commanding stare, and saw no compromise.

I said, "Henderson, get back to the office. I'll call you later."

Henderson rose from the bench and slowly backed away. I don't know if it was my tone or if she recognized the threat in Rex's eyes, but I hoped that it would keep her going.

I slid my hand toward my Beretta; this was the guy who'd tossed Richard Rennseler in the river like an old tire. I didn't want to grapple with him again; if he got the Beretta he'd blow my head off. Even hired killers have gray areas of emotion, but Rex's feelings were solid black. Rage was all he knew, like a football player on steroids, his brain chemistry altered for aggression, and just sitting next to him was altering mine. My teeth were grinding so hard they felt ready to crack. Rex snarled something, and I grabbed him by the collar. Our faces were inches apart, and I could see the venom in his eyes. I tightened the folds of his collar in my fists. "I want some answers."

The answer I got was his forehead smashing into mine. The yellow park light exploded behind my eyes. I shook it off and tightened my grip again. "You killed Brand. Was it because he was a child molester?"

A slow smile of satisfaction crossed Rex's lips. "No more fun for Mr. Brand."

"And Richard Rennseler? Why did you go after him?"

Rex's venomous stare seemed to distill a fresh drop of poison. "He and Tommy took turns with Temple."

I sickened with the thought of those two predators destroying Temple's childhood. I searched for a trace of her in Rex's eyes, but she wasn't in those pools of anger. I couldn't imagine what state she was in, what dreamless sleep or holding pattern in the psyche. And now, suddenly, Rex started to sink, his gaze weakening; he was going back to his own buried chamber like an eel at the bottom of the sea.

"I've still got questions!" I shouted. "Come back, you sonofabitch!"

The venomous glare returned, but Rex had finished with questions. He lunged for my throat, and I managed to block him, pinning his arms against his chest. The energy that was going through his body was phenomenal; I saw my thumb rising and falling from the blood rushing through the artery in his wrist. I was bending him backward on the bench to break his leverage, but his freakish strength was impossible to contain; he twisted to his feet, dragging me with him. We were eyeball to eyeball, and I felt the power rippling through his stance; his arm snapped free and he hit me with a staggering backhand blow, then kicked my legs out from underneath me. I tried to roll away but he grabbed me by the back of the neck and I kissed the pavement. He kneaded my face into it, cutting off my breath. From the corner of my eye, I saw a small white ball rolling toward us. It struck Rex's hand. He stopped choking me and picked the ball up. A peculiar calm came over him as he stared at it. He turned it around in his hand, examining it in silence. I slipped out from under him, breathing hard. He set the ball on the back of his hand and rolled it slowly back and forth with strange deliberation. At that moment, a little girl appeared from behind him and yanked at his sleeve.

"Hey, mister, give me my ball."

Rex looked at her, smiled, and gently set it in her hand. "It's very late. Go to your mommy."

The little girl skipped off, bouncing her ball. I said to Rex, "Why did Helen try to commit Temple?"

"To get rid of me." His sly look returned. "Except I'm not so easy to get rid of." He started to fade again.

"Wait!" I shouted. "Where's the scepter?" But he was gone.

TEMPLE CAME OUT of her therapist's office, her movements clumsy and uncertain, as if she couldn't remember how to use her arms and legs. I'd been meeting her each day the way I met Saul Feldman, as security, but of a different sort.

I walked with her through the lobby to the street, as she steadied herself and regained the rhythm of her own footsteps, a rhythm she lost each time she went to therapy, where, under supervision, she'd begun to let her other personalities out. The night in Washington Square had been the first time the parade had happened in front of anyone, and I had stayed with her until dawn, when the cork finally went back in the bottle, and the Temple I knew returned to take over consciousness again. The next day Henderson found her a therapist, and I'd signed on as a kind of navigator for this hour that followed her therapy, during which she'd walk slowly home, in a fog of overlapping identities. I couldn't think of her as the person who'd three times tried to kill me, because it wasn't she. Was I nervous? Wouldn't you be? Just a little? But the woman beside me was the gentle, caring scholar I'd first met, who wouldn't harm anyone. She hadn't even fired Miss Groome, and probably never would.

She said, "I met Rex today."

"What do you mean—met?"

"When he surfaced, I didn't go unconscious. I hung at the edges, listening to him. He described how he killed Father."

"And?"

"I saw him inject Father with the poison, and I witnessed Father's last few minutes, when the poison was spreading through his system. Father just sat on the floor, gasping for breath and trying to speak. He only got one word out."

"What was it?"

"*Fate.* He was trying to sum up his life, my life. He was trying to say that we were each other's fate."

She lowered her head for a moment, then straightened it quickly. It was a decisive movement, of a kind I hadn't seen her make before, as if she were shaking off her father's interpretation of their relationship. "So now I've recovered the memory of Father's death. Some day I'll recover the rest of it. But not yet. I'm carrying as much remorse as I can handle, just knowing that it was my body Rex used." She turned to me, a weak smile playing on her lips. "My therapist said it could be years before Rex is integrated into consciousness."

"Do you want him in your consciousness?"

"He's not the sort of man I would ever want in my life, much less my consciousness." She looked at her reflection in a shop window, and her look was cautious, as if she didn't know whose face she was going to see. "When I feel him starting to come toward the surface, I panic. But I'm learning to hang in there anyway, because I'm the one who has to control him."

"Shamans have their totem animal. Maybe Rex is yours."

She gave me another faint smile. "It's nice of you to say it, considering that he tried to kill you."

"I'm hoping he's on my side now."

"He is. He appreciates the fact you've never gone to the police about...us."

"Tell him he gets complete client confidentiality." I should have turned Temple in, but I hadn't. My conscience didn't bother me about Tommy. He'd played the Game of Thirty and lost. As for Sheik Vito, he'd fed people to polar bears. And as for Brand, I had a hard time feeling he was any great loss to the world either. The little girls he satisfied himself with were going to have terribly complicated lives; the nightmares of sleeping women would be theirs.

We were on Thirty-third Street, heading toward Temple's apartment. She said there was something there she wanted to give me. We entered through the iron gate into the antique courtyard. And I felt again the quicksilver presences of old New York, the ghostly gentlemen and ladies. Temple herself had quicksilver erupting from her in numerous shapes, mercurial forms that shielded her from the assault life had made on her. She was a courtyard of ghosts.

We entered her apartment. Its atmosphere was no longer charged with premonition; the voices of the statues had been silenced, now that she was hearing the voices within herself.

"My refuge. I don't go out much these days."

"It's a good refuge."

"It could be improved." She pointed to four large, reddish clay jars on a low shelf. Each jar had a different head—falcon, baboon, jackal, and human. "That dream I told you about? In which Father kept saying *Canopus* to me? Those are Canopic—the four sons of Horus. When the pharaoh died, his lungs, stomach, liver, and intestines were stored in them. They're the Protectors of the Dead."

I stared at the baked clay forms. I was pretty sure I knew what they contained. "Do you want me to get rid of them?"

"I didn't know until today that Rex had put Father's organs in them." She drew in a long breath and closed her eyes for a moment. Then she turned to me. "Yes, take them away. I can't have them around, and I wouldn't want anyone else to discover their contents." She put them in two canvas shopping bag from Zabar's, and when she looked up at me I saw her eyes had a faceted quality, her gaze somehow shared. "We're grateful to you, Jimmy," she said. She saw my confusion, and added, "I'm trying to let them all speak."

I took her hand in mine. I could feel Callisto's stony presence, and then Rex's energy snaking through, the hidden protector. And then the little girl, timid as the fairies.

Temple's eyes were tearing over, the facets blurring into a gaze that was less complicated. She said, "It would have been so nice to fall in love with you. But I can't let that happen now." She put her hands on my shoulders and kissed me very lightly on the lips. "Could you love somebody who'd almost killed you?"

"Sure, no problem."

She slipped her hands down the front of my jacket, but a look of regret had come into her eyes. "If the time ever comes that I can safely get involved with a man, it can't be with someone I look on as my savior."

"I'm nobody's savior."

"But you saved me. And that puts you into the image of a father. Don't you think I've had enough fathers?"

I felt a sharp stab of loneliness. I had to look away from her before I fell into those blue eyes again, with their confusing depths. I stared at the wall, where a collection of Egyptian statuary was displayed, a leopard, a boat, the dwarf god who watches over children, many other pieces. They were in three ranks, each piece in an illuminated alcove in the wall. "It's the Game of Thirty."

Temple turned, following my gaze. "Yes, Father designed it when he remodeled this place years ago. The Game of Thirty was his favorite."

I felt the knucklebones rolling in my head, and pointed to the papyrus scroll beneath the rows of statuary. The lettering on it was the same lettering that was inscribed on the bottom of my Game of Thirty. "What does it say?"

Temple stepped toward the wall and ran her finger over the glass-enclosed inscription. "*I will not let you enter unless you speak my name.*"

I walked along the display, from square to square in the life-size Game of Thirty; if there's an Egyptian sage watching over that board I was feeling him now, whispering in my ear, or maybe it was Willy the Wire.

And then I remembered that this house looked different from the others in the courtyard because Tommy had changed it when he'd bought it. Now the most radical of those changes was apparent—one of the interior walls, the wall behind the Game of Thirty, had been deepened, by over a foot, necessitating an alteration to the windows on the outside wall. Why would someone shrink precious Manhattan living space by that much?

I went to the wall, to the beginning of the game board, and checked the first square. The statue in it was a crocodile. When I touched it, it moved, slightly backward, but remained attached to the base of the alcove. The spirit of Willy the Wire said, *Looks like the tumbler of a lock to me.*

"What are you doing, Jimmy?"

"Playing the Game of Thirty," I said, and went to the next square, which had a pair of lions in it, the Executioners of Sakhmet. The lions moved also, just slightly backward.

Temple, stepping in alongside me, said, "I've never been able to figure out why they move like that. It's not really enough to allow someone to clean under them."

"No, it's not. But Willy the Wire says it's enough to set a balance somewhere in the wall."

"Who's Willy the Wire?"

"The god of lockpicks." I checked all thirty squares, and each of the pieces moved. "We've got a primary balance, which is probably when each piece is in its centered position, like so. Then only a few of the pieces have to be moved, to change the balance. This wall is like that little altar your father made, the one in your shop." I ran my hand along the wall. "There are weights that shift inside it, probably lubricated steel and completely silent."

"Father built something into this wall?"

"He was a guy who loved hiding places." I looked at the game board. Thirty squares gave a staggering number of possibilities. But in the Game of Thirty only four of the squares were considered supremely correct. "Square of Hathor, square of Maat..." I slid these figures back and went to the next. "...square of the Leopard, square of the Solar Boat...and... nothing's happening." I stared at the Game of Thirty, and tried to imagine Tommy Rennseler staring at it. I said, "The object of the game is to reach the invisible square, square thirty-one, the square of Heaven. We've hit the favorable squares. What's left?"

You got it backward, said the god of lockpicks.

I shifted all the pieces, putting the balance in its opposite position. Then I brought the four favorable figures back to center, and as I brought the last piece to center, I felt the action move, softly, under my touch. The thirty-first square, the invisible one, was opening. On the wall to the right of the game board a display cabinet had swung forward a few inches. The wall was slotted where the edge of the cabinet had rested against it. A slim metal bolt had dropped down and let the cabinet swing forward on hidden hinges.

"Go ahead," I said. "Open the square of Heaven."

Temple pushed the cabinet away from the wall, and I saw the golden gleam of the scepter of Akhenaten.

"It's all yours, Rafeek." The scepter lay on my desk. The faces had been worn down, their golden features softened by time, but the family resemblance was there— father and daughter. They didn't call it abuse in those days, but you have to wonder if any of the Nile dwellers ever thought maybe it was a little flaky, old Akhenaten up there at the palace, boffing his daughter. We're an ancient people, and we've tried it all, I suppose. But is there a scepter that rules our culture now? And what's carved on it, and will it look barbaric in a thousand years? That's the question that troubles my sleep.

"This is a wonderful moment, Mr. McShane." The Egyptian private investigator stood on the other side of my desk. People don't always look the way you imagine them, but Rafeek's portly form and his bright little eyes corresponded to my long-distance view of him. But his voice had changed, was now more cultivated, and had only the slightest trace of an accent. He'd been playing the fool on the phone with me, probably having learned that people are less guarded around those toward whom they feel superior. His check for a hundred grand was already in Temple's bank account—his finder's fee to her. I'd accepted a somewhat smaller fee for myself.

He ran his dark fingers along the shaft of the scepter, then opened a suitcase and laid the scepter inside, onto a thick piece of tapestry. "The Royal Couple, two thousand years after their reign." He reverently touched the face of the pharaoh and his daughter, then closed the case and twirled the combination lock. "So their journey continues."

"This is a tough city. Be careful."

"I have spent a lifetime in the lively alleyways of Cairo." He smiled again, and lifted the case. "Well, it is time to say farewell." He touched one finger to the brim of his hat and gave me a small bow. As he straightened he noticed the Canopic jars on my windowsill and walked over to them. "You're a collector, Mr. McShane?"

"I've got a few pieces."

He stroked the head of the ancient falcon that stoppered the first jar. "I'd pay handsomely for the four sons of Horus. Do you care to sell them?"

"I like having them around. They have sentimental value."

"I understand. Well, then, goodbye. If you ever get to Cairo, please give me a call. It's not safe for tourists right now, but you'll be safe, I guarantee." He handed me a business card. It had no lettering, only the gold embossed figure of a cobra.

"*You're* the Cobra?"

He bowed.

"You're not a private investigator?"

"Let us say I investigate, on my own behalf. I learned through my sources that you were looking for someone to help you on the Cairo end of this little problem, and I thought, who better than I, since the problem was mine." He put on a pair of mirror sunglasses and walked out. I watched him on the monitor, and then watched him walk up the steps past my window, briefcase in hand. A limo was waiting for him. As he issued directions to his driver and bodyguard, his head turned my way, and his glasses caught the sun and flashed like the cold, impenetrable stare of a snake.

Henderson lit candles in the four corners of my bedroom. They were specially scented candles, containing fifty different aromatic herbs and oils. I'd finally convinced her that our chakras were aligned and that she should spend the night with me.

"There," she said, lighting the fourth candle and placing it on my bureau. "Doesn't it smell wonderful? The scent will permeate the atmosphere and remove the etheric energies of other women who've been here. Of course the hard-core ones require smudging."

"Smudging?"

"With this." She opened her bag and brought out something that looked a little like a whisk broom. "It's made of sage and cedar." She put a match to the tip, and it started to smolder. In about ten seconds the room was thick with smoke.

"Henderson." I coughed. "How about if I just paint the place with quick-drying latex?"

"Ex-girlfriends aren't bothered by latex. You've got them in everything—the lamps, the fabric, the furniture, the rug."

"And I never noticed."

"It's one of the reasons you have such a temper. The energy of your old girlfriends in here stirs you up." She was waving her smudge stick over the bed. "I could never relax in this atmosphere."

"Hey, whatever it takes. You want me to burn the sheets?"

"That won't be necessary."

I caught a twinkle in her eye, of the pixie, and realized that she was playing with me. She was wearing a short white silk kimono, which showed the wonderful Henderson thighs. I was wearing one that matched. She'd bought them in honor of the evening.

As she bent over the bed, the front of her kimono hung open and I saw the round curve of her breasts swaying softly back and forth as she waved her smudge stick. I felt my chakras rapidly revving up.

She paused. "The room should really be framed with a blue ribbon, but I forgot to buy one."

I headed for the closet. "I've got a blue suit we can cut up."

"It already feels better in here. Can't you tell? A cleaner atmosphere?"

My eyes were watering from smoke. "Very clean. Like a hit of pure oxygen." I handed her a wineglass from my bedside table, and poured.

We drank. As she reached across me to set her glass down on the table, her breast touched my arm. I turned toward her, but she pulled away and whispered, "We mustn't even think about sex."

"Excuse me?"

"First-time lovemaking. It requires that we go very, very slowly, and let the energy build, all night if we have to. We should sit close—" She led me into the living room and sat down on the couch, then patted the cushion beside her. "—but pretend nothing is happening."

I sat beside her. Her warm thigh touched mine. I said, "Something is happening."

"Yes, but we're going to ignore it and talk of other things. How was Temple today?"

"She's shaky. But she's getting there."

"I really think she must be a genius, to be able to embody all those points of view." Henderson toyed with the sash of her kimono. "I suppose her sex life must be confusing with so many personalities. Well, you can imagine."

"I don't have to imagine," I said, and immediately wished I hadn't.

"Oh?" Henderson affected clinical indifference, but her thigh was no longer touching mine. "I can't say I'm surprised. I know what a leg man you are."

"It's not what you think. I showed up at her place one day while she was cleaning."

"And you dusted each other off."

"No, no, I cleared out. She was under enormous stress."

After a short pause, Henderson casually said, "Any regrets?"

I hesitated, wondering what the best response would be. "Faint regrets."

She placed her hand on mine. "I've always said you were a gentleman. A gentleman is allowed faint regrets."

The nighttime sound of voices from Christopher Street came through the open window. Wisps of sage smoke filled my bedroom doorway. "So," I said, "what do we do now? Should I sand the floor?"

Her eyes twinkled again, the elf preparing to spin her crystal threads around me, as elves will do to men who fall into their clutches on dark nights. She crossed her legs, the kimono parted, and Viola's voice came screaming down the air shaft: "McShane! I smell smoke!"

I ran to the window and looked out, twisting my head toward the apartment above. "It's okay, Viola."

"The place isn't on fire?"

"No, it's just Henderson driving my ex-girlfriends out of the bedroom."

Viola struck a match to her cigarette, the flame illuminating her face for a moment. "Well, what are you talking to me for? Get back in there."

"You try and get some sleep, Viola."

"Don't blow it, McShane. Love's the best company."

I turned back to the room. Henderson was gone. Then I saw her through the sage smoke in the bedroom, sitting on the edge of the bed. I stepped through the doorway. The white silk of her kimono reflected the glow of the candles. She pushed her hand down on the mattress. "I'm not sure this is at all firm enough for your back."

"Fine, I'll shove it out the window."

She gave her Pekingese smile, her eyelids narrowing and crinkling up at the corners. "Let's test it. You go under the bed and see if my body makes a depression in the springs."

Was she actually asking me to get under my bed? Muttering beneath my breath, I crawled under the bed to look and felt the springs creaking as Henderson stretched her adorable body out on the mattress above me. It occurred to me that I was involved in the most incredible foreplay of my macho-pig life.

I crawled back out. "You're right, the bed's defective. So that's why I get tangled up in the sheets every night."

I sat down beside her. Her head was on the pillow, her hair spread over it. Her dark eyes reflected the sparkling points of candlelight. She said, "I never thought I'd be here."

"On an inferior bed."

"With you." She slid her hand inside my kimono.

Her fingers went into my armpit. "Your latissimus is very rigid."

"Is it because there's a nearly naked woman in my bed?"

"No, it's from carrying a shoulder holster."

I figured we had a ways to go this night, but it seemed we just might get there, after all.

AFTER A YEAR OF THERAPY, Temple succeeded in integrating Rex into her consciousness. She'd gained enough confidence in herself so that Rex's existence had become unnecessary. As her fears dissolved, he'd started to fade; he'd actually said goodbye and told her he was going to vanish. When she asked him where, he'd said, *Into your will.* That day she fired Miss Groome. Temple was still the same sweet person I'd known, but I suspected that no one, man or woman, would take advantage of her, ever again.

As for Henderson and me, we got married, with Ranouka and Manning as our witnesses. "Now that you're married to a chiropractor," Manning had asked, "will your head be screwed on straight?"

I had to tell him this would probably not be the case.

However, I did brush Henderson's hair for ten minutes every evening while she told me about her day. I listened attentively, and was completely accountable, and not just waiting for sex. You believe me, don't you?

Each month Henderson and I drove to Albany, to the state-run orphanage where Rebecca Hewitt resided. The three other girls we'd rescued from the Lab had been united with their families, but the foster parents Rebecca had lived with did not want her back. They'd said they were worried that the abuse she'd undergone had "tainted" her—their word. They'd been afraid that if she were allowed to live in their home again she'd somehow "taint" their own children by what she knew. The mother of the house had even suggested that Rebecca might try and seduce her husband, because "after all, it's what she knows now, isn't it, to have sex with grown men." Her husband would never go for that kind of thing, she said, but it might be best to put Rebecca where temptation wouldn't come anyone's way. But no other foster parents had wanted her either, expecting that she'd be too difficult, for all sorts of reasons.

The truth was she was tough. She'd been hurt, but she grew around it the way a tree will grow around any impediment to its progress; the force is upward. Men like the late Charles Brand had left their mark on her, and it showed sometimes. When she was in pain, she'd start counting, silently, with a faraway look in her eyes, counting the flowers in her imagination which surrounded and protected her. She'd also refused to give up her New York Yankees cap. Her therapist had fought her on it, thinking it might be a reminder of the sick games she'd been forced to play, but it meant something different to her, about which she wouldn't speak. She just wore it, stubbornly and continuously, and finally everyone accepted it. Whatever games she'd been forced to play with grown men who'd cast her in their fantasies as the little American dream, she'd won in the end. So why throw her cap away?

Henderson and I were in Albany now, driving up to the front entrance of the orphanage. Our monthly visits meant a lot to Rebecca, and today's visit was a very special one. The orphanage was a large stone building, covered in ivy, with turrets like an old fortress. The place emanated melancholy, as if the walls were filled with longing. It was summer, and children were playing outside on a rolling lawn, and they showed no outward signs of that longing, but it was still there, like an echo that followed their shouts and laughter.

I parked, and we got out of the car. As we did, the front door of the orphanage opened, and one of the administrators stepped out. He held the door, and motioned someone forward. Rebecca appeared, looking out from under the brim of her New York Yankees cap. The administrator shook hands with her, and said he hoped she'd be back to visit sometime. Rebecca turned our way. She was carrying a little green suitcase. She came toward us slowly, with great dignity.

Got a taste for ancient Egypt?
You may enjoy the following
titles from

CITY of the HORIZON
BY ANTON GILL

Palace intrigues, the murders of royal favorites...welcome to Egypt, circa 1350 B.C. Akhenaten, the "reformist" pharaoh, has died, and his successor is controlled by political schemers with no love for Akhenaten's old supporters. Many of these have lost their lives, but Huy, once a scribe in Akhenaten's court, has lost merely his home and the right to practice his trade.

In desperation, Huy becomes a sort of traveling troubleshooter, the world's first private eye. With his first case he tackles both Egypt's powerful priesthood and a brutal gang of tomb-robbers, all while running from the secret police. The modern world, it seems, has no monopoly on duplicity and corruption.

- The 1st Huy the Scribe mystery of ancient Egypt
- "Huy goes down the mean streets of Ancient Egypt in a fine, swaggering style."—*Glasgow Herald* (UK)

ISBN-13 978-1-933397-11-5
ISBN-10 1-933397-11-X

$14.95

CITY of DREAMS
BY ANTON GILL

Huy (first seen in *City of the Horizon*) was once a scribe in the pharaoh's court. But now he's lost his job to palace politics, and been reduced to freelance problem-solving —working, essentially, as the world's first private eye. And that work has to be kept very quiet if he's to avoid attracting the notice of the secret police.

"Quiet" could be tricky, because Huy's latest case shows every indication of becoming extremely high-profile. A serial killer has been stalking wealthy young women in Thebes, and with every clue that Huy uncovers it becomes apparent that the killer is a person of terrifying power and influence. "Huy goes down the mean streets of ancient Egypt in a fine, swaggering style," said the *Glasgow Herald,* but those streets are getting meaner by the day.

- The 2nd Huy the Scribe mystery of ancient Egypt
- "Exotic, erotic, and compulsively readable"
  —*Gay Times* (UK)

ISBN-13 978-1-933397-30-6
ISBN-10 1-933397-30-6

$14.95

CITY of the DEAD
BY ANTON GILL

The pharaoh Tutankhamun is dead, killed in a mysterious "hunting accident." In theory this should be good news for Huy, who was exiled from court—and prevented from working as a scribe—when Tutankhamun took the throne. Palace intrigue, though, was never so simple. In the years since his exile, Huy has been eking out a living as a freelance "problem solver"—essentially the world's first private eye—and it's in that capacity that he's been hired once again, to find out exactly how Tutankhamun died. If Huy's employer were purely interested in the truth, that would be one thing. But he has an agenda of his own, which doesn't bode well for the suddenly friendless young queen. And in becoming his snoop-for-hire, Huy may have bought himself a lot more trouble than he's being paid to take on.

- The 3rd Huy the Scribe mystery of ancient Egypt
- "A real thriller of ancient Egypt...the characters step from the page fully alive"—*Eastern Morning Press* (UK)

ISBN-13 978-1-933397-66-5
ISBN-10 1-933397-66-7

$14.95

You want to
walk the Mean Streets?
Try the following titles from

SEASON of the MONSOON
BY PAUL MANN

As a police detective in Bombay, Inspector George Sansi is used to struggling for order in one of the world's most exuberantly corrupt cities. But the mutilated corpse discovered in Bollywood – the Hollywood of India – taxes even Sansi's formidable skills. Could the murder have been a cult initiation gone hideously wrong? Was it the work of a serial killer? Was the victim killed as part of a political cover-up?

Answering those questions will take Sansi from Bombay's teeming slums to the film community's palaces of excess and the menacing haunts of India's underworld. It will uncover a web of corruption that stretches from the powerful to the desperately powerless. And it will leave him running for his life.

- The 1st George Sansi mystery of India
- "Harrowing, memorable...with all the elements of a classic noir thriller"—*Publishers Weekly*

ISBN-13 978-1-933397-07-8
ISBN-10 1-933397-07-1

$14.95

BELSHAZZAR'S DAUGHTER
BY BARBARA NADEL

Tourist brochures present Istanbul as a glamorous, modern city, but the brochures don't make much mention of Balat, a decrepit neighborhood of narrow, twisting alleys and crumbling tenements. Until recently it was home to Leonid Meyer, a reclusive elderly Jew who, like many of his neighbors, came here long ago to escape one of Europe's various bloodbaths. But Meyer's refuge ultimately became his coffin, the carnage crowned with a gigantic swastika.

A racist murder? Inspector Ikmen has his doubts, and begins tracking down the few people who might have known the old man, including a faded prostitute, a shadowy family of Russian emigrés, a despairing rabbi, and a high-strung young Englishman in the throes of erotic obsession. The first in a stunningly atmospheric new series from a writer who has deservedly been compared with Michael Dibdin and Donna Leon.

- The 1st Inspector Ikmen mystery of Istanbul
- "Intriguing, exotic, exciting and original"
  —*Literary Review* (UK)

ISBN-13 978-1-933397-49-8
ISBN-10 1-933397-49-7

$14.95

THE FOURTH WALL
BY BARBARA PAUL

Other than a critic, who'd kill a Broadway play? Playwright Abigail James has long been fascinated by "revenge tragedies," those theatrical classics about getting even. But all of a sudden, she's living in one: The set of her latest Broadway hit has been vandalized, actors horribly attacked, a designer blinded with acid, the brilliant director terrified into hiding. Clearly, they have all committed some grievous wrong, terrible enough to prompt this orgy of destruction. But who did they wrong? The police are clueless (and a little too smirkingly eager to chalk it all up to "theater people"'s taste for drama), so James and her colleagues see only one option: They'll examine their collective sins and pinpoint the injured party. And then they'll exact some revenge of their own

- "A boffo thriller...absolutely superb"
  —*Publishers Weekly*
- "Astringent wit, style, and shrewd observation"
  —*Washington Post*

ISBN-13 978-1-933397-47-4
ISBN-10 1-933397-47-0

$14.95